Pamela's manipulation [illegible] stunning. She flicked one fror[illegible] in the air like a boomerang and [illegible] then she caught it in the middl[illegible] cut the deck and walked the [illegible] around her fingers, and demonstrated one-handed versions of three different types of shuffle.

"I want to learn to do tricks with sleight of hand," she said.

"You want to learn, or would you prefer to come and teach?" said Ben.

APRIL'S SHOWER

by Peter Cooper

First published by Peter Ralph July 2020

ISBN: 978-1-8381078-0-2

Acknowledgements

This is the second book about Ben April, but it can be read without having looked at its predecessor, “April's Fools”. Nevertheless, if you intend to read the first one, this one might tell you what happened.

All of the magic tricks in this book (and April's Fools) are real tricks that have been performed by real magicians. I have performed a number of them myself. In general, I have tried not to give away secrets because I think that magic is more entertaining if you do not know how it is done.

Christian Magicians UK is a real magical society and I would like to thank all my friends in that great organisation who have helped and supported me and my family over the years.

Cover design by Seraphim Bryant, bluefalcon1983.com

Special thanks to…

- Sam Thompson who encouraged me to publish;
- Mattie Underhill for her comments and encouragement;
- My son Phil for his proof-reading skills;
- My wife Audrey for lots of things, mostly for putting up with my crazy schemes;
- and to Aliti, the real 'Emily Darkchilde' for lending me her fictional name.

Peter Cooper

1.

Ben April stared at the tennis players as they played their game on the outdoor grass courts of Lockley College of the Arts on a warm and bright summer's afternoon. That is to say, he stared at one of the players. His eyes took in every shapely contour of Emily Darkchilde, a light-haired Asian-looking young woman whose skin, he felt, was golden rather than actually fair or dark. But he was biased.

He would be playing against her out there right now, except that he had no idea how. He didn't even know how to hold the bat, as he was fond of saying. Emily, whose real surname he still did not know, was doing quite well, and with his inability to play the game ("I've got two left foot faults") he was happy just to sit on the side-lines, or whatever they were called, and cheer her on.

He was disturbed by a polite cough to his side, and he turned his head away, reluctantly, from the beauty in front of him to see Professor Michael Kennington, who was trying to get his attention.

"I wonder if I could run an idea by you, Ben."

"Run," said Ben.

"Sorry?" said the professor, who never could get his jokes.

"I mean, go ahead," Ben said.

"Ah," said the professor. "Run. Yes. Well, I was thinking about offering the students some sort of mentoring."

"That sounds like a good idea," he said immediately, without really giving his boss's good idea much thought at all. Professor Kennington was the principal of Lockley College of the Arts, and Ben was a teacher there, so any idea the professor had was going to be a good idea. Then, a few seconds later, Ben actually thought about what had just been said to him. He knew the professor and he knew that when he wanted to 'run an idea' by him he was not looking for a 'yes-man' answer, but he wanted a real opinion.

"Mentoring," Ben said. "What does that involve doing?"

"I don't really know," said the professor. "I always imagined that it was all about sensible advice, a shoulder to cry on, someone to be there for you. I wondered if you were ever mentored, and what you thought about it."

"I'm a professional magician. Obviously, nobody ever gave me sensible advice."

The professor may not have been that good at picking up Ben's jokes, but he got that one. He smiled politely, not finding it particularly funny, and waited for the next remark, which he rather hoped would be of more use.

"No, I wasn't mentored. But I have a loving family and friends. I would say that Emily sort-of mentored me last year here at the college, giving me some support when the pressure was on, or when I had doubts. Although, all she really did was listen while I unwound."

"That's probably all that's needed, most of the time," said the professor. "I would love for the staff to come to me if they needed to talk, but I am the boss, so I can't be the listening ear as well."

"Especially if they want to complain about the boss."

"Do they?"

"No, I didn't mean that," stuttered Ben. "It was just…"

"Oh, yes," said the professor with a smile.

"So, what would I have to do? Is there a course I should go on?" asked Ben.

"For what?" said Kennington.

"Mentoring," said Ben. "You were saying."

"I didn't mean *you*, Ben," said the professor. "In the same way that I can't be the shoulder for the staff, you can't be a mentor for your students. Because you are their teacher. I suppose, because of your particular subject, there is an unusual association between you and your students but you are still a teacher and that means you must have a different relationship with them than a mentor might."

Ben felt silly for a moment, but he was used to that.

"So who would be a mentor?"

"I'm not sure. One or two of the kitchen staff, perhaps, or someone from the village?"

"They would have to volunteer for the role, not be pressed into it. And they would have to be available. They would probably need to go on some sort of training course, too."

"Yes, I know. I'm just playing with an idea at the moment. You have always been good for sounding ideas out. I would have asked Bryn, but I already know what he would say."

Bryn Jones was the art teacher and one of Michael Kennington's oldest friends, but he was a little old-fashioned in his methods and new ideas didn't always seem necessary to him. In fact, the idea of employing a teacher of performance magic seemed silly to Bryn and although they got on quite well, the Welshman thought that Ben's profession was a little odd to say the least.

"Can I sleep on it?" said Ben. "I'll chat to a couple of people, get some ideas. Friends I know in the teaching profession in general think the whole idea of mentoring is a good thing, and it's certainly fashionable right now."

As usual, Ben realised almost the moment he said it that the word 'fashionable' was the wrong word to say to the professor. He was not the slightest bit interested in whatever fashion currently took hold of the world of education. He only wanted to know if mentoring was going to be useful to him and to the college.

"Yes," he said, slowly and thoughtfully. "Well, let me know what your friends say, and any ideas *you* have, too. Any time."

Ben watched as the professor walked away. He did believe that everyone needed someone to turn to. He'd had a childhood friend who helped him grow up, a mother who gave him time, friends who listened to him. The idea of being a mentor or something similar appealed to him. He wondered if he could do something like that himself, not here at the college of course, but for another establishment. He was to teach at the college on Wednesdays and Thursdays, and be available to support anyone who wanted to practise on Fridays. That left him plenty of free time early in the week to visit a school or college in the area as a volunteer.

A shadow fell over him. It was cast by Emily Darkchilde, who had finished her game. He looked up at her. She seemed to glow. Somehow, even the hot and sticky exertion of playing tennis in the summer heat didn't make her sweat.

"You look like you're deep in thought," she said, "and that's never a good thing."

"Are you trying to say I don't normally think?"

"You said it."

"Did you win?" he asked.

"You mean you didn't notice?" she said. "You've been sitting here watching me play and you don't even know who won?"

"I take it that's a no, then."

"I'm getting better. I'll win one day."

Ben told her about the professor's idea, and she also thought it was worth investigating. Then he told her about his own idea of becoming a mentor somewhere else.

"I know it's not the same thing," said Emily, "but I heard someone at the nightclub say the hospice just outside Stevenbridge is looking for visitors. They might like you to do a magic show some time."

Ben's ideas clicked into place. He did not really want to be a mentor but he did want to do something useful. Emily knew him, knew his imagination and his need to do some kind of good in the world around him and her idea was just right. He did not need to make a long-term commitment; all he had to do was offer a free show. Then, if he settled with the idea of further commitment, he could deal with that when the time came.

"That sounds just my kind of thing. I'll look them up later on."

He got up and accompanied her towards the shower block. They weren't at the 'public show of affection' stage of their relationship just yet, so they just walked together. Everyone else at the college had known about their feelings for each other long before Ben had worked it out, but they were still two teachers at a college so, although they had not discussed it with each other, they were happy to be in each other's company without making a fuss about it. Even if Ben seriously wanted to 'make a fuss about it' sometimes.

Lockley College of the Arts was an unusual college a couple of miles from Lockley village in Norfolk. The building was a beautiful converted Georgian mansion set in its own grounds. It was a residential college that also accepted day students from nearby towns and villages. Although it had been heavily in debt and relied on regular generous grants and donations from various sources, it was beginning to make a little money at last. A number of London-based politicians were now sending their children to the college, some of whom might have needed bodyguards to keep an eye on them while their parents were engaged in negotiations in politically unstable parts of the world. The security staff, provided by the government, also lived on the premises, providing essential extra revenue for the college.

Some new classes had been included in the year's syllabus. One of them was a short, one-term session on stagecraft and performance support. The creative writing class had increased its range, expanding to include creative reading and dramatic storytelling. There were to be other short courses, particularly throughout the first term, on catering for the film and television industry, including a general food hygiene certificate which about half the college had signed up to. The college had excellent kitchens, including brand new (and not yet used) ovens. Ben's own syllabus (although he thought 'syllabus' was rather a grand word for what he did) had now stretched to two years and was going to include more on clowning, circus skills, puppetry and other associated arts as well as a great deal on actual magic tricks and how to perform them.

This year, he had a class of nineteen young people, most of them new students, although two of last year's class had returned. Mark Tyler was back, of course. He was a magic fanatic, and the inspiration for Professor Kennington's decision to have a magic class in the first place. Mark was an untidy-looking young lad with a mop of unruly hair, but he was beginning to build up a repertoire of quality magic performances. Juliette MacIntyre was also back in his group, although her real interest was Emily's singing class. She was an attractive, confident young woman who always dressed conservatively and spoke politely. She had a fantastic stage presence and whether she sang or performed magic, she always held everyone's attention. The others, of course, he had not met yet.

On the two days before the term started, most of the boarders had arrived. Ben was among the staff who greeted them. One or two wanted to see the 'magic room', but Ben had not yet set out any props, so, apart from looking comfortable and welcoming, it was just another classroom.

On the two *nights* before the term started, Ben realised there was something he should have done before now. He had, for the last year, stayed at a room in the great old building. It was a small room, but apart from a huge collection of magical props which were kept in a locked storeroom adjacent to his classroom (or 'the cellar' as people called it), he did not have many possessions here in Lockley anyway. Nevertheless, Emily had already advised him that it would be a good idea to move out of the college and have some space of his own and now he realised how important that was.

The number of residential students had more than doubled over the last year and the noise they made at night before they settled down kept him awake. He could not remember struggling like this last year – perhaps he was just lucky and had some quieter students near his room. In fact, there may not have been any students very near his room last year, but now that the college was filling up, they had to use rooms closer to where the residential staff were staying.

Tuesday, he thought. On Tuesday, I have no lessons and I am prepared for the first six sessions anyway. I will look for lodgings then. And I will get in touch with the hospice in Stevenbridge and ask if they need a visiting magician.

On Monday, the professor delivered the opening address and introductions were made. Downstairs, Ben surveyed his classroom and realised he had already set it ready for action on Wednesday so he did not need to spend any more time on it. Nobody new came to sign on to his class today. The program this year had more to choose from and the new students had been encouraged to choose and sign up for all of their options before the term started. Still, Ben thought, it would have been nice to have met one or two of his new class before the actual session on Wednesday. Mark Tyler, of course, came and spent some time with him, enthusiastically telling Ben how much he had missed the lessons over the summer, and what he was looking forward to about this year's work.

Mark had Asperger's Syndrome, which was a form of high-functioning autism. It meant that, while he was very clever and good at a small number of things, he also found it difficult to relate to the outside world. Mark loved chess, computers and magic, and he would talk about his favourite subjects until Ben's ears fell off. However, down here with Ben, Mark was also hiding away from the rest of the college – Ben's cellar was a safe place for him to go so that he did not have to cope with the strange new world that was going on outside. There were new friendships forming and lots of new people to meet. Mark would not be able to cope well with this, so he valued the privilege of being out of the way for a while. Nevertheless, Ben would have to wait until his first lesson to meet any of his other students.

On Tuesday, Ben started the day by telephoning St Mark's Hospice in Stevenbridge.

"Could you do with a magician to come and entertain your children?" he asked them.

"Can you make accountants disappear?" came the sharp-witted reply.

"I do magic tricks, not miracles," he responded. After he explained that he was offering his services for free, they arranged for him to visit on the following Saturday morning, which was sooner than he expected. However, he was getting excited about the prospect of this new project, so he was eager to get started.

Then he drove his car into Lockley to look for a place to stay. Unfortunately, the village was a small place and the only flat available was above the little local bakery. He did not fancy the idea of being woken up at four o'clock in the morning when they started the ovens up for the day's baking, even if his room would always smell of freshly baked bread.

On Wednesday, he was in his classroom ready for the first lesson. He had a small performing table in front of him and the desks had been moved to the back of the room, leaving just cushioned chairs for his students to sit on. There was plenty of space and he had set out exactly nineteen chairs in addition to his own for his students.

As people made their way into the class, Ben put his empty hand into one of the open boxes in front of him. He took out a bright red light, which he held between his finger and thumb, and put it in his mouth. Then he took another light, this time from out of the air, and put it in his mouth. He carried on, apparently taking lights from all over the place – his pockets, his ear, Mark's mop of unruly hair, one or another of the boxes in front of him. After four or five red lights, he took green or blue lights, and seemed to eat them.

When he had counted that all nineteen students had arrived, he looked at them as if he had only just noticed them there.

"Sorry," he said. "I was just enjoying a light snack."

Mark Tyler laughed uncontrollably and a newcomer called Martin Kent thought it was funny, too. Most of the others just smiled politely. One smartly-dressed young man looked at Mark, who continued to giggle at the joke for some time, as if he was an idiot.

Ben realised that this children's party trick was not the most impressive opening for a bunch of intelligent, mature young adult students like this, so he moved on. Unfortunately, he moved on to a lecture about secrecy and confidentiality and then respect for props. He did a little card magic at the end, but nobody was too interested in card tricks by then. He realised he had probably lost the whole group by the end of the morning, and it would take some effort to regain their interest.

During their first session together, poor as it was, he managed to take a good look around the group to see if he could pick up a little information about his new class. He noticed that a couple of them tried to chat up Juliette during the lesson and she politely redirected their attention back to him. John Stockton, the smart young man who didn't like Mark's enjoyment of the opener, kept casting derisory sideways glances at Mark, who didn't seem to notice. There were four smart, VIP-looking lads in the class, but Ben only noticed John Stockton in his smart shirt and tie and one of the others, Rich Collier, who stood or sat apart from the others as if he was some kind of inspector, checking the group out.

The one other person who laughed at his opener, Martin Kent, was obviously a bit of a comedian himself. He made little quips all the way through the session, but most of them were on the point and supportive, so Ben did not want to suppress him – this college was about creativity, after all.

At the end of the session most of the class left quickly. It was nearly lunchtime. Mark, as usual, stayed behind, and so did the only young lady (apart from Juliette) in the group. She was a very short girl, slightly chubby, with a pretty round face and mousy hair. Her hands were well looked-after and she had unusually long fingers for such a short person. She made to pick up the deck of cards on Ben's table, then looked up at him.

"May I?" she asked, remembering what he had said about respect in the class.

"Please," said Ben.

"Please may I?" she asked, a little nervous now.

"No, I mean, *please* go ahead. Feel free. Be my guest. Er... Yes."

She smiled, relaxed, and took the cards.

"Pamela, isn't it?" said Ben. "Pamela Grice."

Pamela beamed. "Have you memorised everyone's name in your class?"

"No," admitted Ben, "only yours."

"Really?" she sounded encouraged.

"Yes. There are only two girls in this group, and I know Juliette already, so you must be Pamela."

"Oh," she said, deflated again. Ben thought, I'm really not very good at this.

"I quite liked your card tricks," Pamela said, shuffling the deck. Then she shuffled and cut it with one hand. "But they were simple tricks, maths tricks. There was nothing, well, *clever* about them."

Her manipulation of the cards was stunning. She flicked one from the top so it flew in the air like a boomerang and returned to her, and then she caught it in the middle of the deck. She cut the deck and walked the cards around her fingers, and demonstrated one-handed versions of three different types of shuffle.

"Maths is clever," said Ben, rather weakly.

"I want to learn to do tricks with sleight of hand."

"You want to learn, or would you prefer to come and teach? Your moves are pretty impressive."

"Thank you," she said with a smile. "I can do lots of spectacular stuff with card *shuffling*, but I want to learn *tricks*. I actually only know a couple of real, actual magic tricks. I want to learn something that will make what I do with the cards *useful*."

"We'll probably spend a little while on the simple tricks to start with, but I promise we'll spend some time on clever stuff, too. In fact, if you drop by any time during the day on Friday, I'll show you something you can work on in the meantime."

She seemed to be happy with that, thanked him, and left.

In spite of that last positive moment with Pamela, Ben felt he had not connected with his class from the start. Last year, he had been disappointed when he discovered he had only eight students, but now he had nearly twenty, and from very different backgrounds and perspectives. The little 'light snack' magic trick on the way in had not grabbed their attention or drawn them together as he had wanted. He decided he would have to enlist Juliette's help.

Juliette MacIntyre was the daughter of a retired Ambassador to the Middle East, now an advisor to Downing Street. She was always smart and well-dressed, her brown hair mid-to-long and perfectly groomed. When she was not at home, she liked to wear a blonde streak in her hair – that was the closest she got to rebellion. She wore only a little make-up and it always looked like it had been put on by an expert. The way she dressed was reserved but attractive. She had been in Ben's class last year and had been an accessory to one of his outrageous schemes. He thought he might ask her to help with another one. He met her at lunch after his first lesson.

"I wonder if you could help me," he asked her. "I've got a comedy magic trick I need your help to perform. It's a little personal, so I thought I should ask you first."

"That's very kind of you," said Juliette. Ben felt they were more like friends than teacher/student, but she still talked in her usual formal and polite way. "Of course I'll help."

"It's a bit out of character for you," he started to explain, "which is what will make it funny."

"Yes, that's fine," she said. "I've done stuff like this before."

"And the fact that you're an attractive young lady is, of course, a factor."

"Why are you taking so long to get to the point?"

"It involves your bra," said Ben. He spoke quietly, because he was in the dining room which was bustling with people. It was also bustling with noise, which was good, but he did not want to be saying "your bra" to one of his young students at one of those times when everything goes embarrassingly quiet. Luckily, he got away with it.

Juliette, unperturbed, smiled.

"What is the purpose of the trick?"

"I didn't feel I connected well with the new class. I want an ice-breaker at the beginning of the next session to get to know them."

"And you doing something with my bra will break the ice," she said, more loudly and clearly than Ben would have preferred.

Now *that*, thought Ben when he realised just what she had done, was a perfectly timed line. Juliette was really good at delivering lines like this, but this was a corker. Not just because she said it, of course, but because Emily Darkchilde was about to join their table at that very moment. Juliette was one of Emily's star students, and the young lady must have seen her approaching the table.

"And what," said Emily, with a little over-dramatised shock in her voice, "does my Ben want to do with your bra? Will you be wearing it at the time?"

"Yes," said Ben. "No, not exactly. It's a secret." Ben realised that secretly doing something with Juliette's bra was not the actual message he wanted to convey. "I mean, it's private." Neither was that. An image of a graveyard set with a place just for him entered Ben's mind. Mark, who was sitting at the four-seated table with them, nearly choked on his burger.

"A trick," said Juliette, to put him out of his misery.

The following day, when the group were all there and ready to go, Ben showed them the two large blue silk handkerchiefs which he was going to use to perform the first trick. Nearly half of his class were late, so he had to start by reminding them that they should start on time, which was a shame, because he wanted this session to be fun and upbeat. Perhaps he had bored them all so much yesterday with his introductions that they decided they did not really want to turn up at all today.

He waved the handkerchiefs about a bit and then he tied them together. Then he made a fuss about where he should put them so that they were on show.

"I don't want them hidden, so I need to put them where they can be clearly seen." His eyes finally rested on Juliette. "Juliette, would you help me, please? You seemed to draw more attention than I did yesterday," (slight chuckles from one or two who worked out what he meant) "so I wonder if you could put this…"

Then he acted out an embarrassing moment where he started to make a lunge for her front, and then held back. She was wearing a blouse which had the top couple of buttons undone. It was a little more casual than she would normally wear, but most of the students did not know that, so nobody was suspicious. She indicated for Ben to tuck the two tied handkerchiefs down into her blouse, but he fumbled and got a better laugh than he had the day before. She finally took them from him and tucked them down there herself, in spite of offers from three of the lads, including Martin Kent and Rich Collier.

Ben let the disruption die down as he picked up a small yellow handkerchief from one of his boxes and played it through his hands.

"We are going to look at making things disappear today," he said. He balled his hand into a fist and started to feed the yellow handkerchief into it. While he was doing it, he talked on. "I think making something vanish is a bit of fun, but making it appear somewhere different is really… magic."

Upon the word 'magic', he opened both of his hands to reveal that the yellow handkerchief had vanished. A couple of the students clapped politely.

"I think, perhaps, that we should make the handkerchief reappear between the two blue cloths I just tied together. They should be quite warm by now."

He took hold of one end of one of the tied blue cloths and gave a little tug, pulling them away from Juliette's blouse. The little yellow handkerchief was there, tied between the two large blue silks, but that was not all. A bra was also there, tied to the yellow handkerchief on one side and the other blue cloth. Upon seeing this, Juliette gave a little squeal and covered her chest with her arms.

The trick had the desired effect, and the class became animated and excited about learning new stuff. Ben still had a lot to learn about this bunch of students, though. It wasn't going to be like last year.

2.

St Mark's Hospice was a large, friendly building set in pleasant parklands right on the edge of Stevenbridge. St Mark's Church, from which it derived its name, was the big parish church that seemed to watch over the town from its place on the hill just off the town centre. The hospice (unlike the church) was a new, modern structure which was all ground-level buildings. It had wide corridors and doors and no steps.

In the main entrance, Ben was met by Mrs Engles and a cat. Mrs Engles was a stout woman with a smile so huge her face didn't seem big enough to contain it. The cat was a black and white house cat that watched Ben as if he was an intruder. It followed at a wary distance as the woman led him through to a large, brightly coloured, positive-looking play area, where a pretty young lady showed him where he could set up ready for his performance.

"I'm Sally," she said in a sweet voice. She almost looked as if she was young enough to be one of the children he was to entertain that morning, except that she was wearing the 'not quite a nurse' uniform that all of the staff in the hospice wore. She was fairly short with a curvy figure and she had a round, child-like face framed with dark hair which he guessed would probably have been longer than shoulder length, except that it was tied up for hygiene and working convenience. She also had big brown eyes which paid him a lot of attention.

At 11 o'clock, he started his show. There were more than 20 children of all ages in the audience. The youngest was a little girl of about six years old, and the oldest was a boy who was probably over 16. Some were in dressing gowns because they couldn't stay out of bed long enough to get dressed. A small number were day visitors, and there were a few parents there. A couple of the older lads kept saying “I know that one” every time Ben took a prop out of his box and one of the two kept saying “I know how you did that.” Ben put up with this, partly because he had done loads of children’s parties, and partly because they were ill and he wanted to help.

He did his ‘light snack’ joke, which went down better with them than it had with his class earlier in the week. He made a large wooden dice disappear into a box, amid lots of shouting as to where it might be. He pulled the heads off of a bunch of fake flowers, made them vanish, and then he magically returned them to their wire-and-feather stalks.

He was slightly distracted by one young lad who was not laughing or joining in. The young man looked around twelve years old, with dark, sunken eyes and no hope of smiling. In spite of the brightness and positive attitude exuded by this place, it was probably hard for some people to smile, he thought. He carried on with his show, trying not to be too aware of sad the boy in the corner.

“I have a really old trick,” he announced as he came to the end of his performance. “It was invented by a man who lived more than a century ago by the name of Professor James Sally. It is known as Sally’s Bottom.” He looked directly at young Sally, who began to colour up a little.

“There is a story among magicians that this little trick only works if the person who does it has a helper called Sally. Is there anyone called Sally here?”

Ben had realised that Sally was a popular care assistant among the children. She seemed to be the type of person who always had time for people, who would give that little bit extra to assist or to listen. He hoped she was up for a laugh; she certainly seemed the type. All of the children pointed to her and egged her on to volunteer to help him. Reluctantly, she began to get out of her chair.

“It’s alright; you don’t have to get out of your chair. So, your name’s Sally, is it? That was lucky. What I’m going to do is make something appear on a blank card.”

He showed them a stack of calling-card sized blank cards which were tied with an elastic band, and he took a pen and drew a dotted line on the bottom of the top card and bowed as if he had just done something amazing. By this stage in the show, the children knew what to expect and some of the adults also gave mock groans of disappointment.

"What?" he said. "I said I was going to make something appear on a blank card, and I did. I didn't say I was going to do it *magically*." They jeered and giggled a bit more.

"I'll tell you what. As this trick is called Sally's Bottom, I'll just ask Sally to sign on the dotted line." He went over to where she was seated and handed her a pen and the stack of cards, where she signed as he had asked.

"Now, Sally, what I want you to do is sit on it." He pulled the top card away from the rest of the banded set and made to put it under Sally. She took it from him and slipped it on the seat under her. Then he returned to the front and pulled out a deck of cards.

He did a little comedy card trick where he had one of the children pick a card from the middle of his pack. He asked the sullen young lad at the back if he would help, but he didn't want to so Ben picked someone else. The card chosen was the Ten of Clubs, which was shown to everyone except Ben and then returned to the deck.

"Now I want everyone to think of the card you have chosen," he told his audience. "Say it in your heads over and over again. Ten of Clubs, Ten of Clubs, Ten of Clubs."

Some of them looked surprised that he knew what card they had chosen, and then he turned over the top card to reveal that it was, in fact, the Ten of Clubs, the card he had just put in the middle of the deck.

"I know that magicians aren't supposed to tell you their secrets," he said over the applause, which died down quite quickly, "but I thought, as it's you, I'll tell you how that was done." He leaned towards them all and looked around as if to make sure nobody else was watching. Then he said in a quiet, conspiratorial voice, "It's Sally's bottom."

Everyone turned to look at Sally, who got a little redder.

"Would you show us your signature on that card you're keeping warm for me?" he asked her. She stood up a little, took the card from her seat and looked at it. She did a double-take. Her signature was there, just as she had written it, but there was also something else written on the card that had not been there before – it was the words 'Ten of Clubs'. She showed everybody, and Ben told her she could keep it as a souvenir. Then he took his final bows and began to pack away as people left.

Some of the children came up and talked to him afterwards. One of the mums asked for his details so that she could book him for a party and he gave her his business card. He would normally feel really good after a good show like that one, and Sally had been the perfect foil for that final trick. There was just one hiccup in his thought processes, and that was the young lad who had sat through the performance of some of his best and funniest children's material without laughing. Or even responding in any way at all.

When the children had gone back to their rooms, or wards (or homes in some cases), Sally asked if he needed any help tidying up.

"No, I'm fine, thanks," he said. "Except, that lad in the corner. He wasn't all that entertained, was he?"

Sally's big brown eyes looked into his, displaying her emotion a little.

"No," she said. "Harrison Bell doesn't seem to be entertained by very much, I'm afraid."

"He disappeared back to his room quite quickly after the show," said Ben. "Any chance I could visit him?"

"You don't need to apologise," said Sally. "I'm sure it's him, not you."

Ben smiled. "It wasn't my intention to apologise. I just thought I might give him a little private show."

"Best of luck," Sally said, and led him to the young man's room. Ben knocked on his door.

"Hello, Harrison? I'm Ben April. Can I come in?" Ben had in his hand a ring and ribbon for his favourite close-up trick. Harrison, who was dressed and sitting in the small armchair by his bed, looked up at Ben, but said nothing.

"I brought along a little magic trick," said Ben, holding the ribbon which dangled the ring.

"I don't like magic," said Harrison.

"But you came to my show," Ben said.

"I was being polite," said Harrison. "Actually, they have a go at me if I don't turn up to their little events."

He was quite grown-up sounding for a child of his age, thought Ben. Not to mention, horribly honest.

"What *do* you like to do?" asked Ben.

"I read," he answered, a small hand movement indicating the huge number of books on shelves and stands surrounding his bed. There were books by Douglas Adams, Eoin Colfer and Spike Milligan, as well as a number by people he had never heard of. Ben looked at the ring and ribbon in his own hand, and put it away in his pocket.

"Tell me about the books," said Ben.

"Well," said Harrison, "they've got words in."

"I mean, what's in them? What do you like reading best?"

"I'm getting a bit tired," Harrison said, apparently not trying to be rude. "Would you mind if I rested?"

"Yes. I mean, no, of course not. I'll see you again, perhaps."

"For another magic show?" Harrison asked and there was almost a hint of disappointment in his voice. Ben was not sure how to react.

"Goodbye, Harrison."

Sally sympathised a little as she escorted him from the building.

"Thank you so much for coming," she said as he loaded his equipment into his car. "I hope we'll see you again."

"Would you really want me here again?"

"*I* would," said Sally, focussing her attention entirely on him, "as long as you don't mention my bottom again. And the children loved it, too."

"Except for Harrison."

"We haven't found out what entertains him yet," said Sally. "He reads and watches videos. He turns up to a lot of the events we put on, but he doesn't connect with anything. He just sits there and puts up with it all."

"Except his books."

Sally touched his arm. "I don't think he enjoys his books or his films, either. He just exists."

"What's wrong with him?" asked Ben. "I mean, if you're allowed to tell me how he is ill, that is."

"He has leukaemia. All the treatments have failed. We just have to make him as comfortable as possible now. He probably won't last out the year."

Ben looked into Sally's big eyes, wanting to say something helpful or supportive. He could not think of the words. You're a better person than I am, he thought about this young lady, dealing with sick children like this every day. He opened his mouth to try a word of encouragement, but closed it again when he realised his brain wasn't going to provide him with any. She smiled a 'goodbye' to him, and returned to the building. Ben got into his car and sat there for a while before starting up the engine. He looked back at the bright building. The cat was looking back at him from the inside, where he was sitting on the window sill of the foyer.

He drove on into Stevenbridge. Being Saturday, the town was busy, so Ben was grateful that Emily had previously showed him a great place to park cheaply. He had arranged to meet her at a little café in the town centre. Emily occasionally worked a little voluntary shift on Saturday mornings at the college, giving singing lessons to the local children, so she had not joined him at the hospice. However, she had offered to help him afterwards as he looked for a place to stay in Stevenbridge, his search in Lockley having been unsuccessful.

The café was St Mark's tea rooms, and it was nearly 1.30pm when she got there. Ben was pleased, because he was a little later than he had expected to be, but he was still there before her. He was able to examine his surroundings as he sipped his mineral water while waiting for her. The tea rooms were run on Fridays and Saturdays by volunteers, and were set in the large halls of St Mark's Church, the same church that gave its name and large sponsorship to the hospice. A little notice by the counter said that all profits from the tea-rooms would, in fact, be donated to the hospice.

"How did it go?" she asked after she arrived and they had kissed each other in greeting.

"I thought it was quite good," said Ben.

"But..." said Emily, who had got to know Ben and his feelings quite well over the last year. She knew he wanted to say something else, to unwind a little.

"One of the kids there wasn't entertained."

"You can't win 'em all."

"If there was just one I wanted to win, Harrison Bell would be the one."

"And he didn't like your show?"

"He doesn't like magic,"

"Do you do anything other than magic?"

"Well, there's cornflake stories."

"What," asked Emily, "is a cornflake story?"

Ben smiled. "Tell me your surname and I'll tell you what a cornflake story is."

"Okay."

"Go on, then," said Ben.

"You first," said Emily.

"No, you first. I've asked you what your name is before, but you won't tell me."

"My surname is Darkchilde."

"I mean your *real* surname," said Ben. Emily used her stage name all the time. She had inherited it from her father, who had played guitar with a rock band called Darkchilde in the 1980's and was now retired and lived somewhere on the south coast of England. She had always refused to tell Ben her real surname. The staff photographs presented in the college foyer had her photograph labelled as 'Emily Darkchilde', and the other teachers he had asked had not been able to tell him otherwise. He had not asked Professor Kennington yet.

They sat and chatted, laughed a lot, drank their fill of coffee and left it very late before hunting for a place for Ben to stay. When they did look, however, Ben quickly dismissed everything he saw as 'rather expensive'. He had been used to saving up lots of money in the last year, and his savings would diminish quickly if he took on some of these properties.

"You must really enjoy living at the college, then," said Emily.

"Actually, I like it less and less now that the students are there. I remember when I could go to sleep quickly because it was quiet."

But Emily knew that there was something else on his mind that was stopping him from concentrating on the job of flat-hunting. Young Harrison had touched his heart, and he could not properly concentrate on other things until he had dealt with it. He wanted to go back to the hospice to make an appointment to return the following week, or, at least, sometime soon. Emily drove her car and followed him back there at the end of the afternoon. She joined him in the main entrance hall of the building, looking around at the fabulous, bright décor and the children's pictures on the walls while Ben went to the reception desk.

Mrs Engles looked like she was packing away to go home. She looked up from her job of tidying away the paperwork, and recognised Ben. She was still smiling that enormous smile.

"How can I help you, Mr April?"

"Thank you for remembering my name. I wonder if I could book to come back sometime soon?"

"Have you arranged anything with Sally?"

"Is Sally your entertainments officer, then?" he asked. "Could I speak to her?"

Mrs Engles pressed a button on her control board, which contained a vast array of buttons for her to press, and very shortly afterwards Sally arrived.

"Mr April! Back so soon."

"Hello, Sally. Please call me Ben."

"Of course, *Ben*," said Sally. "We ought to be on first name terms after what you did with my bottom." Ben was slightly aware that Emily's attention was redirected from looking at children's pictures. He imagined his neck felt warm from being stared at.

"I wondered if I could come back some time."

"Another magic show?"

"Well, do you do anything else, other than have children's entertainers in, I mean?"

"We do as much as possible," said Sally. "We have craft times or board games on Saturdays when we don't have people in, that is, and story times on Wednesdays, and…"

"Story times!" said Ben, "I would love to come and tell a story. Does Harrison come to the story times?"

"Well, yes."

"Wednesday?"

"4.30 in the afternoon. Can you make it?"

"Definitely. What about this coming Wednesday?"

"Fine. But you live out at Lockley, don't you? It's a long way to come for a twenty-minute story slot. Perhaps you'd like to stay for tea with us?"

"If you wouldn't mind."

"We'd be happy to have you," said Sally. "Do you want us to provide a story for you to read or will you bring your own?"

"I'll bring one of my own," he said. Having seen that Harrison's books included a number of humorous writers, he thought he knew just the right kind of story for him: a cornflake story.

Then she looked at him for a moment or two. "Look, we run a volunteer visitor scheme here. Maybe when you come on Wednesday we can talk about it with you. You come in every now and then, not as a performer, but as a visitor for one of the kids. I know you've taken to Harrison, and he could do with a friend right now. Would you think about giving it a go?"

Ben wanted to say 'yes, please' straight away, but he gave way to an uncharacteristic display of common sense. After all, as much as Harrison had struck his heart, he had hardly hit the jackpot himself as far as the young lad was concerned.

"Perhaps we could talk about it then."

"It's a date," said Sally.

Ben was aware that Emily had moved closer to him, and was now near enough to whisper in his ear.

"A date?" she said, quietly enough for him to be the only one to hear it. They left together and started walking back to their respective cars.

"I can see why you want to go back there again," said Emily.

"Yes, it's a really nice place."

"I was thinking of the young nurse," said Emily with a wicked grin. "She's very pretty. And perhaps you could tell me about what you did with her bottom sometime?"

3.

Ben woke up rather late on Sunday morning. Or, to put it more accurately, he woke up early on Sunday afternoon. He had not slept well, because some of the new residential students had decided that Saturday night was party night. Last year, he recalled, many of the students went home at the weekends. Perhaps they would this year, too, but not on the first weekend of the new term. He really must, he thought, find somewhere to live away from the college soon.

When things finally quietened down in the early hours of the morning, he still had not settled. Harrison Bell was on his mind. He would just love to become a visitor at the hospice and make friends with the young lad, but he had no idea how to break that barrier of misery that blocked out all desire to enjoy himself and relate to the world outside. But then, if someone told Ben that he had a terminal illness, how would he feel?

Thoughts buzzed through Ben's head, and daylight was just about finding its way through Ben's curtains before he finally drifted off to sleep. After that, nothing could wake him until after midday.

He was late for lunch, but the cook was happy to serve him. He was popular among the staff from the village, and they would always save him some food if he was late for a meal – which was more often than he would have liked.

He looked around the dining room for any of his students, in case there was someone from his class he could have a chat to. His attention at the beginning of this term had been more focussed on volunteering at the hospice and finding a place to stay than starting a healthy relationship with his class, so he thought it might be a good idea to correct that now, while it was still early in the college year.

He noticed the short girl Pamela, who was chatting with a couple of lads from his class and some other young people he had not seen before. They were animated and involved in whatever they were discussing, and he did not feel it was appropriate to interrupt. Juliette would have had her lunch early and gone off to study or something. She was a disciplined and organised young lady, so Ben would have missed her, coming in this late.

He spotted a couple of students who had been in his class last year, but had not signed up this year. Shelley and Xander were sitting at a table on their own, opposite each other. Ben had run a one-year course last year. In discussion with the professor, he had changed his course to cover two years, because as well as magic performance, he wanted to cover circus, clowning, puppetry, ventriloquism and a number of other arts related to magic in his two lessons a week. He decided to start from the beginning again, so Juliette and Mark would have to cover ground that they had already covered, but neither of them seemed to mind. Juliette was really in it for the performance experience rather than the magic, and Mark loved magic so much that you could do the same thing twenty times and he would still be enthralled by it. Dancer Shelley had only signed up for the class last year because she had been a subject short on her compulsory subjects list, and Xander had discovered he had terrible stage fright, so this year they had signed up for the stagecraft class instead.

Ben asked if he could join them. They were delighted to see him. He stood by the chair they indicated for him for a few seconds and looked at them. He tried to read their body language. They were both popular with their peers, and they had their fingers on the pulse of what was going on around them. It was natural that the two of them should spend time together, possibly to compare notes. But was there more to them than that? It seemed to Ben that they were possibly getting involved with each other. He sat down at their table.

"How are you both getting on?" he asked.

"Fine thanks," said Xander, with his customary confident manner. It was only on stage that he lost that confidence.

"Yeah," agreed Shelley. She was letting her hair grow a little longer. All last year she had kept it cropped short. "We are doing stagecraft."

"I know. I think you'll both do well there," said Ben. "We miss you in magic, though."

"You can't possibly be missing me," said Shelley with a smile. "I was the world's worst magician."

"And the world's best beautiful assistant," said Ben.

"I miss the close-up magic," said Xander, "but I love the backstage stuff – better than standing in front of an audience, anyway." Xander was now comfortable owning up that he suffered from stage fright. Ben was disappointed that he had run away from it rather than try to deal with it, but that was his choice.

"How are things with the rest of the world?" asked Ben.

Shelley looked as if she was about to say something, then she cast a glance at Xander, who looked, with his expression, as if he was telling her that it would be better not to.

"We've got to go," said Xander, quickly. "See you."

The two of them left together without a further word, as if Ben had scared them away. They didn't start talking until they were out of sight, and Ben was not aware of what they were saying then.

Ben sat on his own with his lunch, which was also his breakfast. He reckoned that there was some student stuff going on that Shelley wanted to share with him, but Xander didn't. He smiled to himself. He was young enough, almost, to be one of them and as his subject was magic sometimes he could get away with not being treated like a 'real' teacher, which he rather liked. Still, it was his own fault (or the fault of the partying last night) that he was the only one left in the dining room as the others drifted off to whatever social activities they had planned for the Sunday afternoon. He wished Emily was here today. Perhaps he might drive over to her house this afternoon and say 'hello'.

Mrs Bailey from the village started tidying up around him. She was an older woman who had a 'farmer's wife' look, with permed white hair, rosy cheeks and lines around her eyes.

"Mr April," she said.

"Please call me Ben."

"Ah, good," she said, "Ben. I hear you're looking for a place to stay."

"That's right."

"Have you found anywhere yet?"

"No. I went looking in Stevenbridge yesterday, but it was very expensive."

"Towns often are, aren't they? And it's a long way to drive to work every day. You want somewhere a bit closer. A lot closer, possibly."

Ben worked out where this was going.

"Do you have somewhere in mind, Mrs Bailey?" he asked, taking a sip of his coffee.

"Seeing as we're on first name terms, you can call me Hayley."

Ben nearly spat his coffee over the table – Hayley Bailey? He quickly swallowed what wasn't leaking out of his mouth.

"Hayley," he repeated, barely keeping a straight face. He hoped she hadn't noticed.

"My mother had a little fall a couple of years ago," she said, talking as if she had not, in fact, noticed his rudeness at all. "She was quite a sick woman, you know. Anyway, while she was in hospital, my husband made a little granny flat for her. It was converted from the barn right next to the house. Unfortunately, Mum died in hospital, and we never got to use the place. It's got its own bathroom and kitchen, chairs and a bed, and everything. We were going to rent it out, but we didn't want it to go to a stranger, so we never got around to it. But you're not a stranger, not really. It's yours if you want it. It'll be a lot cheaper than Stevenbridge, and, in my opinion, a lot nicer, too."

"That sounds fantastic. Can I have a look at it?"

Hayley Bailey beamed a smile. "I'm off in half an hour. If you're ready, we can go then."

"Will I need wellies?"

"No, I don't think so," said Hayley with a grin. "It hasn't rained for days."

Ben had imagined that a converted barn on a farming estate would be muddy, of course, but this was not so. He followed Mrs Bailey's car in his own, in which he had put some overnight luggage because he had a good feeling about this. When they arrived at the house with its converted barn, he was very pleasantly surprised.

The Baileys had recently retired, and sold their fields to a neighbouring farmer. They kept their house, and had resurfaced the driveway, giving themselves enough access and parking space for six vehicles. The house and its attached 'granny flat' were clean and spacious, and there was no farmyard mud for him to wade through.

He parked his car next to what was to become his new residence, and stared at the building, not being able to believe his luck.

"I'll take it," he said to himself, before he even got out of his car.

He thought the rent they were asking for was far too low, and tried to talk them up, but they wouldn't have it. They explained that they were happy with their current income and as long as he kept the place in good condition, they would have a good property which they would still own when he moved on. They had no mortgage to pay and they felt that he had made a good contribution to the community. He didn't understand why they thought that, as he saw himself as an ordinary person doing a job he was paid for. They explained that everybody in the village loved Mark Tyler and his mother, and Ben had given him a lot of time over the last year, and that's why the locals loved him. Hayley actually used the word 'love', which embarrassed Ben a little. He *cared* about a lot of people, but he struggled with big, deep words like 'love'. Nevertheless, he accepted their generous offer and moved his stuff in immediately, making another two journeys in his car to move the rest of his things from his room at the college. He was surprised that it had taken so few journeys to move. He had less, apart from his vast collection of magical props which were to stay in his storeroom at the college, than he thought.

Ben ended up not visiting Emily on that Sunday afternoon after all. Never mind, there was always Monday morning.

Ben was going to like Monday mornings. Emily started her first session of the week by singing to her students, and Ben had no duties at that time, so he took a chair and sat outside her room. This Monday morning was the best possible start, as she sang 'Love Changes Everything'. Ben was sure that the four lads who had signed up for her group were only there because they loved her singing as much as he did (and they would be in a room full of girls, of course). Actually, that couldn't have been completely true, because nobody could love her singing as much as he did.

She had an interesting style, which Ben had spent some time thinking about. He had heard a recording of Michael Ball singing the song, and there was a difference. Firstly, Ball was a man. Secondly,

Ben didn't fancy him. But Michael Ball built up the song to a booming and triumphant-sounding crescendo, while Emily treated it differently. It was as if she was making it more personal. Even the great line "Nothing in the world will ever be the same," which most singers would build up to a grand finish, was different when Emily sang it. When she sang it, it was as if she was standing in front of you, singling you out from the rest of the audience, and singing it, gently and sweetly, from her heart to yours. Ben couldn't imagine a single man in the audience not falling for her when she sang that way. Ben would close his eyes and imagine there was nobody else in the room and she was there, whispering the line to him in her beautiful, musical voice.

In fact, his eyes were still closed when Professor Kennington came up to him. The professor politely waited until Emily had finished singing before speaking.

"I'm not into music much, Ben, but I can certainly appreciate a voice like that," he said.

Ben jumped out of his seat and stood to attention.

"Good morning Professor," said Ben. "Sorry, I was miles away."

"Yes," said the principal. "I noticed. Now that Emily has finished, I wonder if you can spare a few moments."

"Of course." And they walked together out into the grounds of the old building.

Both Ben and the professor liked walking the grounds, which were particularly beautiful in the September sunlight. It was still warm, but not uncomfortably so like it had been for that part of the summer holidays when it hadn't been raining. The sunlight reflecting off of the trees emphasised the many shades of green in creation. Some yellows and browns that were beginning to break through heralded the end of summer and the coming of autumn.

On those few occasions when the two of them actually went walking at the same time, they had developed the habit of patrolling the perimeter, starting at the car park on the east side and walking towards the brook past the large trees.

"I'm glad I found you this morning," said Ben. "I wanted to tell you that I'm moving out of my room in the house."

"Yes," said the professor, as if he had just been distracted by something. "You said you might move out this year."

"Hay… Mrs Bailey has offered me their granny flat."

"And when will you make the move?"

"Yesterday."

"Ah, yes," said the professor. "I'm afraid I often struggle with your use of English. You tell me you are *going* to move out, when you already have, and you tell me you are glad *you've* found *me* when, in fact, *I* found *you*."

Ben looked at his boss, who was smiling. He knew that Michael Kennington struggled with his sense of humour, but sometimes Ben struggled with what the professor found funny, too.

"Anyway," said Ben, after what he hoped was a suitable pause. "You wanted to see me."

"Yes," said the professor. "I wanted to talk to you about one of your students. Martin Kent."

"Yes. Martin. Pleasant lad. Very witty. I think he might be good stand-up comedy material."

"He uses his humour to cover up the fact that he can't read."

Ben was not surprised. He had not guessed that Martin had problems, but it seemed to be the thing that his class had people in it who did not fit the usual 'further education' category of student. He imagined that was because he didn't have a 'further education' type of subject.

"Does he know you're telling me?"

"No. If you could give him some support without making a fuss about it, it would help him. He's embarrassed about it. I have told his other teachers, and they are doing the same."

"Not being able to read doesn't have to be an embarrassing problem," said Ben.

"I know. But he is embarrassed about it, anyway."

"There is not much reading and writing to be done in my class. Sometimes I offer books to read, but it's optional. Sometimes we try to unravel complicated instructions, but I think I can control situations like that so it doesn't single him out."

"That's probably why he chose your class," said the professor. He left Ben at the top of the hill and walked on down to the brook. Ben started making his way back to the main house. He wanted to tell Emily What's-Her-Name about his move to the Bailey's annex. About halfway across the playing field, he stopped still. I should have asked Professor Kennington what Emily's real surname is, he thought.

He managed to get to sit with Emily at lunch, which was something they did occasionally, and he broke the news about his move to her then. She was delighted, and eager to see his new home, which he promised to show her after the college day was over. He tried to look out for Martin, but did not see him that day or the next.

On Wednesday morning, he introduced his class to mentalism.

"I have a number of friends who are mentalists," he said. "It is currently one of the most popular forms of magic, possibly because of performers like Derren Brown. Some people believe that it is different from other forms of magic, because there is more to it than just doing tricks. I'm going to let you decide whether that is the case. Some of you may feel it is the best thing that ever happened to the performing arts, some might end up saying it is simply another 'branch' of magic."

He started by having conversations with some of them to manipulate them into saying certain things, which he then revealed on cards he was carrying in his hands as he went around the room. It was light-hearted with a comedy element, because that was his style ("You don't know what's printed on this card, do you?" "No." "Correct."). However, he then went on to show how reading body language, manipulating choices and what he called 'seriousing up' some basic magic tricks could draw people in to believing you had real mental powers.

"Don't try that on Mark," said John. "He stutters so much it would take hours to get him to say anything." A couple of John's friends laughed at the comment.

Ben had encouraged light-hearted banter, but he was not keen on the way some of the students were treating Mark. In fact, he noticed that his stutter had got worse the last couple of times he had spoken. He also noticed that Mark hadn't actually spoken as much as he normally did. When they first met a year ago, Mark was a shy and withdrawn young man whose confidence Ben had worked hard to build up. It almost seemed as if he was taking a step backwards.

"Let's keep it pleasant, please, lads," he said, but decided not to make any more of it than that. He would have to keep an eye on this situation. They pursued mentalism a little more. Ben noted that many of the new students really took to it, and Martin and Mark, who preferred their entertainment to be a little lighter, stood back a bit for this one.

"Tomorrow," he said at the end of the lesson, "we are going to do something on escapology. I don't want anyone trying to get out of it."

Ben went 'home' for the afternoon. He was enjoying the peace and quiet of being away from the college. As he sat in the big armchair which the Baileys had provided, he thought about lots of things. He thought about Mark and his stutter, and about whether he might have to intervene if some of the other students were bullying him. He thought about getting a television for his new lounge. He thought about the story he was going to tell this afternoon, and he thought about whether he should take the idea of being a regular visitor to the hospice seriously.

He left early in the afternoon. When he got to the hospice, he found the place he had performed on Saturday was also the place where he would tell the story. There were scatter cushions gathered around a little child's seat where he was supposed to sit for his part. He decided to move the seat, because he was going to tell the story standing up, and he moved the cushions back a bit to give himself room to move and so that the smaller children did not have to crane their necks to look up at him. He decided that there was one cushion he might not move. The black and white cat was sleeping on it. The cat opened his eyes, still curled up as if he had not actually woken up, and looked at Ben, as if to challenge him about a cat's right to a cushion. As he (Ben, that is, not the cat) was moving the furniture, Sally came and joined him.

She looked different today. Her dark hair was down, framing her young, round face in an eye-catching way, and the top button of her 'uniform' blouse was undone.

"The children will come in for the story in just a few minutes. Have you got everything you need?"

"Yes, thanks," he said. The way she poured her attention on him was almost distracting. She went to get the children, who reacted positively when they saw it was him. The cat moved off his cushion when the children arrived, and watched from the side of the room like a matron watching over her charges. Harrison and the older lads sat on chairs at the back.

As Ben told his story, he moved about in front of the children, miming actions and making silly gestures whenever he thought it was appropriate. This was a story he used to tell to his Cub Scout group, back in Birmingham, before he ever got into magic.

"In a cornflake factory, somewhere in the middle of the country, at the bottom of a huge pile of cornflakes, there was one cornflake who was different from any other cornflake. He was an *adventurous* cornflake. There he was at the bottom of the pile, wondering why he was surrounded by other, more normal cornflakes, who just sat there going 'boop' like cornflakes do."

At the word 'boop' which he said in a high voice, he hung his hands by his side and swung them like an ape, doing an impersonation of what he thought cornflakes might do in a factory. He got a little laugh out of the younger children. Harrison just sat and watched him politely.

"'What am I doing at the bottom of a pile of cornflakes?' he thought to himself. 'I should be at the top.' So he climbed up through all the other cornflakes, who just sat there, going 'boop', like cornflakes do. Then, he got to the top. He looked around him, and started to explore this new world in the cornflake factory. Then a huge metal scoop came down and whisked him up, dropping him and the other cornflakes into a cornflake box. So there he was, at the bottom of a box of cornflakes.

"'What am I doing at the bottom of a box of cornflakes?' he thought to himself. 'I should be at the top.' So he climbed up through all the other cornflakes, who just sat there, going 'boop', like cornflakes do. Then, a mechanical loader lifted the box he was in and loaded it on to a lorry. Upside-down. So there he was at the bottom of a box of cornflakes.

"'What am I doing at the bottom of a box of cornflakes?' he thought to himself. 'I should be at the top.' So he climbed up through all the other cornflakes, who just sat there, going…" and he paused.

Half of the children said "Boop" in a high-pitched voice. Ben stood up straight, leaving his storytelling pose for a moment.

"Oh," he said, feigning disappointment. "You've heard it before."

Out of the corner of his eye, he got the slightest impression that he saw Harrison smiling. He carried on.

"The lorry was unloaded and stacked on the shelves of the supermarket. Upside-down. So there he was at the *bottom* of a box of cornflakes.

"'What am I doing at the bottom of a box of cornflakes?' he thought to himself. 'I should be at the top.' So he climbed up through all the other cornflakes, who just sat there, going…"

"Boop," said most of the children, including some of the older ones who, after all, could always have claimed they were only encouraging the younger ones. Harrison was quiet, but at least he looked interested.

"…as cornflakes do. Anyway, he got to the top, and a lady came along to do her shopping. She picked up the cornflake box, paid for it, and loaded it into her car. Upside-down."

The children started laughing at the fed-up tone of voice he used when he said 'upside down'.

"So there he was at the bottom of a box of cornflakes.

"'What am I doing at the bottom of a box of cornflakes?' he thought to himself. 'I should be at the top.' So he climbed up through all the other cornflakes, who just sat there, going…"

"Boop." Everyone except Harrison this time.

"…like cornflakes do. Anyway, to cut a short story long, he ended up on the breakfast table. So there he was at the bottom of a box of cornflakes.

"'What am I doing at the bottom of a box of cornflakes?' he thought to himself. 'I should…'"

"…be at the top," said the children, catching on.

"So he climbed up through all the other cornflakes, who just sat there, going…"

"Boop."

"…like cornflakes do. Somebody opened the box, and he saw daylight. Somebody poured the cornflakes into the bowl, and he was the first to leave the box! He landed in the bowl, and all the other cornflakes landed on top of him. So there he was at the bottom of a bowl of cornflakes.

"'What am I doing at the bottom of a bowl of cornflakes?' he thought to himself."

"I should be at the top," they all said. Except Harrison.

"So," continued Ben, "he climbed up through all the other cornflakes, who just sat there, going..."

"Boop."

"...like cornflakes do. Then, from the top of the bowl of cornflakes, he saw the milk. Someone was about to pour it over him. 'Oh, no,' he thought, 'I'll drown!'"

Ben paused for a moment.

"And that's all we've got time for – it's a cereal."

One or two of the older children got it straight away, and the others caught on when the first lot started laughing. He did not want to look directly at Harrison, but he glanced quickly, and was pleased to have made him smile. It was a start.

There was still time to fill, so Sally read them a short story, a 'real' story, as she put it, and then they tidied away ready for the meal. A number of the children wanted to sit with Ben and some asked him to do some magic for them.

"Later, perhaps," he said. Harrison had not left his seat straight away.

"How are you today?" Ben asked him, not sure that this was the best greeting under the circumstance.

"Today has been one of the better days," Harrison said in a flat tone, coldly polite. "Thanks for asking."

They sat together for a couple of minutes, Ben not knowing what to say. When he had sat in silence with Emily, it was a relaxed, comfortable silence. It was one of the many things he loved about being with her. This was nothing like that. He got up after a short while and went to find Sally.

'Little Sally', as some of the patients at the hospice called her, was busy. She always seemed busy. She was lining people up for tea in a bright, clean, open-plan dining area. She would join them to eat, and invited Ben to do so, too. She sat him on a different table from herself, so that the largest number of children could be served, and he got two of the children that asked for him to do some tricks. He had in his pocket the ring and ribbon trick he had brought on Saturday and not got around to showing anyone.

Harrison was on his eight-seater table, too, so he did the one trick and said they would have to wait for more. He tried to include everyone in conversation, aiming for Harrison in particular, but the young lad was little more than polite.

Afterwards, Sally had a word with Ben.

"Would you like to know more about our visitors' programme?"

"Do I get to visit Harrison?"

"Yes, please," she said. "He needs a visitor. His parents live some way away and can only visit on weekends. They both work during the week. He gets a bit lonely. And he has taken to you."

"He doesn't look like he has taken to me."

"He's always like that. In fact, he's worse than that, but he was okay with you."

"Were his parents there on Saturday?" Ben asked.

"No. They make it most Saturdays, but not always."

"If they live so far away, why don't they choose a different hospice?"

Sally leaned towards him and stared with her big, brown eyes into his. She said, slowly, "Because we are very, very good."

"I'd like to give the visitor's programme a try."

"Ah," said Sally, thoughtfully. "That's the thing. Trying is a problem. We get some people who come in here for a bit and then give it up after a short while. That lets the children down. I wouldn't want you to be like that."

"I promise," said Ben, "that when I say try, I will try really hard. But if Harrison doesn't want me, I won't bother him."

"Fair enough," she smiled. "But don't give up on him until you are absolutely sure."

4.

Mark failed to turn up to the lesson on Thursday.

This was serious. Ben was distracted during the whole session and he wondered if the bullying he thought he had witnessed on Wednesday had anything to do with it. Mark was never absent from the lesson. His mother had told Ben that he never gets ill and he would never miss an opportunity to do magic stuff even if he *was* ill.

The class covered more on mentalism, and touched on a bit of escapology as Ben had promised. He also promised a more serious look at the subject next week. The students were good and attentive, which was just as well, as Ben was not at his best. He fancied he might even have taken on Mark's stutter once or twice.

At lunch, Emily joined Ben, who was, for the first time in a while, sitting on his own.

"Hi, Ben," she said, studying his face for a minute. She wanted to say something to him, but it could wait. "How are you?"

"A bit concerned about Mark," he said. "He's not here today."

"Where is he?"

"I don't know. He seems to be off sick."

"I don't remember him being ill before."

"He isn't, normally. In fact, I think he would normally have come in even if he *was*."

"You want to go and visit him."

"Yes, I thought I might go this afternoon."

"Give his mum a ring, first."

"Good idea."

Having made his mind up, he stopped feeling downhearted and looked up at Emily. Who could feel bad when he was seated opposite the most beautiful woman on the planet?

"It's my father's birthday soon," she said. "It's on 1st October, in fact. It's a Saturday this year. He'll be having a big party that day. He says I can invite a guest if I want."

"So, who will you invite?" said Ben, his customary cheek returning.

"Oh, I don't know," said Emily, "that little girl from the hospice with the nice bottom, perhaps?"

Ouch, thought Ben. He ought to know by now that he was not going to win against Emily, but that didn't stop him trying.

"A hospice with a nice bottom?" he said.

"First Juliette's bra, then what's-her-name's bottom. I think you have a one-tracked mind."

"Sally."

"I thought you might remember her name," said Emily, scoring another point. "Anyway, would you like to join me for my father's birthday party in Southampton on Saturday the 1st of October?"

Ben loved the idea of a rock star's party, so he eagerly said 'yes'.

"What should I bring him as a present?"

"You don't have to buy him a present. He likes funny cards, though, but not rude ones."

"I'd like to get him something."

"He collects teddy bears. Small ones."

"You are joking," said Ben.

"No, honestly. There's a series of collectable teddy bears in a shop in Stevenbridge. I'll show you which ones he hasn't got."

"You're winding me up. I'll give him a teddy bear in front of all his rock star friends and end up embarrassed. You're just getting back at me because Sally couldn't help falling in love with me."

Emily laughed, her eyes sparkling. "Ben, I am not winding you up about the teddy bears. He really does collect them."

"So what *are* you winding me up about, then?"

"You'll have to wait and see."

"It really is his birthday?"

"Yes, really."

"And it is on that day? And there will be a party?"

"Yes, and yes," said Emily, "and his friends will be there. And he would love to meet you, and he will appreciate a particular type of teddy bear as a present. Honest."

In the afternoon, after a telephone call to Mark's mother, Ben visited the Tyler house in Lockley village. It was an old cottage on the main road going through the village, although the word 'main' was probably a little grand to describe this well-made but not-too-wide road. The cottage was a short walk from the local post office and not far from the bakery where Ben had looked at a possible flat.

Inside the house was cosy, with lots of books and magazines and un-emptied wastepaper bins. Mrs Tyler was not a tidy person. The living room was cluttered with armchairs, a sofa and a small television set. Mrs Tyler took Ben through to the dining room, which was big and spacious with a large polished dark wooden dining table in the centre of the room, surrounded by eight upright lightly-cushioned chairs. It was much tidier that any of the rest of the house. She called Mark from his room.

He was dressed in an old, scruffy tee shirt that he might well have slept in and his hair was even more untidy than usual. He did not greet Ben with his customary happy greeting.

"Oh, hello," he said.

"Hello, Mark. We missed you this morning."

"We?" said Mark.

"Some of us. Is everything alright?"

"I didn't feel t-too good this m-morning," said Mark, sitting on one of the dining chairs. Ben sat down opposite him.

"I'm sorry to hear it. Flu?"

"N-no."

"Food poisoning? Headache? Ear ache? Nose ache? Bubonic plague?"

"No," said Mark, only slightly cheering up.

"John Stockton?"

Mark did not answer, but his head drooped down even further and he didn't want to make eye contact.

"You know I'm on your side," said Ben.

"I know."

"Has he been having a go?"

"E-every t-time he sees m-me. I'm only in there th-th-three t-times a w-w-week and he's alw-ways there, as if I-I, as if h-he's, h-he's f-following m-me around."

Mark's stutter was worse than ever Ben had remembered it. Whatever John Stockton had said and done, it appeared to have taken apart in one week everything Ben had done in the last year. Ben's anger built up in him. He was ready to throw Stockton off the course immediately, although he was sensible enough not to do that straight away. He wanted to charge into Professor Kennington's room as if it was his fault, and demand that he does something about it. He actually wanted to hit somebody. All of those actions were wrong, of course, and he knew it the moment they crossed his mind. He took a deep breath.

"I need to have a chat with young Mr Stockton," he said to Mark. "May I have your permission to tell him about you having Asperger's Syndrome?"

"W-will it help?"

"Sometimes, when people are properly informed, they aren't so..."

"Obnoxious?" suggested Mark without a stutter.

"Prejudiced," said Ben.

"Or it c-could m-make him w-worse," said Mark.

"It's possible. You know I wouldn't lie to you," said Ben. "Well, I might lie to you, but only if I was showing you a magic trick."

Mark was silent in front of him, still not making eye contact. He was thinking it over.

"We need to make sure that you are happy coming back to the class. Happy, I mean, not just putting up with it. I'm not going to ask you to cope with John Stockton's ignorance – I want to help you deal with it, get rid of it, even, so that you can enjoy your life, lift your head high. I want you to be what you have become over the last year. Don't let him take it away from you."

With some considerable effort, Mark raised his head to look at Ben. There were the beginnings of tears forming in his eyes.

"You really *are* on m-my side, aren't you, Ben?"

"You don't need to ask," said Ben.

"Y-you can t-tell them if y-you want to. B-but I d-don't know if it w-will stop them."

"I will stop them somehow," said Ben, then he worked out what Mark was trying to say. "Them? Is it more than John Stockton?"

"John, Rich, the L-London lot. Th-they are all in it t-together."

Ben thought about it. It was a little early to say, but it was worth asking the rest of the staff about it. There were some students from rich and privileged backgrounds, mixing with 'commoners'. It might have been an enriching experience for everyone concerned. Certainly, that was how Juliette the ambassador's daughter had found it last year. However, John Stockton was coming from a different angle. Perhaps he thought that the people from the village were beneath him.

And for that matter, thought Ben, perhaps he was being a reverse snob himself, assuming that rich people had no time for the likes of him.

"I will speak to John, and see if anything else needs doing," promised Ben. He left Mark feeling a little better, and promising to come back to the college tomorrow. Ben thought that, being a Friday, John himself might not come to the practice session, which was optional. At least, that was probably what Mark was hoping.

Back at the college later that afternoon, a little before tea time, Ben found John Stockton, who was with Rich and a couple of others. He noted that their group consisted of people who were all from well-off London families, and there were no 'commoners' among them. When John looked up at him, he nodded as if to say he'd like a word with him. John presently excused himself from the crowd, and approached Ben.

"Hello, sir," he said, with well-spoken politeness.

"Hello, John. You can call me Ben. I wondered if I could have a word with you."

"Yes, certainly, sir. Ben. When?"

"Now, if you have the time."

John looked around at his friends, as if weighing up how convenient it was for them. He looked a little tense. They shrugged their shoulders, as if to say it was alright with them.

"Okay," he said.

"It's about Mark Tyler. He feels you have been bullying him."

John relaxed, as if he had been caught, but not for the big crime he thought he had been caught for.

"Not exactly bullying. We tease him about his stutter and that, that's all."

"Mark has Asperger's Syndrome."

"I don't think I've heard of it," said John.

"Well, it's a form of autism. It's not exactly a disability. Well, it is, technically. But there's more to it than that. It doesn't work the way most people would imagine a disability. It's different. When people think about autism, they might remember something that they've seen on television, about people who can't talk or go to the toilet on their own, that sort of thing.

"People with Asperger's Syndrome aren't like that. They can be clever, some of them get jobs, and they can look after themselves, although they might need help there. Mostly, people with Asperger's want to relate to the outside world – they are just not very good at it. Your job, John, would be to help them. At the moment, what you are doing is making things worse for Mark, not better."

John thought about it for a while.

"He's just a kid with a disability."

"Listen," said Ben, who had the distinct impression that John had switched off for his clumsy autism lecture. "Mark can't read body language or tell what you're feeling from your tone of voice. People with Asperger's can't read the instinctive, intuitive stuff that most people can. But he's a highly intelligent young man. Like all of us, there are things he can do well, and things he can't. I would hope we all work as a team to support weaker areas."

"So is he just a kid with a disability, or is he normal?"

"He's a normal kid," said Ben, "with a disability."

"This is a college," said John. "It's about education after you've left school. It's for *clever* people. What is it doing entertaining people like Tyler?"

"Mark Tyler is a clever person. He's a chess champion, he builds his own computers, but he…" said Ben, frustrated that nothing he said seemed to get through. "I know your father might have wanted you to go to university or something, but did you choose this particular college to exercise your brain power?"

"No. I chose it because it would teach me to be a better politician. One year here looking at performance skills, then three in Uni studying politics."

"Why here?"

"Because I need to be able to do decent presentations to the people. A good politician should be a good performer, too."

"And magic and politics are similar, of course," said Ben as if he had just had some kind of revelation. "They are both full of deception."

John wisely did not take the bait.

"I believe in our political system," he said. "It's certainly a lot better than those countries who are led by dictators, or places where they train children to fight as soldiers, or have you thrown into prison for your beliefs. I want to be a good leader of men. I imagine you don't vote, then?"

"I always vote, and I encourage other people to vote, too. I don't always like what I get. Would you keep your election promises?"

"I would try to," John replied with some genuine honesty. Unless he was trying out his 'performance skills'. "It's not all cut-and-dry, you know."

"I imagine. How would you go about winning my vote? Performance skills, or something else?"

"I would use my performance skills to get your attention," said John. "I would hope you would agree with my policies, and vote for me."

Ben smiled. In spite of his anger of John's treatment of Mark, he found himself beginning to like this idealistic young lad. He (Ben) was not a fan of political argument, but he was desperately trying to reason out Mark's case for this young man to consider.

"What about *my* policies?"

"What policies?" asked John.

"Do you just make up a load of policies yourself? Do you always go along with your party policies without thinking? *Or do you listen to the people?*"

"People don't know how to run the country. You need training and experience."

"That was the wrong answer."

"What was the right answer?"

"*That* was," said Ben. "Asking for my opinion, not just telling me what yours is. I've got a challenge for you, John. I'm not a supporter. I don't like your attitude towards Mark. But I want to be open-minded. Do something to make me 'vote' for you."

Ben let him get back to his friends. He had the impression, somewhere in the back of his mind, that there was some tension going on between them that had nothing to do with Mark. He made a note to speak to the professor about it. Perhaps Emily had picked something up, too. She was more sensitive than he was about what was going on in the student world.

The following day was 'free study' day. There were no lessons, but the classrooms were all open and staffed so that the students could spend some time working with what they had learned during the week. Mark turned up early and started to work on one of Ben's 'big props'. John turned up a short while later, without any of his friends, and picked up some equipment they had been working on the previous week. He was eager to show Ben what he had learned in his class. After a few minutes, Ben noticed that Mark had slipped out 'for some air'.

John showed Ben how he could make a small yellow handkerchief fly around the room. Then he picked up the soft rope and wrapped it a couple of times around his neck, tying it and pulling it tight. The rope seemed to pass through his neck and out the front, now tied in a knot. He did it smoothly and slickly, standing in exactly the right position so that nobody would see how it was done.

He fiddled with a deck of cards patiently while Ben watched Pamela do some spectacular shuffling moves, constantly turning over the King of Hearts, hiding it in the deck and bringing it out to the top again. Then, when Ben was ready to watch him again, John showed him a trick with sponge balls which seemed to vanish from one hand to various different places in the room. He was quite good for someone who had only been here for two weeks. Ben had to admit, albeit grudgingly, that he was quite a talented young man.

"This practice and performance," said Ben to John when they took a break. "It's all about 'getting my vote', isn't it?"

"Well, I think I should work hard at my subjects, don't you?" came John's clipped answer.

"Even if you don't care about magic, but you are only here to further your political career."

"I signed up for this class. And you said you'd have an open mind."

"I said I'd try," said Ben. "Do you feel that, if you excelled at my class, it would get my vote?"

"If you have a truly open mind, yes."

"But," said Ben, "I don't have a truly open mind. I didn't lie to you, I promised to be as open-minded as possible, but you need to find out what I was looking for in you. And a great magical performance wasn't it."

"What was it?"

"It was all about Mark," said Ben.

"I've got nothing against Mark. He's okay."

"And you won't be bothering him anymore?"

"I never bothered him in the first place. Like I said yesterday, he's just some disabled kid."

Ben was struggling to come up with a response to that, when he was saved by the sound of a bump on the stairs just outside the classroom. Rich Collier appeared at the door.

"Oops," he said with what he obviously hoped was a winning smile. He stumbled into the room and John looked particularly embarrassed by his friend. He went to help him, though.

"Idiot," he whispered to Rich as he helped him stand up straight. "You should have stayed in your room."

"I wanted to practise," said Rich. Ben thought that his words were slightly slurred.

"Go for it," said Ben. "Show me what you've got."

Rich went to unzip his trousers, but John elbowed him in the ribs. Rich tidied his dishevelled clothes and walked in a more-or-less straight line towards the props table. He fiddled through the items on the table and tried making a sponge ball vanish from his hand. In a manner of speaking, he succeeded, in that the ball didn't stay in his hand for long, but fell onto the floor.

Ben made sure he came as close to Rich as possible as he stepped forward to pick up the sponge ball. He wanted to see if he could smell alcohol on his student's breath, but he could not. Perhaps the lad was just larking around.

Mark was at the door looking in. He had obviously seen Rich stumble down the stairs and had decided to return to the classroom to find out what was going on. Ben saw him.

"Care to show them how it's done?" said Ben, holding up two sponge balls for Mark, who came back into the room. He smiled and took the balls, including a third one which Ben slipped him without the others seeing. Mark started a slick, well-practised routine, far superior to John's, which, of course, they would not have been able to work out without knowing about the third ball. Mark never showed more than two at a time.

When he finished, Ben and Pamela started to give him a loud and enthusiastic round of applause, which John and Rich, with reserve, politely joined in. Then Rich seemed to change moods rather suddenly, and he left the room in a sulk, knocking the door frame heavily with his shoulder on the way out as if he had aimed at the opening and missed.

In the evening, the staff met at the Tin Whistle, which was the Lockley village pub. This was a regular Friday night event, where the college staff met to unwind at the end of their week. Sometimes they might discuss any big issues involving work, or on other occasions just enjoy each other's company. Professor Kennington turned up occasionally, but he often left the others to their fun, as he felt the 'boss's presence might be a hindrance rather than a help. As well as the teaching staff, one or two of the domestic staff joined them sometimes. This Friday they were also joined by Gordon Franklin, one of the security guards who was off-duty tonight.

Among the usual range of subjects for chat, the tutors talked about how well, or otherwise, the students from the City were mixing with the others.

"Rich Collier looked drunk this morning," said Ben. "Although, I didn't smell alcohol on his breath."

"Perhaps it wasn't alcohol," said Gordon Franklin.

"Do you think the mix of affluent and, well, not so affluent is not working, then?" asked Bryn Jones, the art teacher.

"What is it like in your class, Bryn?" asked Emily.

"I have mostly the usual suspects," he said. "The posh people of London are looking for something a little more exotic than my painting classes." Bryn had felt a little less than special since the professor had put performing arts into the curriculum.

"The singing class is okay;" said Emily, "but the London girls and the locals don't mix much. There isn't any actual animosity, and they seem polite enough with each other. They just don't make strong friendships."

"Last year Juliette really benefited from going to the Tyler's house for Christmas lunch," said Ben. "Perhaps we could find a way to mix the two types of people."

“Halloween,” said Emily, just getting an idea. “We could have our Halloween show in the village hall instead of the college. Perhaps we could entertain the locals.”

“We need a volunteer to put that to the professor,” said Bryn.

For some reason, everyone looked at Ben.

5.

Ben and Emily went to the teddy bear shop in Stevenbridge on Saturday afternoon. It was a convenient time to go as Ben wanted to visit Harrison at teatime and both of them were performing at the Shining Star nightclub in the evening.

The teddy bear shop was, surprisingly, called 'The Teddy Bear Shop'. It was a tiny shop in the middle of a row of shops just off the high street. It was long and thin from the outside, and equally long and thin on the inside. You would have to know it was there to find it, which must have been hard on them for passing trade. All the stock was down one side of the elongated shop, with a counter by the door. There were six or seven customers in the shop when they walked in. That effectively made the shop crowded.

The teddy bears were mostly of one type, soft and fluffy with sewn-on clothes, about large enough to fit on one open hand. There was a huge collection of different clothes and shades of fur, and they seemed to represent different nationalities and professions.

"And your dad collects these?"

"Oh, yes," said Emily. "I won't let him come in here, in fact, because he would simply buy the place up. He tells me what to look for, and I get him one or two every now and then. At the moment, he wants a fisherman."

She looked in the place she thought she would find one. Ben, in the meantime, found a set of rock band teddy bears, complete with drums, guitars and a saxophone. He imagined that Emily's father would already have that one. One thing that caught his eye, however, was a smartly-dressed teddy bear with bow tie and magic wand. There was a top hat sewn into one paw with a tiny white rabbit poking out of it.

"Would he like a magician?" asked Ben.

Emily, with a fisherman teddy bear in her hand, came over to join him.

"I've not seen that one before," she said. "It would be perfect."

So he bought the magician, and she bought the fisherman. The church tea room was closed when they got to it, so they had a short break at a rather crowded 'normal' coffee house, before Ben went to the hospice, and Emily made her way to the nightclub to have a chat with the owner, who was an old friend. They were both going to meet there later and have something proper to eat before their respective performances.

Sally was delighted to see him at the hospice. Her hair was tied up and her uniform fully buttoned up this time. She had a cup of tea in her hand, from which she was about to pour some into a saucer.

"Hello, Ben," she said. "I wasn't expecting you."

"I hope it's not inconvenient," said Ben. "I just wanted to say 'hello' to Harrison."

"That's great," said Sally. "His parents aren't here this weekend, so it's a good time to visit."

"I'm not sure I'll be able to make every weekend," said Ben. "I was thinking Wednesdays would be the best time to visit."

"Yes, Wednesdays would be good," said Sally. "Harrison's mum and dad normally make the weekends. We put them up on Saturday nights here so they don't have to pay expensive hotel bills. Sometimes they even take him out to the cinema or something, if he feels up to it."

"You're very accommodating."

"I could be," said Sally, quietly.

"Sorry?"

"I said, 'it's important to look after the whole family'," she said. She went back to pouring the tea from the cup into the saucer. She looked up at him watching her, and decided it would be a good idea to give him an explanation.

"It's for Seefer."

"Seefer?"

"The ship's cat," she said. "He likes tea." She put the saucer down next to the entrance desk, where the black and white cat, Seefer, stalked it for a moment before starting to lap it up.

Harrison looked miserable in his room. Perhaps, Ben thought, he got miserable when his parents weren't there.

"Mind if I come in and say 'hello'?" asked Ben with a cheerful smile. Harrison nodded, almost imperceptibly. Ben came in and looked around his room.

"Do you read much about history?" asked Ben, thumbing, apparently idly, through the young lad's collection of books.

"No, not really," said Harrison.

"I love history," Ben said. "Did you know that Alexander the Great invented the first wristwatch? It wasn't a real wristwatch, of course. At least, it wasn't the kind of thing we would recognise as a wristwatch."

"Wristwatch?" said Harrison, just slightly suspicious.

"Yes. It was made of strips of cloth, soaked in… you see, Alexander the Great never lost a battle. But, strangely enough, he nearly always used the same strategy. It was customary in those days for the general to lead the battle from the centre of the front line. Alexander didn't do that. He led from the right-hand side. All his superior cavalry, called 'the companions', were there with him. He would charge, with them, towards his opponent's weaker flank, beat them thoroughly and easily, and then join the next part of the enemy's line from the side. By then, the rest of his army would have already engaged them. It would not take long for them to be routed or destroyed, so they would combine forces and take on the next lot, and so on.

"The thing is, it all needed careful timing. Without Alexander being in the centre, his junior officers needed to know what to do and when they should do it. They couldn't shout orders, because sometimes the battle line could be as much as five miles long. So they planned it all beforehand, and timed when they should move. Alexander developed a timepiece made of strips of cloth soaked in various plant extracts so that it would change colours as it dried out. At each certain colour, the army would manoeuvre as they were instructed.

"Obviously, they couldn't hold the cloth in their hands, because they had swords, spears, shields, and half of them were riding horses. So they tied the strips around their wrists so they could see the signal to move as the cloth dried. Hence: wristwatch.

"Of course, they didn't call it a wristwatch."

"What did they call it?" said Harrison.

"Alexander's Rag Time Band."

Harrison smiled, which was his version of laughing. Ben had been afraid that he might not have heard of the song 'Alexander's Ragtime Band', so the joke might fall flat. But Harrison seemed to enjoy the story, as much as Ben could tell from the worn-out expression that was normally there. It seemed, for a moment, as if the tiredness began to leave his eyes. Ben was sorry he could not stay very long, but he had to go and take Emily for a meal before both of them performed at the Shining Star that night.

During the week, Ben talked to the professor about the idea of having the Halloween show in the town, to enable the Londoners among them to see a bit of country life. He explained that he felt there was a gap between the rich and not-so-rich students at the college, and this might help strengthen relationships. Professor Kennington had heard that there were one or two small concerns, and was pleased to organise the event with the town council.

He was quite shocked, however, to hear from Ben that Mark had been bullied, and that Ben felt he had to take action to intervene. The professor was very fond of Mark, and would not tolerate him being treated badly. He was happy with the action that Ben had taken and so he would do no more than keep an eye on the situation.

On his Wednesday lesson, he made careful note of any interaction between John and Mark. There was nothing particular, either positive or negative, that he could identify. However, there seemed to be a little atmosphere of unpleasantness. John and his friends didn't exactly do or say anything to Mark, but they just didn't seem to accept him. One of the characteristics of Asperger's Syndrome was not being able to read body language, so if they did not make it obvious that they were having a go, Mark would not notice it. That was alright for Mark, but not for Ben.

Ben got some handcuffs out of his box. It was an unusual-looking set, consisting of an elongated loop of metal about 25cm long and half as wide, with chains and small padlocks on the ends. He asked the nearest students to help him get into them by padlocking the chains to his wrists as tightly as they could. He made out that they were cutting off his circulation as they pushed and shoved to make the first padlock tight, then, as they picked up the second padlock, he was already out of the first set of chains.

As the helpers sat down, he explained.

"Escapology is an art associated with magic, but there are differences. You can get escapology-related magic tricks, of course, but some sets of handcuffs, straightjackets, boxes and so on, are real. It's not always a gimmick, not a trick, sometimes it is just skill."

He put the chain handcuffs back in its box, and smiled.

"Possibly."

After the lesson, Martin stayed behind with Mark and Ben.

"Can I have a word?" he asked.

"Certainly."

He glanced at Mark.

"In private."

"Mark, don't worry about tidying up. I'll see you upstairs for lunch in a minute or two."

"Can I s-stay here?" asked Mark. He did not want to go upstairs where John and his friends would be in the dining hall without Ben by his side. Ben had to think for a moment.

"Yes, of course you can. Would you tidy things up for me in the storeroom? Martin wants a word in private, so we'll go over here."

Ben took Martin to the other side of the classroom, but he was concerned about Mark not wanting to roam the grounds without an escort. He did not know what kind of strategy he could form to help Mark build up his confidence again and he doubted that he could enlist John's help to undo the damage he had done.

"I wanted you to know, because you help people," said Martin, nodding over to the storeroom where Mark was working. He spoke in a very quiet voice, his tone far from the comedian he presented in class. "I can't read."

"Do your other tutors know?" asked Ben. That was a dishonest question, of course. He should have asked if Martin had *told* his other teachers. Ben already knew that they all knew.

"You're the first one I've told. Mrs Cleese doesn't need to know; we don't ever read or write in her class."

"You dance?" said Ben, incredulous.

"You get tied up in straightjackets, mister, so don't have a go at me!" said Martin, his comical side coming out again.

"You belong in the last century," said Ben, "you are the perfect music hall star."

"I hear it's coming back," said Martin.

"I think you should tell Mrs Cleese," suggested Ben.

"That music hall is coming back?"

"About your reading problems. Tell all of your tutors. If they know, they can help, and nobody will look down on you. Lots of people these days can't read, and in a college like this, it's not going to be a problem. The professor might be able to help, too."

"He knows, of course."

"I know," said Ben.

"What?"

"The professor," said Ben. "He knows everything." He hoped that covered his slip. "Look, if you want me to keep it a secret, that's fine. But I wouldn't want you to keep it from the tutors. You're not in Miss Darkchilde's class as well, are you?"

"Oh, yes," said Martin, grinning. "I can't sing, but I just like to watch her performances. If I wasn't in her class, I would have to sit outside her room and listen from there like a lovesick puppy."

Ben was found out! Should he get angry at the young lad for passing that comment, or would it be better to make a joke about it? For that matter, was *he* the joke?

"No, you can't do that," said Ben. "The lovesick puppy award is mine."

"No, I'm not in her class, I'm in Mr Jones' art class. We have to read up on artists. I was hoping it would just be about painting."

"Are you any good? Mr Jones would not have a problem with your reading skills if you were a good artist."

"Not really. I enjoy doing it, but I don't think I'm ever going to sell a painting."

"If you like, I'll speak to him. Try to get him in a good mood."

"On a Friday night, down the pub?" Martin asked.

"Tell me, do you know Xander Harris and Shelley Hickman?" asked Ben.

"Yes, why?"

"You seem to be well-informed about my activities. They know everything. They have their fingers on the student pulse, so to speak."

"They certainly seem to," agreed Martin. "They know stuff you and I don't know, too."

“Like what?”

“Not sure,” said Martin, “but something is going on, and they’re trying to deal with it.”

“Among the students?”

Mark came out of the storeroom and called across to them.

“It’s dinner time,” he said. “We don’t want to be late.”

“No,” answered Ben. “We don’t. Not again.”

The rest of this conversation, wherever it was heading, was lost. Over the next couple of days, he discovered that Martin had, in fact, told his other tutors about his reading problems. Ben managed to speak to Bryn Jones, and Bryn had been sympathetic, in spite of believing that Martin would have less trouble “if only he was straight up about it in the first place.”

Ben looked for Xander and Shelley, the founts of all knowledge in the student world, but did not see them around over the next two days. He kept a close eye on Mark, who had no particular trouble from John Stockton and his friends, but he was still unsure about that situation. Neither John nor Rich turned up to his practice session on Friday and the other tutors did not say anything about any further incidents of bad behaviour or apparent drunkenness on behalf of Rich.

Emily knocked on Ben’s door at 7 o’clock on Saturday morning. Ben was ready. He was rather looking forward to meeting a real, live, albeit retired, rock star.

“We’ll be leaving to come back after breakfast on Sunday,” Emily had told him.

“We could be home in time for lunch, then,” Ben had said. “I could visit Harrison in the afternoon.”

“No, I’m afraid not,” said Emily. “My dad rarely has breakfast before noon on a Sunday. When I say ‘after breakfast’, I mean early in the afternoon. We’ll be back by teatime.”

Ben loaded his small overnight bag into Emily’s car and she drove them South. It had rained a rather cold rain over the last couple of days, but today the sun shone and it was a pleasant journey. It could have been hail and thunder and Ben the ‘lovesick puppy’ would have found it a pleasant journey in Emily’s company. He told her about Martin’s remark and Emily laughed.

A lot.

For several miles.

"Martin seems to think that there's something going on among the students, and Xander and Shelley are trying to deal with it," he said when he thought she had calmed down.

"The student soap opera," she said.

"The what?"

"The student soap opera. There is always something going on. I think this one might be about the nature of the party life. The professor won't allow the consumption of alcohol on the premises, the tutors all go to the local pub, so the students have nowhere to drink."

"Something they knew before choosing Lockley as a college."

"True enough," said Emily, "but will that stop them? They are nearly all over 18, and they should be allowed to act like grown-ups."

"I don't think that Rich Collier was acting like a grown-up the other day."

"Yes, and Juliette doesn't have a high opinion of him, either. She may be one of the rich kids, but she is squarely on the side of the locals."

"Is the 'locals versus Londoners' problem serious?"

"I don't know," said Emily. "Perhaps that's what Shelley and Xander are trying to deal with."

Southampton, or at least the part of Southampton that Emily's father 'Johnny Darkchilde' lived in, was an affluent and pleasant place. There were wide, tree-lined streets – typical 'leafy suburbs'. Her father's house was quite large with a paved driveway big enough to park four cars. The house itself was painted white with a weather-proof sanded textured paint. It was not a mansion, but was a spacious, pleasant place for a retired rock musician to live on his own.

Emily knocked on the door, because she no longer had a key, and he was there in a second or two, as if he had been waiting for them. He was a tall man with short, tidy fair hair that was very similar in colour to Emily's. His skin was not dark like Emily's, as Ben had expected. In fact, it was quite pale, hardly even tanned in spite of his living in a seaside town at the end of a reasonably warm English summer. He was dressed smartly, although he did not wear a tie.

He gave Emily a fatherly hug and shook Ben's hand. His handshake was firm and polite. Inside the house, just like the outside, there was no sign of the 80's rock star. The living room was well-decorated with a certain reserve. There were no rock memorabilia. In fact, there was hardly any memorabilia at all, apart from a few pictures from the 'old days' of him with a few friends on one wall. The fireplace framed a smart gas fire and a rich red wooden mantelpiece. On the mantelpiece, there were just two items – a small wooden cross on a stand to the left, and a photograph of an outstandingly beautiful dark-haired Asian woman on the right which Ben guessed was Emily's mother. Ben could see that with his fair skin and her dark, they had produced Emily's fabulous golden complexion. He looked at the picture for a moment, wondering what had happened to her mother. Was it his wife? Was she still alive? He berated himself for not asking before now.

Against the far wall, the one without the window, there were two large glass cabinets. One of them was full of the collectable teddy bears that Emily had told him about, and the other was not quite so full, but not far off. There must have been more than a hundred teddy bears there altogether. Sure enough, the rock band was there, pride of place on the top shelf of the full cabinet. Ben was relieved that Emily had told him the truth about his collection.

Ben caught Emily glancing in his direction. She had said she was winding him up, and Ben had been looking for the 'how'. This was it. She knew his image of her father was long hair and wild parties. But Darkchilde senior was not like that at all, and Emily had never said.

Johnny Darkchilde was a polite and pleasant man, who expertly kept Ben feeling included, whilst at the same time spending some quality father-daughter time with Emily. At one point, Emily went out to the kitchen to make them all some tea. Ben seized his chance.

"So what's your real surname?" Ben asked, hoping he was sounding natural and conversational.

"Rumpelstiltskin," Johnny Darkchilde answered.

"I beg your pardon?" said Ben.

"Emily, which, by the way, is her real name, has told me that she hasn't told you her real surname yet. She suggested you might try and get the information out of me, so she asked me to go along with her little scheme. Personally, I think she's being horrible to you. But I never could say no to her, so I'm not going to tell you our name either."

He grinned that big friendly grin, and the sparkle in his eye matched something Ben had seen often enough in his daughter's eyes.

"Sorry," he said, then, as an afterthought, "If it helps, my first name isn't Johnny, either, although all my neighbours call me that. It's Eric."

"Eric Darkchilde."

"No, Johnny Darkchilde. Eric something else. Good try, though."

The dinner party that evening was a pleasant, casual affair with no loud music and lots of middle-aged and older friends around to help Johnny/Eric celebrate his birthday. Ben was introduced as 'Emily's guest', and one or two had heard he was a magician, so they asked him to show them something. He did a trick or two, but politely did not allow it to dominate the party.

None of 'Johnny's' old friends from his rock star days wanted to talk about the past, even when Ben asked them, and, as a lot of them knew Emily from when she was a baby, they were eager to learn about what she was doing these days. One older man (older than her father, Ben guessed) said that he had once seen her perform at the Shining Star in Stevenbridge, and complimented her on her singing talents.

It was approaching midnight and there was no sign of the party finishing, when people started to give their presents to Darkchilde senior. Ben was surprised that they were all small gifts, like a pen or a paperback novel. It seemed that Johnny didn't like to make a fuss. He was particularly delighted with Ben's teddy bear magician, saying he would have to rearrange one of his cabinets to give it a place of honour.

The room that Ben was given for the night was spacious and comfortable, and he slept late into Sunday morning, but not as late as the others. He got up and wandered the house for an hour or so before they made an appearance.

As Emily had predicted, it was nearly two in the afternoon on Sunday before they were on their way home. On the journey, Ben asked Emily if it was alright to do a little diversion so that he could visit Harrison. She said that would be fine, but she said she wanted to get an early night, so not to be too long.

When they got there, they discovered that Sally didn't work there on Sundays. Emily didn't seem disappointed at that. Ben knocked on Harrison's door.

"Hello, Harrison. I'm just passing and I thought I'd pop in and say 'Hello'."

"Hello," said Harrison, looking past him at Emily.

"How are you today?" said Ben.

"I'm a bit tired. Mum and Dad came this weekend, and we've done lots of stuff. They took me out yesterday. I think I'll regret it tomorrow." He didn't stop looking at Emily.

"This is Emily Darkchilde."

"Darkchilde?" said Harrison. "What a cool name."

"That's her stage name," explained Ben. "Her real name is…" and he looked at her for confirmation.

"…a secret," she said.

Harrison continued to look at Emily. Ben had discovered that Harrison was not twelve years old, which was how his illness had made him look, but rather, he was fourteen. He certainly had a fourteen-year-old's healthy interest in looking at beautiful women.

"Is she your girlfriend?"

"Yes," said Ben, "so hands off."

Harrison smiled.

"She's nice," he said. "You should marry her."

He didn't look into her face for the whole journey home.

6.

John, Rich and a couple of their friends were handing out leaflets in the cellar. Ben had been in his storeroom preparing 'today's secret weapon', as he called it, when they all started to come in, and there was a buzz among the students. Some were making jokes, some were starting serious discussions, and some were ripping up the leaflets, which got an angry response from John Stockton.

Ben came out to see what all the fuss was about. They were all looking at the leaflets, and there was the start of some lively debate.

"May I see?" said Ben, making a point of taking the leaflet that Martin was holding in his hand.

"'Vote for John Stockton?'" he read out loud. "What's this about?"

"I'm in the creative writing class," said John. "Mr Hunter said that, as there are so many children of politicians in the class, we should try to create a campaign. Rich and I are creating one for me."

"That sounds brilliant. Another opportunity to make me vote for you, John. Although, it wouldn't have been a bad idea if you had asked first before campaigning in my class."

Rather than apologise, John looked daggers at Ben.

"I'm supporting this," Ben continued, waving the leaflet in his face. "I think it's a great idea, and if you had asked, I would have said yes. But at the *end* of the lesson, not right now. Can we put all the leaflets away so that I can introduce our subject for the day?"

He turned to the door of the storeroom and nodded to Mark for his assistance. Mark helped him wheel out a number of large boxes and other such devices, including a guillotine and a rack of long, shining swords. The class quickly sat in their seats and waited for the show. John sat where Mark would normally sit, but Martin signalled for Mark to sit next to him on the second row.

"Pamela," said Ben. "I'm sorry to do this to you, but it's customary for magicians to have a beautiful assistant. I only have two to choose from. I have already used Juliette, and John is just not beautiful enough, so would you help me, please?" John did not find the comment amusing. Perhaps, after rebutting him at the start of the session, Ben should have picked on someone else for the 'beautiful' remark.

"Ladies and gentlemen, may I present my beautiful assistant, Pamela."

Pamela made much fuss of bowing to the audience and curtseying, while Ben put some music on. He then took her hand and led her to the first box, which was open-topped and big enough for her to get into. It was made of hard plastic, coloured and textured to look like wood from a distance. It had slits in the sides, but not the front and back. He whispered instructions for her to stand inside the box and pose for the audience again. He took a lid and asked her to curl up inside the box.

"It's a bit tight," she said.

"Shh," he responded, "we're doing a performance." This remark got a giggle from the audience, although most of them were prepared to make allowances for what obviously, to them, appeared to be lack of rehearsal on Pamela's part. At least, even if Pamela was not fully rehearsed, they hoped Ben knew what he was doing.

Pamela got down into the box and Ben put the lid on it. Before he could fasten the metal clips at the side, Pamela popped her head up a little as she adjusted herself, pushing the lid up a bit. Ben paused and waited while she settled and then went about fastening the lid on the box.

Then, as the music built up, he pulled a sword from the rack and swished it about a bit for dramatic effect, before easing it into the box. Then he pulled another sword, and another, each time pushing it into the box where Pamela had just squeezed herself. Four more swords went in before the music began to fade. Realizing that the music was running out, Ben rushed the eighth and final sword, and it seemed to get stuck, so he gave it a hard push.

From inside the box, Pamela screamed and a trickle of blood started to come out of one of the sword holes. The shocked audience sat in stunned silence, while Ben hurriedly pulled out all the swords in an untidy fashion, throwing them across the floor in his haste and panic. Mark slipped out of his chair to turn the music off.

Ben pulled the lid of the box off as fast as he could, and Pamela, all smiles, popped out of the box with a triumphal and well-over-exaggerated pose. The audience started breathing again, some of them laughing, and one or two remembering to applaud.

When the commotion died down, Ben let them in on the secret that Pamela, who was normally slick and well-rehearsed in her own, more close-up area of card magic, had to practice the clumsy act for nearly two hours on the previous Friday in order to convince the audience that she wasn't in on the trick.

"And it was worth every minute of it," she said. "I just wish I could have seen your faces."

"Today," said Ben, "we are going to look at big props."

Ben was happy that Pamela had done such a great job, because the beautiful assistant job had gone to the good-looking Juliette far too much and Pamela's moment in the limelight had obviously given her confidence a decent boost.

"Pamela's Oscar-winning performance will show that, even with a big prop, you still need a performance to make it look good. When I stuck the swords in, you all had an idea that you knew what was going to happen. When she screamed and squeezed the fake blood through the hole, all of a sudden you were transported into the realm of the unexpected."

It was usual for Ben to explain a trick – after all, it was a magic class, but with big props he did not like to give too much away. If any of the class wanted to perform this trick, they would have to shell out a lot of money, and then they would have the right to know how it worked. Rather, he talked a lot about 'bigging it up', making the showpiece worth the investment of time and money.

He allowed Mark to show his performance of the guillotine trick which he had developed last year, with Juliette as a helper. Ben felt that the two young ladies were going to get a lot of attention this year, and wondered if there was a way around that problem, other than putting John and Rich in dresses.

Some of the box props he had involved getting people into fairly tight spaces, so using a slim girl was usually the practice. There was also the misdirection angle. Having a beautiful woman on stage gave the audience something to look at when the magician himself might not have wanted them to examine his own actions too closely. As Ben told them, the women in the audience would want a sparkly dress like that, and the men would want a woman like that! However, as there were some slight or athletically flexible men in the class, Ben would try to use them in the future. It wasn't going to stop him calling the young men his 'beautiful assistants', anyway.

John was impatiently patient throughout the lesson, not as drawn in as the others were. Ben noticed this, and put it down to his dislike of Mark getting to do the guillotine routine, although it was more likely that his enthusiasm for his political 'campaign' outweighed his interest in magic. At the end of the lesson, he gathered his friends around him and showed them his voting papers.

The rest of the class started to leave. A thought struck Ben. He didn't like John very much. He had taken a side in the locals versus Londoners battle, and that was wrong. He wanted to do something to make peace between them.

"Hang on a minute, everyone," he said out loud to the ones that were leaving. "I shut John up earlier, so I think it's only fair if I gave him his platform now. Let's all have a look at his leaflet and give him a chance to get our vote."

That didn't stop one or two from leaving anyway, possibly because they might not have been interested in politics, or maybe they simply didn't like John's arrogance. But others stayed, and commented on his 'vote for me' leaflet.

Ben had a good look at it. It was words in black on a sheet of white paper, saying very little more than 'Vote for John Stockton' and a few fairly bland words about him. One or two of the students commented that colour and different fonts would enhance the attractiveness of the leaflet. They drifted upstairs, and John and Rich stayed behind for a few minutes to pick up the abandoned leaflets.

"Would you mind a comment from me?" asked Ben.

"It's your class," said John, shrugging his shoulders. Now what did that mean, thought Ben. Does he mind a word, or would he not care one way or the other?

"I mean, would you *mind*? Would it be helpful, or would you ignore anything I said?"

"You tell me," said John. "Would you be helpful?"

"I would try."

"Okay. You gave me my bit at the end of your lesson. It's only fair I give you your turn now." That was not exactly the attitude Ben wanted, but it would have to do for now.

"You have some friends who would support you because they are your friends. You don't need to convince them. There are others who just don't like you. I'm sure that can't be helped, nobody is going to be loved by everyone. But what about the floating voter?"

"He wants you to campaign in the swimming pool," said Rich, but John was listening.

"There are people, and perhaps I am one of them, who haven't made their minds up yet. Maybe your leaflet could target people like that. Say something more than 'vote for me'. Tell me *why* I should vote for you."

"Will I convince you?"

"I don't know," said Ben. "To be honest, I think you might have a hard job. But I did promise to try and be open-minded."

"Okay," said John, obviously thinking this through seriously. "I'll give it a go."

Ben was still not sure he had made the peace between them, but if John was going to go into politics, he would need to try to understand ordinary people, not just impress his mates. Mark stood by Ben as John and Rich left for lunch. Rich glanced back at Ben as if he was completely unable to work him out.

The regular foursome met for lunch. Ben and his star pupil, Mark, sat at a table with Emily and her star pupil, Juliette. Ben liked to think of this as a regular foursome but, in fact, it did not happen as much as he might have wanted. They chatted a lot as none of them had a lesson to go to that Wednesday immediately after lunch. Ben noticed that Emily made a special effort to talk to Mark, although she normally struggled with people who had Asperger's Syndrome. There had been a chill in the air signifying the end of summer, and the kitchen staff had decided to put a hot stew on the menu rather than the usual lunchtime fare of burgers and salad stuff.

When most of the students had moved off to whatever they were going to do next, Ben asked Juliette about the 'locals versus Londoners' situation. She was, after all, from a rich and well-connected family in London.

"I have always been brought up to think the best of people, and, my father having been an ambassador, to think about making peace between people."

"But you have an opinion," said Ben.

"Which I keep to myself," said Juliette with the politest of smiles.

"I'd like to think that you and I have a stronger relationship than tutor to student," said Ben. "I have seen you 'let loose', so to speak. I'm asking you for your honest opinion, in spite of your habit of cool and calm."

Juliette thought for a moment before replying.

"Rich is a spoiled brat and John is full of himself. Nobody else is good enough for them. There isn't really a 'locals versus Londoners' situation at all; there is only Rich and John against the rest of the world."

"They've got their group of friends," said Ben.

"They've got their followers, their little toadies who will do whatever they want. You know in these musicals like Grease where there's a ringleader, some cheerleader or rich girl who is all vain and has a load of other girls at her beck and call? Well John Stockton is like that, except that it's worse – he's not a girl."

Then the lights went out.

It was the middle of a fairly light day, so the place wasn't exactly plunged into darkness, but in the kitchen, which had no windows, all the working lights and ovens and water heaters and ventilators went off. A fire alarm over-ride sounded somewhere in the building. A little while later, Ben heard that the computers had gone off in the computer room (which was normally open for student use) as well as the office, where the professor's part-time secretary was working at the computer. The groundsman, who also passed as a handyman around the site, was not in today, so Bryn, who was probably the most practical of the teaching staff, had a look at the fuse box. It only took him a few moments to discover that nothing was wrong.

"I-it could b-be the c-computers," suggested Mark. "I think the c-computers are all at-tached to the rest of the electrics. If s-someone crashed them, then it m-might be p-possible for everything to b-blow."

"Can you have a look at them?" asked Ben, and Mark agreed. Mark was a computer expert. He had built his own computers at home during the summer holidays, and his devotion to computers was almost as fierce as his commitment to magic.

Ben took him through to the main computers, where he spent half an hour or so looking at various systems. He discovered that not everything was computer controlled. The shower blocks weren't, or the upstairs room lights, all of which were still working. In fact, it was the computers and the kitchen that had had gone, along with the fire alarms. He fixed them quite quickly, and everything started up again.

In the afternoon, Ben and Mark were sitting back in the dining room, sipping an afternoon tea. This is to say, Ben had tea, and Mark had cola. John Stockton approached them.

"May I join you?" said John.

"Certainly," said Ben without thinking. Then, a second or two too late, he *did* think, and looked at Mark. "If it's alright with you?"

Mark shrugged, but didn't look too happy. John sat opposite Ben, and leaned towards him, speaking in a low voice.

"I'm not sure who to go to, so I'm hoping you are the right person."

"About what?" asked Ben.

"I think it was me who crashed the system after lunch."

"How?"

"I'm not sure, but I was working on my voting paper. I wanted to improve it, but I'm not very good with computers. I tried to get into the programmes to help me get a coloured layout, and then the whole thing went down."

"Mark?" Ben turned to the computer genius.

"It's un-unlikely that it was you," said Mark. "G-getting into a p-programme wouldn't c-crash the whole s-system."

"I heard it was you who fixed it. What happened?"

"S-something overloaded," said Mark. "The k-kitchen p-people think it was b-because they used the b-big ovens for th-the first t-time s-since the s-summer."

"Our hot meals have been cooked in the older ovens up to now," said Ben. "But they were being used for tonight's meal, so the kitchen staff turned on the new oven for our hotpot today."

John sat back in his chair and relaxed. It was not his fault after all. Ben was interested that John should take his worries to him. Perhaps the animosity between them was not as great as he thought.

"Look," he said, "why don't you ask Mark to help with your leaflet? He's really good with computers, and he can make your designs come to life."

"It's okay, thanks," said John, getting up to leave.

"You're big enough to use some disabled kid to help you, aren't you, John?" said Ben, probably ruining any chance of improving their relationship any further.

"I'm doing it right now, now that the computers are up and running again," said John. Ben looked at Mark.

"I'll help if you w-want," said Mark, who did not know how to hold a grudge. Ben wondered, as Mark and John got up to leave together, if they needed a chaperone. He gulped down the rest of his tea, which was now cold, and returned the cup to the counter. Mrs Bailey (Ben still couldn't say her first name without wanting to laugh) took it from him with a polite 'thank you'. She looked at Mark and John leaving together.

"I thought they didn't like each other," she said.

"This could be the start of a beautiful friendship," said Ben.

"Really?" asked Mrs Bailey.

"To be honest, I doubt it," said Ben. He walked outside into the afternoon air. He wasn't going to go very far, in case Mark needed a bit of support dealing with John.

Across the front field, he saw Shelley and Xander together. He had not thought that the two of them would link up. It was true that both of them had lots in common. They both had eyes and ears on what was going on in the college, and they were, in their own different ways, well-liked among the students in general. Xander was a bit of a ladies' man, at least in his own opinion, and Shelley was always looking for ways to help and support people. He was planning on running across to talk to them, but they were moving out of sight behind the trees, so he decided to give them a bit of privacy. Anyway, it wasn't far off time to go to Stevenbridge and visit Harrison. He thought he might just leave it a few minutes longer and then stop at the computer room before he left.

Emily was at the door of the computer room.

"They're getting along fine," she said when he got there. "You go. I'll be around, just in case."

Ben got to St Mark's hospice while Sally was telling the story, so he stood at the back and listened. It was a story for younger children from a book full of pictures, so he imagined that Harrison was not going to be that impressed. He joined the lad for tea afterwards and asked him.

"I watched some of the children," Harrison said. "And they liked it." He did not sound enthralled, however. "I slept a lot today. I can't sleep now, though. I probably won't sleep well tonight, either. I don't if I sleep too much during the day. I am so bored."

"Well, the children wouldn't like what I heard today. It was on the news, about the soldiers that got lost in the desert. They all thought they were going to die because they had no food or drink. Luckily, the captain had field glasses and could see that, just over the next couple of sand dunes, there was a bacon tree."

"A bacon tree?" said Harrison. His mouth was curled in a bit of a smile because he was trying to guess what was coming next.

"That's just what his men said," said Ben. "'A bacon tree? There's no such thing!' they said. 'It must be a mirage.'

"'No,' he said, 'mirages have blonde hair and long legs. It's definitely a bacon tree!' Well, the men thought that the captain had been touched by the desert sun, so he said he would prove it. He sent a small scouting party to find out whether or not there was really a bacon tree over the next couple of sand-dunes. They went out of sight over the first dune, then up and over the second."

Ben paused for a moment, as if he was waiting to see what happened.

"Then they came back. Only something terrible had happened. They were cut and bruised, with arrows and spears sticking out of their flak-jackets, and their arms and legs.

"'You idiot,' they said to the captain. 'That wasn't a bacon tree, it was a ham bush!'"

Ben walked with Harrison for a while after they had eaten, and he talked about his favourite writers, the comedy ones. He said that sometimes he read late into the night, and sometimes he didn't feel like reading at all. The stories, even the funnier ones, didn't make him laugh, but he liked feel-good stories where things ended well.

Ben had not read most of Harrison's favourites, and he was not sure he would have the time to read what the lad was recommending. But Harrison was beginning to open up a little, which felt good. When it was time to watch some television, Sally took Ben aside.

When she stood quite close to him, he realised how short she was. She was almost as short as Pamela, but a little slimmer and very shapely. Ben particularly noticed her figure when she did that thing with her buttons.

"Harrison actually talked to you today," she said, her big brown eyes once again paying him much attention.

"He *normally* talks to me."

"An actual conversation, I mean," she said. "Back and forward. You must be a real magician."

Ben smiled down at her. "I cast a spell on him."

"Not just him," she said, wistfully.

"What?" he said.

"I'm sorry to say that the children want another cornflake story," she said in a mock exasperated manner.

"Next Wednesday?" he suggested, and she agreed with her 'it's a date' line. He made a mental note to tell Emily that he had arranged a date with Sally, but he would try to find exactly the right time to tell her for the best comedy effect. Possibly when she wasn't near any heavy or sharp objects.

On the way home, he thought about Harrison quite a lot, but he also worried that he had left Mark and John together. He would not see Emily to ask her if everything was alright until tomorrow.

He got in early the following day. Emily had not actually arrived yet, having further to travel to get to the college than Ben did, so Ben went downstairs to prepare his room for the morning's lesson. Both of Ben's lessons were late morning, finishing a few minutes before lunch. Ben was happy with that, as it felt like a good learning time. It was late enough for people to be awake, but they were not lethargic from just having eaten.

When he got down to his cellar, he found a notice on the closed door. It read; 'Welcome to Hogwarts'. Ben went to take it down, but he changed his mind and decided he might leave it there. If someone wanted a bit of fun, he would be happy to oblige.

Back in the staff room, Emily told him that Mark and John had got on okay yesterday. John had got a little frustrated with him over the layout he wanted, which Mark had struggled to understand, but the final piece of work was slick and good-looking. Most of all, John had said 'thank you' when they finished, which was, in Emily's opinion, progress. Emily was keen to point out, however, that while she felt this was a step in the right direction, it was by no means 'problem solved'.

In the class later, they talked a lot more about big props. Ben was trying to work out what big props each of the different students might like. Pamela was not sure, because, although she had enjoyed working with Ben on the sword box, she still preferred close-up tricks. Martin had taken to the guillotine because of Mark's comedy presentation. In fact, Martin and Mark looked like they were becoming good friends as they discussed comedy moments and timing, and had started sitting together. Martin was considerably more patient with Mark's stutter than some of the others.

Ben suggested that, when they did their performance at Halloween, they could take a single big prop; the spookier the better, but they could only take one because of transport problems to the village hall. The other performances would have to be with smaller items. John pointed out that the props weren't spooky at all; it was what you did with them that made them spooky. Ben complimented him on his observation, and asked the class how they could make something suitable for Halloween.

Rich, missing the point, wanted to do a lighter item, something that got a laugh, such as the bra trick. Ben wasn't sure whether Rich was slow or what, but it seemed that he frequently talked about something that had happened a couple of weeks earlier. He wondered if the Londoner would apologise for his previous bad behaviour in a week or two's time.

The group deteriorated into separate conversations speculating on what they could perform at the Halloween show and what would make something dark and spooky, or whether comedy would be a good alternative, or if the two could be mixed. Ben told the group that they could start putting a show together during tomorrow's practice sessions, bearing in mind that they would probably only get a chance to do one or two pieces, so not all of them would get a go. Quite a few were willing to contribute outrageous ideas, as long as someone else was doing the actual performance.

Ben was happy to let the conversations flow. It seemed to him that most of them (unfortunately not all) were on the point, and that the group was developing its own dynamic, and, after a shaky start, was beginning to fill with enthusiasm for the subject. He did note, however, that John and Mark politely stayed out of each other's way. Mark was no longer as stressed as he had been, and his stutter was not as bad as it was a couple of weeks ago, but Ben felt he still had some work to do.

7.

There was a new sign on the door of Ben's cellar on Friday morning. It read, "Warning: may contain nuts."

It was printed out in the same way as yesterday's little sign, in clear black letters on thin white card, and stuck to the door with pieces of sticky tack. Surely it isn't John, thought Ben. He hasn't got the sense of humour for this kind of thing. Martin has, but he can't read, so he wouldn't go for a printed joke. Mark might, but why start now? And anyway, this was not really Mark's kind of humour. Shelley and Xander, especially now that they were no longer in the class, might be prime suspects. Still, it was not exactly a bad-taste joke, so Ben left it there.

A group of students arrived early to prepare what they might perform in the Halloween show. Ben just sat around and watched as they started to get their ideas together. The general idea was that the big prop item would be the sword box, because it was not as big and bulky as the guillotine or one or two of the other props, but it was scary. They were talking about Pamela doing her clumsy assistant bit, and trying to work out who would be the magician, so Ben suggested that they might want to find their own way of performing it rather than copying his.

Rich Collier had decided what he wanted to do in spite of Ben's advice, and asked Ben for all the equipment needed to perform the bra trick. Ben showed him how to prepare the props and, in particular, how to hold his hands when tying the larger silks together so that the audience did not get a peek of anything they shouldn't. They had all practiced making the small silk disappear, so Ben decided not to go over that ground again. If Rich messed up that part of the trick, Ben would use it to reinforce the need for all of them to practise the basics.

Rich held up two large blue silk handkerchiefs. Although this was only a practice session, all of the students stopped what they were doing and formed a small audience to watch. Juliette, a little reluctantly, had been persuaded to join in for this version of the bra trick.

Rich made a good job of tying the two cloths together and Ben wondered if he would do as well making the small yellow silk vanish after all. However, he was not going to find out today. As he started to tuck the tied silks down Juliette's front, she struck out with an almighty slap around Rich's face. The sound echoed around the classroom.

He spun away, holding his face. Juliette had struck him so well Ben couldn't help wondering if she had practised it.

"Akta Gamat!" she said, angrily spitting the words out while Rich was still reeling from the strength of her blow. Ben thought it must be Arabic, as Juliette's father had spent some time in the Middle East. It might be an Arabic swear-word, he thought, as she was such a disciplined and polite young lady that she would never swear in English. Rich looked up at all of his classmates, including his friends. None of them looked as if they were on his side. He left the room immediately. He seemed to be making a habit of this.

"Are you alright?" Ben asked Juliette. She smiled, completely composed, as if nothing had happened.

"Yes, I'm fine, thanks. I take it nobody else wants to do the bra trick?"

Martin raised his hand a couple of inches, and then he pulled it back quickly.

"Perhaps I'll ask Pamela," he said, sheepishly. This little piece of comedy was much appreciated by Ben, as the tension in the air was relieved by the joke. Pamela, unfortunately, was not around to comment.

"I did my performance for Halloween last year," said Juliette, "so if everyone will excuse me, I have a song to practise."

"With Miss Darkchilde?" said Martin.

"Yes."

"Ben will be up in a minute."

One or two people laughed, Mark didn't understand the joke and, a few minutes after Juliette had left, John also excused himself, possibly to go and help Rich.

"Does anyone understand Arabic?" said Ben. Mark didn't understand that remark either. The rest of the session was a little weak, and people drifted in and out for only a few minutes during the day. There were periods of time when it was only Ben and Mark. Mark played with a set of metal handcuffs. He had not been that interested in escapology, at least, not as interested as he was in most aspects of the magic spectrum; he was just fiddling with Ben's 'toys' as Emily called them.

"Akta Gamat," Mark said under his breath, with a little chuckle. Ben heard him.

"What?" said Ben.

"What Juliette said."

"Yes, I thought that's what you said," said Ben. "I wouldn't say that kind of stuff without knowing what it means. It might be really rude."

"It isn't rude. It means, 'Never without my permission'," said Mark.

"I didn't know you could speak Arabic," said Ben.

Mark grinned. "It's not Arabic."

"What is it then?"

And Mark told him.

Ben could hardly wait until lunchtime. His mind boiled over with ideas, plots and reasons. He very much wanted to speak to Juliette and would probably end up having to speak to Rich, fairly soon. With any luck, Emily and Juliette would be eating together.

Unfortunately, that was not the case. Emily had a number of students who liked to sit with her at meal times, so she felt that too much quality time with one of them would look like favouritism. When the girls around Emily's table saw Ben coming, one of them offered him her seat.

"Thank you," Ben said to her, "you're a gentleman. But I won't take your seat." He and Emily had an unspoken agreement that they would not make a fuss of each other when they were at work. Students should be the priority, so while they did not make a secret of their deepening relationship, they did not put any emphasis on it, either. He just nodded a greeting to Emily, who nodded back, and looked around the dining hall for Juliette. He asked at the counter, and one of the servers there told him that Juliette had collected a sandwich and left for her room. Ben also collected a sandwich and went outside.

'Deepening relationship', thought Ben. That was how he would describe his friendship with Emily, and he would, of course, be wrong. He wasn't keen on using the word 'love' because it meant so many different things to different people. He loved ice-cream and pizza, but not at the same time, he loved his mother, but he would not use the same word to describe how he felt for Emily Darkchilde. He loved the name Darkchilde, even, so that, while he was having some fun trying to find out what her real name was, he didn't really want to try too hard. He loved his students, well, most of them, but he wouldn't go up to Pamela and say 'I love you'. He simply preferred not to use the word 'love' at all with reference to or about people – although he had no trouble using it for so many other mundane things. There was so much to misunderstand. Not to mention that he did not really understand the kind of love he had for Emily anyway.

A late heatwave had come to Lockley. It was not really a heatwave, but felt quite pleasant after a few chilly days. It should probably be called a warm wave. Some of the staff had referred to it as the calm before the storm. Apparently, this happened before some serious heavy rain in this part of the country, sometimes. Students were taking advantage of it anyway, playing on the tennis courts and fields. Bryn Jones had a couple of his students, having set up their easels, painting the big house. Over by the trees at the other end of the field from the house, Ben saw Shelley arguing with someone. Looking closely, he saw that it was not Xander as he had thought, but Rich. It seemed quite heated, and he wondered if it was about the incident with Juliette, or if he should go across and intervene. It seemed that Rich was upsetting a lot of people.

John had gone into the kitchens, got a cup of coffee and came out to where Ben was standing. John also saw the argument.

"I wouldn't interfere with it if I were you," suggested the student, as if he could read Ben's thoughts.

"Something to do with what happened between Rich and Juliette this morning?" asked Ben.

"No," said John with certainty. Then he changed his tune a little. "Probably not."

"Is there something we can do to help Rich?" said Ben.

"Like what?" said John.

"I don't know. You're his friend. I thought you might have an idea."

"Sometimes," said John, then he stopped. It was almost as if he was ready to confide in Ben, then decided they hadn't got to that point, not yet. He shrugged his shoulders, and then walked away, both from Ben and from the heated exchange going on at the other side of the field. Ben could not make up his mind whether John just didn't care, or whether he cared deeply but felt there was nothing he could do, or even if he really believed it was none of his business.

Ben watched for a while, and then he returned to his classroom. The phantom sign writer had not changed the message. Ben thought that perhaps it was done late at night after he had gone home so that there was no chance of him catching them.

Pamela came in during the afternoon. She showed Ben and Mark some of her card moves, and they were suitably impressed. Ben had tried to find her favourite moves and provide tricks for her to do with them, but he had also given her a few new things to learn which she was working on. As she was working the cards, she fumbled, and apologised.

"Oops. Sorry, that one needs a bit more work."

"Don't apologise," said Ben. "You need to be doing new things. You'd go stale if you only kept to what you know."

Ben found that he was often saying things like that to Pamela. Her self-esteem seemed to be quite low. She spoke in a quiet voice and apologised a lot. Ben had treated her as work, someone to be taught, and had not given the time to get to know her more personally. With nobody else in the room except Mark, who was happy to be left while Ben looked after someone else, now was the time to correct that.

"Have you settled in here okay?"

"More or less," she answered.

"Tell me about the 'less'."

"I haven't slept very well since I got here," she said. "I'm the kind of person who likes an early night, and it's a bit noisy in the corridors. Or rather, it was."

"That's changed?"

"Do you know Shelley Hickman?"

"Yes. The dancer. She was in this class last year, but stagecraft was more of her thing than magic."

"She noticed me. I felt a bit singled out and alone, and she spotted that. She asked me about how I was settling in, like you just did. I told her about the sleeping problem, and she went to Professor Kennington, who sorted it out."

"Did he? How?"

"He let me change rooms to a quieter part of the house, and started to have staff patrol the corridors in the evenings. I think he also opened one of the old dormitories on the south wing and made it into a late-night lounge for students. I've never been there but, whatever the others are doing, I'm starting to sleep a bit better now. Shelley has been really good to me."

"I know what you mean," said Ben, looking up at Mark, who had heard what Pamela said and was nodding. Shelley had been a great support for him, too, helping him to settle in and protecting him from people who might not understand Asperger's Syndrome and how it affected him. "If there was a student union, she would be the president."

They set to work. Ben watched as she learned how to manipulate a chosen card throughout the deck until it came to the top, then flick it into the air in a spinning arc and catch it in the deck so that it was the other way around from all the other cards, facing the 'audience'. It was a lovely way to present the volunteer's chosen card at the end of a trick.

That night Ben lay in his comfortable bed in his granny flat. He never called it his 'granny flat', of course, but Emily did whenever she got the chance. It was peaceful and quiet, and he began to feel the sleepiness creeping in. He was definitely sleeping better now that he was living here, and he was beginning to feel that he was performing better as a teacher because of it. However, with flat-hunting, a couple of shows in Stevenbridge and the time he had given to Harrison Bell, he was beginning to think that he had not spent enough time at the college to be aware of what was going on.

He had decided not to go to Stevenbridge this weekend. He had been planning to have a lazy weekend anyway, with no shows, no visits and as little actual work as possible. However, he now thought it might be a good idea to spend some more time at the college, not as a tutor, but trying to gauge the mood of what Emily had called the 'student soap opera'. There was a tension in the air which Ben could not help feeling was unhealthy and he wanted to know if there was a need to intervene. The incident in his classroom earlier in the day was only a small part of it and Pamela's comment about the noisy nights disturbing her peace also bothered him. Juliette's part in all this was not as straightforward as it originally looked and he was glad he had not seen her or talked to Emily about it before having some proper thinking time. And the professor's solution of opening a late-night lounge for the students was an excellent idea but Ben was surprised he had not heard about it before now.

He had not gone to the pub that evening, and perhaps he should have, but he did not want to discuss his thinking with the rest of the staff until he had a clearer idea of what he was actually thinking. He wanted to take a good, unbiased look at what the students were up to. Possibly he could get a word with Shelley when Xander was not there to stop her speaking freely. Perhaps he might decide it was none of his business after all, and would take Emily's advice and let the students sort it out. Did she say that? He wasn't sure. Perhaps she was doing the same as him, and trying to work it out herself. She had the edge over him. Her classroom was at the centre of the college, while his was beneath it, and she had the bright, talented and socially 'with-it' Juliette MacIntyre to link her to the student scene, while he had Mark, who never knew what was going on.

He thought an apology to Mark for his harsh thoughts, and went to sleep. Eventually.

The October warm-wave continued, although there were clouds in the sky on Saturday morning when Ben turned up at the college. Emily had already started her class for the local school children, aided by three or four of her students, including Juliette. He could hear them singing one of their duets through the door. Aware of a few of his own students nearby, he found himself a little embarrassed, so he did not stay around to listen, but went downstairs to his cellar room. The sign had been changed to read, "Always finish what you st..."

He tidied up a bit, which wasn't really necessary, and went upstairs to find out where the students' late-night room was. He found it, and the professor was there.

"Hello, Ben."

"Hello, Michael," said Ben. The professor liked the use of first names as much as possible. The room was quite large, and was one of the small number of rooms that they had decided not to use as a bedroom, as they preferred the students to have individual, private, lockable rooms in which other students would not be allowed. One of the other large rooms had been turned into an upstairs theatre, and yet another was Bryn Jones' art room.

This one was a bit untidy. There were papers and cola cans on the floor and chairs. The tatty old carpet in the centre of the room (it didn't go all the way to the walls) was bunched up and torn in two places. One of the smaller chairs was upturned. There was an unpleasant smell which was hard to identify. Ben looked at the professor to try to read his body language.

"Should I get the students to tidy up their own mess?" the old man said, thinking aloud rather than drawing Ben into the conversation.

"They are grown-ups," said Ben, answering anyway. "At least, that's what they would like us to believe."

"I came up here because the Saturday cleaners complained about it. We set the room up just last week. I feel like taking it away from them now."

"I don't think you should. I would talk to Shelley Hickman about it. See if she might come up with a solution."

"Ah, yes. Shelley Hickman," said the professor. There was a father-like fondness in his voice. "She's the reason this room is here. Well, I suppose the builders who built this room are the reason this room is here, but, well, you know what I mean. When I wanted to restrict the late-night activities in the corridors, she asked for an alternative. I put a few staff on patrols on Friday and Saturday nights, and the corridor situation has improved."

"At a cost," said Ben.

"Yes, this," said the professor. "But you are right. I should put the problem to the students, and see if they can come up with a solution." He turned to Ben. "Did you want me?"

"Not especially. I wanted to see this room."

"It's out of bounds to staff after 8 o'clock at night, the same way that the staff room is out of bounds to students."

"That sounds reasonable," said Ben, with some doubts. "They *are* grown-ups, after all."

Ben thought about the word 'staff' and an idea came into his head. Some of the students were from rich and influential London families, some of them working in political situations in other countries where the lives of their children might even be in danger. As a result, the government paid for three bodyguards to be stationed at the college to oversee any security issue. The rest of the college had grown to accept these three people, two men and a woman, as part of the scenery, and there was no longer any thought of real danger – the guards were there 'just in case'. Two of the three guards remained out of the way and invisible most of the time, so that the people at the college hardly knew whether they were on duty or not, but the senior of the three, Gordon Franklin, interacted well with the staff. But he was not a staff member himself and, being part of the security provided by outside agencies, would not have been prevented from going anywhere in the college, not even somewhere that might be out of bounds to staff after 8 o'clock in the evening.

He excused himself from the professor and went to look for Gordon, who had joined them at the pub on a Friday night once or twice. He did not find the security man, but did see Martin Kent, sitting on the low wall of the front garden area, playing on a hand-held games machine. He went up to say 'hello'. Martin was playing a reading and writing education game on the little device.

"I should get you a Dictaphone," said Ben.

"A what?"

"A Dictaphone voice recorder. They're like phones or mp3 players, but specifically to be used as a recording device for making notes. It would be good for helping you to make a note of stuff in class."

"Mr Jones would tell me off for talking in class," said Martin.

"Not if you recorded anything in a Welsh accent," said Ben in a poor approximation of a Welsh accent. "Or, better still, in Welsh."

"I've got a really good memory," said Martin. "That helped me through school, at least when I was able to turn up. But a voice thing would be a good idea. Thanks."

Children started leaving the front entrance, having finished their hour's free lesson with Emily and her student helpers. Ben waited until the last one had gone, and then he made his way into their music studio (he gets a cellar, she gets a 'studio', he thought with some amusement). Juliette was the only student left there, helping Emily pick up and sort out the sheets of music.

"May I join you?" Ben asked.

"You don't need to ask," said Emily.

"I wouldn't sit here without Juliette allowing me. 'Never without her permission'."

Juliette suddenly looked up at him, not afraid to make eye contact.

"Ah," she said, realising that she had been found out.

"Something is going on," said Emily, "but everyone is speaking in code."

"Did she tell you about the incident in the cellar yesterday morning?"

"The cellar?" said Juliette. "You mean your classroom?"

"That's what I meant," said Ben. "Don't change the subject."

"She told me, briefly," said Emily. "But if she hadn't I would have heard. I think it's all around the college. Juliette here is a local hero."

"She staged it," said Ben. Juliette, normally perfected poised and cool, started to look a little uncomfortable. She was an accomplished actress and a first-class performer, but her act had been discovered.

"What?" said Emily.

"I think it's me who's supposed to say that," said Ben.

"What do you mean, I staged it?" said Juliette, her tone of voice controlled, and not displaying any emotion or offence. "You saw what happened."

"And I heard what you said, too. I thought it was Arabic to start with. But then Mark told me."

"Ah," Juliette said again. "It would have to be Mark. He *would* be a geek, of course. I should have guessed."

"Geek?" said Emily, apparently even more lost.

"When she slapped Rich, she said something. I thought she was swearing in some Arabic language. She said 'Akter…"

"Akta Gamat," Juliette confirmed.

"It means, 'never without my permission'. It's not English, Arabic, or even any human language. It's a from the film 'The Fifth

Element'. It's an imaginary language. Would you believe it, our Juliette here is a science fiction geek?"

"Not all science fiction – I just like that film," Juliette explained without apology. "It's an artistic masterpiece."

"So does Mark, luckily for me. But the only way you'd say something like that was if you had planned to."

"Well," started Juliette, thoughtfully forming a proper reply. "Not exactly. I said 'yes' to Rich's suggestion because I thought he would be clumsy about how to perform that trick, and maybe try something on. Somebody needed to bring that boy down, and I got the opportunity. I thought I was doing the right thing. The rest of the college thought I was doing the right thing."

"But they don't know you planned it," said Ben

"I only planned to respond if it was necessary. It turned out that it was. Are you going to tell me off for that?" Juliette's poise was such that, although she maintained her usual confident and aristocratic manner, she showed that she really did respect Ben and did not want to get on the wrong side of him.

"I should," said Ben. "If I thought I could do it and keep a straight face, I would give you the 'respect' lecture. But..."

Emily said, "Look, this is between you two, but Juliette, you're a student here. In spite of the privileged position we seem to have given you, you are still a student. If this is a part of the student soap opera bit, tell us to butt out. If it is something we should get involved in, let us deal with it and don't take it on yourself."

"I don't know," said Juliette. "I think it's something *we* should deal with. The students, I mean. But I'll call on you for help and advice if it gets to that. I promise."

"I quite like the Fifth Element, too," said Emily trying to disarm a tense moment, "although not enough to have recognised that 'gamut' phrase. It was spoken by the most perfect woman in the universe, did you know that?"

"That would be me," said Juliette, with only the slightest hint of humour in her voice.

"I couldn't agree with that," said Ben, looking directly at Emily. "Second most perfect, perhaps."

8.

Ben spent the rest of the weekend relaxing on his own, except for cooking a meal for Emily and himself at his new accommodation. This was his equivalent of a housewarming party. Ben was not actually the best of cooks, and he left the kitchen in a mess, but he would be spending a non-working evening with the *real* most perfect woman in the universe, so he thought he should make the effort. After the actual cooking effort, Sunday late afternoon and evening was a really easy-going and pleasant experience.

They had agreed not to talk about work, which Ben found a little difficult, because there was a lot going on and Emily was normally the person he would unwind to. But they were able to find out a great deal about each other because they left work out of it. Ben did not ask for her real surname, because he was fairly sure she would not tell him anyway, but they discovered their similarities and differences in taste, and simply enjoyed each other's company. Ben would have liked to have asked Emily about what happened to her mother, but their time together was so upbeat and positive, he didn't want to spoil it.

On Monday morning Ben went to the college as usual, and found that the label on his classroom door still read "Always finish what you st". Perhaps the phantom door labeller only changed the signs on the days when he was actually running a lesson.

Ben frequently used the days when he was not teaching to do preparation. As well as his college life, he did shows at the Shining Star nightclub and a few old people's or children's parties. He sat in his room looking at his props. He was not pleased with the preparations the students had made so far for the Halloween show.

There seemed to be so much to choose from, but they had not exercised their imaginations about doing anything better than showing off the props. They needed to produce a *performance*. He would have to spend more time on that. He went back upstairs.

During the morning, the rains came. It was a little warm and clammy inside the house, while the skies darkened and the rains came down heavily against the roof and windows. This was something he did not remember happened often in his childhood home in Birmingham – warm inside, pouring with rain outside. Students (the ones that were out of bed, that is) who had no lessons for that part of the morning came into the canteen, where the kitchen staff made hot drinks for them in the midst of their business of preparing lunch. Shelley was one of the young people sheltering from the deluge.

"Hello, Ben," she said, sitting in a seat next to where Ben had planted himself to watch the rain splashing into the reed pond which was just outside the window.

"Hello Shelley," said Ben. "We miss you in the magic class."

"Who needs me when you have the mighty fists of Juliette?"

"That story is getting around," Ben said. *Not the whole story*, he thought.

"Nobody does that to a lady," said Shelley with some anger in her voice.

"Never without her permission," said Ben.

"What?" said Shelley. Ben had noticed that one or two people had picked up his habit of saying "What?" He often mused about the effects of being a role model, but he would have to speak better in future.

"Never mind," he said. "How is the new student lounge going?"

"It's tidier now."

"You organised it to be cleaned up?"

"Not me," said Shelley. "John Stockton got a few of his friends together, and they did it. It's not perfect, but I think we all wanted to show the professor our gratitude for letting us have a 'party room'."

"John did it?"

"Yes. I think he thinks you don't like him."

"He's not stupid," said Ben. "But I am *trying* to like him. Honest."

"He's not clever, either. He finds it hard to see the other person's point of view. He's good in a debate because he can be so single-minded, but I'm not sure he'll ever be the great politician he sees in himself."

"I saw you with Rich on Friday. Were you giving him some support?" asked Ben, remembering that they looked like they were arguing 'hammer and tongs'.

"I was asking him to drop out," said Shelley, going all serious.

"Drop out?"

"That's right."

"Of the magic course?"

"Of the college."

"That bad?"

"'Fraid so."

Was this some kind of competition to see who could hold a conversation with shortest possible sentences, thought Ben.

"You're a supporter, Shelley. You don't ask people to leave."

"That's very kind of you, Ben," she said. "But if I wanted to support this whole college and everyone in it, getting Rich to leave would be a good strategy."

"This is a different Shelley from the one I knew last year," he said, and he took a good look at her. She had the same compassionate face, with caring eyes and, if there could ever be such a thing, a kind expression on her face. Her hair was getting a little curly, deliberately frizzed to match a bubbly, fizzy personality. She had an excellent dancer's figure, which she quite often showed off with some confidence by the clothes she wore. She was, in fact, a striking young woman. Xander was a lucky man, he thought.

"I'm the same person. This is a different college."

"Do you miss the old, smaller college?"

"Yes, I think so. But I know it couldn't have survived the way it was. It had to grow. Nothing stays the same."

These were old words coming from so young a mouth. It was as if she had shares in the college, or at least a serious interest in its success.

"And you think Rich doesn't deserve to be part of it?"

"Deserve?"

The conversation fell apart. The wind started rattling the windows and the rain fell harder. Shelley excused herself, as she had to go to her first class. Ben was left wondering what Shelley had not told him. However, he had someone else to find, so he got up from his seat and started to try and find a member of the security team.

He found the person he was looking for on the landing at the top of the stairs above Emily Darkchilde's studio room. There were the sounds of people singing and chatting as they prepared their various voice exercises below. Somebody had put a chair outside the room and written "Ben's chair" on it. This made Ben slightly embarrassed and more than a little annoyed, but he tried to see the funny side of it.

Gordon Franklin was only about the same age as Ben, which was, in the teacher's opinion, a little young to lead a security team. He looked very athletic and fit, but in his job, Ben supposed he would have to be. His head was almost completely shaved, lending a greater intensity to his deep blue eyes. He did not seem to carry a gun or any kind of weapon, but he wore a loose jacket, so Ben was not sure. He greeted Ben with a friendly handshake.

"Mr April," he said by way of a 'hello', "I've been meaning to come and have a chat with you."

"You have?"

"Yes. I believe you are responsible for the decision to have me and my team here at the college."

"Me? I wouldn't say that. I have always supported everything Professor Kennington has done." Always. It is interesting, he thought, how a little over a year has become always. Nevertheless, Ben had been involved in the secrecy around Juliette MacIntyre's safety last year, which resulted in the college becoming a place where political VIPs would send their children and could be assured of their added safety because of the three bodyguards (or the three amigos, as Ben called them when they were not within hearing distance).

"Well, your position in the college is interesting. Having only a small number of classes, I am told you have your ear to the ground," said Gordon.

"I don't even know which of our students are the ones in danger that you are protecting," said Ben.

"We're protecting *all* of them," said Gordon. "There may be no danger at all to any of the students. Miss MacIntyre's father is quite influential, *extremely* influential, and this bodyguard idea is his way of piling financial support into the college."

"It was his idea?"

"Not entirely, but his influence in the matter was considerable. You see, there doesn't have to be an actual threat for us to be deemed a necessary precaution. There are a lot of people who just feel better about putting their children into a college with this kind of support. So we might be told of a particular situation to watch out for, when one of these students' parents are out in a politically volatile country, or when there may be news of terrorist activists threatening our leaders' families, but, in general, we are just here to help our leaders feel that their families are secure."

"So you have a cushy number at the moment?" said Ben, who was accustomed to opening his mouth and putting his foot in it. Fortunately Gordon, who probably knew sixty different ways to kill Ben with his little finger, did not take offence.

"My last assignment included taking three invalids out of a hospital which was being bombed as I was doing it. So yes, you might say I have a cushy number at the moment. But we try to act as if it was a serious situation, just in case it ever *becomes* a serious situation."

"Well, I'll tell you what. Why don't you call me 'Ben', rather than Mr April? I'm happy to call you 'sir', if you like."

"Gordon will be fine," laughed the bodyguard, leaning over the railing of the landing and looking out across the entrance hallway below him. "You looked as if you wanted to speak to me."

"Yes," said Ben, thinking through exactly how he was going to phrase this next request. "There's something going on among the students. Some bad feeling. You and your team are out and about quite a lot, and I wondered if you could let me know your take on it."

"Obviously, quite a lot of what we do is confidential, and I wouldn't be able to keep you informed of anything," said Gordon, "but the way we work is this: two of us are normally off-duty, with the third one on. We roam the house and grounds and keep our eyes and ears open, and meet once a week to debrief. Any one of us can call an additional meeting if we feel it's necessary. We've recently decided that two of us will be on duty on Friday and Saturday nights."

"Party nights," said Ben.

"That's right," confirmed Gordon. "We have a duty to protect the parents of these kids as well as the kids themselves. From scandal, for example."

“And what scandal do you think is going on?”

“We think one or two of the students are bringing some, er, illegal substances into the college. We haven’t been able to confirm it, yet. John Stockton and his friends all go home to London on the same weekends, and the following weekend the parties are a bit wilder than the normal festivities. It’s slim evidence, and as long as nobody gets hurt we are not authorised to take any action. We haven’t seen any actual drugs – we think it might be mephedrone – but we are keeping watch for the moment.”

“That’s what I wanted to ask you to do. I appreciate you telling me.”

“In complete confidence and only because Professor Kennington said I could. Should.”

“I was going to ask if he knew,” said Ben. He felt quite good that the professor said that Gordon should tell him. The next classes began to leave their various rooms and Gordon once again shook Ben’s hand, and vanished down the corridor. He liked not being seen too much by the students. Ben stood at the top of the stairs for a little longer, while a number of girls from Emily’s class made their way past him. One or two of them took a good long look up at him before going on their way. The rain had not lightened up much, so most of the students would go to their rooms or to one of the common areas in the college.

He heard Emily laughing fiercely in her room, so he went down to find out why. Two more girls left hastily when he entered the room, leaving Juliette and Emily, who was sitting down with tears streaming down her face. She struggled to compose herself when he came in, with limited success.

“What’s so funny?” he asked. Juliette made to answer, but was interrupted by Emily.

“Don’t,” she said.

“You *must* tell him,” said Juliette.

“No, I mustn’t,” she replied, “not ever. And neither must you.”

“Like Ben said before, we are friends. We’ve been through a lot together. We *have* to tell him.”

“You do now,” said Ben.

“No,” said Emily to Juliette, surprisingly sharply.

“Tell him now, or I will,” said Juliette, not giving way.

“I’ll throw you off my course if you do.”

"No, you won't," said Juliette, taking on quite a stern voice, as if she was in charge and not Emily. Ben was quite fascinated by this unusual exchange between them.

Emily looked at Juliette, and decided to give way. Then she looked at Ben, and collapsed into laughter again.

"Ginny and Cheryl," she said, but the laughter took hold of her again and she could say no more. Juliette, who was obviously far more disciplined, took over.

"They fancy you," she said.

"You're not serious," said Ben.

"*They* are," Emily said, just about getting the words out.

"And why is that funny?" he asked. At that point, Juliette joined Emily in uncontrolled laughter. Ben decided he should be somewhere else, so he went to the canteen. Unfortunately, not knowing who Ginny and Cheryl were, he thought that every young female student in the college was looking at him. He went to the cellar to get a few things ready, and then went back to his rooms in Lockley village to do some preparation in peace.

For some reason, the humour of the situation did not grab hold of him. In fact, he was quite annoyed about it. He thought that the 'Ben's chair' note and stories about girls fancying him (and tutors and senior students laughing at it) undermined his authority and his damaged his credibility as a tutor. When he had been at school, he had the least respect for teachers who people insulted behind their backs, and at teacher training college, he had been told that all teachers should maintain their integrity in order to keep discipline in the classroom. However, he had also been told to stay aloof, and that was a rule he broke regularly. By the end of the day, he had lightened up a bit, and also had prepared his lessons for the next two weeks. Perhaps he would do his preparation from here more often.

The following day he went into the college as usual, but it was fairly uneventful. The joke appeared to be over, and people were normal with him. He still didn't like the way one or two of the girls looked at him, but he put that down to his own self-consciousness. Emily had a word with him to make sure they hadn't hurt his feelings, and he said he was fine. She also said that she had tried to telephone him yesterday evening, but he had left his phone off *again*. He had frequently missed calls because he kept his phone off for lessons and meetings, and forgot to put it back on again afterwards.

On Wednesday, there was a new sign on his classroom door. It read, "Be Alert! Your country needs Lerts."

Today's lesson was on comedy magic. Ben wondered if he'd had enough comedy for one week, but he went ahead with the lesson as planned. They looked at comic timing, slapstick or 'physical comedy', as Ben called it, and wordplay. Mark showed them his version of Tommy Cooper's multiplying bottles, and Ben was pleased to note that John Stockton led the applause. He also noted that John looked at Ben while he supported Mark, as if to make sure Ben saw him. He was still vote-hunting, then.

They also looked at how comedy put-downs were not always as helpful as people thought.

"The point of going to a show is to have an uplifting and entertaining experience. I wouldn't want to go out for the evening to be insulted."

"What about hecklers?" asked Martin.

"Are you asking as someone who has suffered hecklers, or as someone who has been one?"

"Well, both," admitted Martin with a sheepish grin.

They discussed how to disarm hecklers in a way which made the whole audience laugh, including the person who had interrupted. When they brainstormed ideas, some of them were original, and some were from performers which members of the class had seen before. There were one or two suggestions which were a bit harder on the audience member, too.

"Jesus loves you, but I haven't made my mind up yet."

"This isn't a ventriloquist act, but there's the dummy."

"Don't talk with your mouth full. Come to think of it, why don't you keep your mouth full?"

Rich suggested that Martin should be making notes as this was his kind of thing, and Ben remembered that he was going to get him a voice recorder, but he had forgotten about it the last time he was in Stevenbridge. He was going this afternoon, but his intention was not to go all the way into the town, just to visit the hospice where he was going to tell his next story.

They also talked about magical one-liners, like, "Don't try this at home – go around your friend's house and try it there."

They did not spend much time, beyond the repeating bottles, doing actual comedy tricks. They talked about tricks that looked like they were going wrong, but turned out alright in the end or 'sucker tricks' that made the audience think that one thing was happening, when it was really something else.

"But don't call them sucker tricks to your audience," Ben told them.

Martin sparkled in this lesson, most of his humour being verbal. It struck Ben that, although he could not read, he was very clever with words. He wondered why Martin was unable to read, whether it was a form of dyslexia, or poor education, or he just wasn't clever. Actually, it was obvious that Martin was extremely clever, so evidently that wasn't it. Ben remembered that Martin had mentioned about not being at school all the time.

Ben tried to summarise at the end of what he felt was a rather disorganised and ragged lesson.

"I like the way we've worked together on presentation, even though we haven't actually done much actual magic. I must tell you that, although your magical skills are coming along well, I have been feeling we need to work more on the presentation side. You copy me, or other magicians you have seen, rather than creating a performance of your own.

"When Mark did the Tommy Cooper routine, that was different, because his performance was a tribute to the great comedian and magician. When he did the guillotine trick, it was his own work, assisted and encouraged in its creation by his classmates last year.

"Tomorrow, I'd like to brainstorm like we did today, but this time, not about comedy magic. I'd like to see us all create something for Halloween that we can perform at the village hall – something that has never been done before."

That created a buzz of excited conversation that continued as the students left for lunch. Martin left quite promptly, so Ben did not get a chance to talk to him. That was a shame, because he wanted to say 'thank you' for his contribution today.

When Ben got to the hospice later that afternoon, he was greeted as usual by Sally. Her shapely petite form was all dressed up in a party style today, and she was not even wearing her uniform coat. It was not a special occasion, she told him, except, of course, that he was there. She had a lovely way of making him feel welcome, he thought. Even Seefer brushed up against his leg today. He thought it was the first time the cat had gone near him.

He went straight to the story area, and got himself ready for his bit. Some of the children were already there. Harrison, unfortunately, did not turn up for this session.

"Edward had a grizzly bear. I know that's not the kind of animal you would normally have as a pet, but Edward did. Every morning, when Edward went to work, he would leave his beloved grizzly bear at home. And when he came home in the evening, the grizzly would be there, grizzling. He was a very sad and lonely grizzly bear.

"'What's the matter?' Edward would say. Between heart-wrenching sobs, the grizzly bear would say, 'You leave me all alone every day, and I get soooo lonely'."

Ben put on a silly 'goon style' voice for the grizzly bear, which made some of the younger children laugh. He was disappointed that Harrison was not in the audience, as he thought the lad would like this one. Nevertheless, he carried on, trying not to be distracted.

"'I know,' said Edward. 'I'll go to the pet shop and buy you a friend.' So Edward went to the pet shop, and asked if he could buy a new pet.

"'What would you like?' they asked.

"'A lady grizzly bear, if possible,' he said.

"'I'm sorry, we don't have any lady grizzly bears,' they told him, 'We've got hamsters, mice, kittens, puppies…'.

"'They are all rather small,' said Edward. 'Haven't you got anything bigger?' And they showed him the biggest animal they had in the shop. It was a pig.

"'I'll take it,' he said. So he brought the pig home to see if his pet grizzly bear would like it."

Ben paused for dramatic effect. All of the children seemed spellbound, as if they were listening to a *real* story.

"The bear was delighted. Edward watched them play, and, when he went to work, the pig and the grizzly bear were happy. They played together like brother and sister. Edward was pleased that his grizzly bear was happy again.

"But one day, something terrible happened. He went to work as usual, leaving the grizzly bear and his new pig friend playing together, but when he got home that night, the pig was nowhere to be seen and the grizzly bear was sitting in the middle of the room, crying.

"'What's the matter?' said Edward. 'And what has happened to your pig?'

"'Someone had stolen it,' said the grizzly bear. 'They sneaked in while I wasn't looking and took him away.'

"'That's terrible,' said Edward. 'But please cheer up. I'll sing you a song to make you happy.'

"So he sang this song," said Ben, putting on a singing voice. "Today's the day that Eddie's bear had his pig nicked."

Nobody actually laughed, but the groans were satisfying enough. Sally took over for a real story, and Ben nodded to her and indicated that he was going to visit the absent Harrison. She looked up at him, the deep pools of her eyes fully focussed on him for a moment, and she gave a little negative shake of her head, as if to tell him not to go. He waited for her to finish the story.

While everybody was getting ready for tea, Sally escorted Ben to Harrison's room, walking quite slowly so that she could say her piece first.

"Harrison's had a bad day today," she said. "It happens sometimes. He's been quite ill. We've had the doctors out to him, and they say it's just one of those bad days. He's sleeping right now, so I don't really want him to be disturbed. I don't think he's rested properly for a day or two."

Outside the closed door of his room, on a cushioned chair against the opposite wall, Seefer the Cat sat upright and watched everything as if he was Harrison's own personal guardian angel. When they got to the door, Sally turned and faced Ben, standing close so that she had to crane her neck to look up at him.

"You don't have to see him like this," she said in a quiet voice. "If you go off home now, I'll tell him tomorrow that you dropped by."

"Thank you," said Ben. "But I would like to see him anyway."

"I thought you might," she said.

“Which was why you walked me here to his door before saying I didn’t have to be here,” he replied, also talking quietly in case the voices outside Harrison’s door disturbed his sleep.

“I must warn you,” she whispered. “He doesn’t look good.”

She opened the door gingerly, as if the slightest movement would disturb him. Ben looked at him from the doorway. Sally was right. He looked worse than usual. The dark areas around his eyes seemed even darker than normal, and his cheeks seemed hollow. His hair was matted as if he had been sweating, and his bedclothes were untidy from his tossing and turning. Ben felt quite distressed to look at him – he almost felt like he wanted to cry. Sally noticed, and put her hand on his arm for comfort.

Harrison had three pillows, but they were dislodged. One had been thrown almost completely off of his bed by his restless movements, and had landed on his bedside table, and the other two were askew, putting his head at a slightly uncomfortable-looking angle. Ben wanted to go in and adjust the pillows for him.

“Don’t,” whispered Sally, both arms now wrapped around his now as if she, too, needed some comfort. “He wakes up very easily. He needs as much sleep as he can get right now.”

Ben stood looking at him for a few minutes, but his legs felt weak. This was Harrison’s life – good days and bad days, sleep and no sleep, always looking rough, often feeling rough.

After a few minutes of leaning against the door frame, Ben returned to the dining room, where he went around the children and said ‘hello’ to some of them. He did not feel as cheerful as he was pretending, and he did not stay to eat with them. He soon went out to the car park, where he sat in his car for half an hour staring at nothing before he eventually drove home.

9.

The sign on Ben's classroom door the following morning said, 'Abandon hope all who enter here'. Ben ripped it down and threw it into the recycling bin he kept in the cellar. He was not in the mood for that kind of humour today. But neither was he in the mood for the macabre and that was what he had set for the lesson. Still, thoughts like 'the show must go on' went through his mind and he started to prepare the room.

Mark joined him a short while later, looking at where the sign should have been as if he was missing something. He helped Ben clear the room of all props and put up a large easel and pad. The chairs were set, all the lights turned on for comfort and a clean slate was created so that the class had no visual impetus to start them thinking. We have some clever people here, he thought, so it's time to give them a chance to *be* clever.

"Ladies and gentlemen," he said to them all when they had all arrived. "Thank you for getting here on time. We have nothing for you this morning. I am not allowing you to copy one of my performances at the Halloween show this year. What we are going to do is think of a trick, *invent* a trick, ourselves. No, not just a trick, a whole *performance*. Any volunteers to take notes? Someone who can write quickly and clearly."

He held up a marker pen for a volunteer. One young lad, Charles (*not* Charlie), who was one of John and Rich's friends, volunteered, possibly in the hope that, if he was writing, he might not have to contribute in any other way.

"Now, let's start with a theme. Anyone?"

"Halloween," said someone.

"Ye-e-e-s," said Ben, thoughtfully. "I don't suppose we can be more specific?"

"Vampires?"

"Horror."

"Ghosts."

"Bunny rabbits," said Martin.

"Something with lots of blood," said someone seated near to Martin. "Martin's blood, possibly."

"Serial killers," said someone from London, "out in the wilds of Norfolk."

"I could murder a bowl of cornflakes," said Martin.

"Poison."

That last suggestion got a few people's attention, especially as Charles had written 'poison cornflakes' on the board.

"What are we going to do with the poison?" asked Ben.

"Drink it."

"Make someone from the audience drink it."

"How do we show them it is really poison?" said Ben.

"I know something that dissolves that oasis stuff they use in plant shops," said Charles. "Some chemical stuff."

"You would know about chemicals," said Rich with a snigger. John elbowed him in the side. Ben thought that John's elbow and Rich's ribs were probably well acquainted.

"Is it safe?" asked Ben, ignoring Rich's remark. "It doesn't create poisonous fumes or anything?"

"I can check, but I think it's pretty much household chemicals."

"Household chemicals can still create poisonous fumes, so yes, please check it out. Then we need to make it into a magic trick," said Ben. Enthusiasm was gripping the whole group. They talked about whether they should force a member of the audience to choose the right drink, or make it a free choice, then switch bottles at the last minute. They wanted to make it as clean-looking as possible, with no cover to hide a switch, but also with no cheesy or complicated method of choosing so that the audience did not suspect they were being manipulated. How could you force a free choice? What should you do to make it impossible to detect where the trick was actually a trick?

Some of the ideas were outrageous or impossible, of course, and the group had lots of laughs eliminating the impossible, leaving only the improbable to keep them in business. Ben tried not to interfere, but there were times when he knew methods that would fit their ideas, so he contributed his ideas, many of which were dropped by the group anyway. John and Martin seemed to take control of the brainstorming, both making sure everybody who wanted a say was heard. This was strange, thought Ben, because neither was best of friends with the other. Nevertheless, they had some respect for each other and somehow managed to work well together in spite of their differences.

"What about the mood?" said Martin, forgetting his comedy façade for the moment. "We need to create a performance, remember, not just a trick."

"We could tell a story," suggested Juliette, "illustrated by the magic."

"Like last year," said Mark.

"We don't want anything like last year," said John. "This has got to be unique."

"It could still be a story," said Martin. "A unique story."

"Somebody is after you," said one of the local lads.

"You dare not go to sleep," said someone else, "or they'll get you."

"We know what you did last summer," said one with a laugh.

"Or last week," said Martin, "and we're out to punish you."

"Are you a saint or a sinner? Drink the potion and you will find out. We will *all* find out."

"If you can survive until morning."

Time went by very quickly, and the excitement of what they were in the process of creating captured all of their imaginations. Ben was sorry to have to bring them to a close, but he was pushing his luck with the kitchen staff, so he stopped them in time for lunch. They all turned up the following morning for more. Although only a few of them would be actually in the performance, every single one of Ben's nineteen students turned up.

Their job on Friday, however, was to make their ideas work. Martin started them off.

"I was offered a magic potion yesterday. Someone came to my room and said, 'I have a magic potion. It's a truth potion. Would you like to drink it?'

"'A potion of truth?' I asked.

"'Yes,' he said. 'If you drink it I guarantee you will be compelled to tell the truth.' So I agreed.

"'Wait,' he said. 'It will cost you £60.'

"'Sixty pounds?' I said. 'That's a lot of money.'

"'It *is* a potion of truth. It's not just any old potion.' So I paid the money and drank the potion.

"'This is just water!' I said.

"He said, 'That's the truth!'"

After that, they put some serious work into making the trick work. They worked all morning, and by midday they had a solid plot and a reasonable trick to perform. They were able to free themselves up by the afternoon for whatever other preparations their different classes required.

So Ben was on his own, apart from Mark, as usual, and a little visit from Pamela, who came just to show him her progress with the last couple of card tricks she had learned.

"You are quite a quiet sort of person, aren't you?" he asked.

"I suppose."

"Almost shy, in fact."

"Yes, a bit," she answered.

"So why did you choose one of the performing arts?"

She thought about it for a moment.

"Because I hate being shy," she said. "I don't want to be like this anymore. The subjects I have picked here are geared to what I can do – painting, creative writing, although I'm not too good at that. I've picked magic because I want to stand out in the crowd, to be different, to be confident."

"Oh, you'll be all that, Pamela, I promise you."

That night at the pub, the tutors got together for their regular 'Friday Night Unofficial'. One or two of them wondered what their students would get up to while they weren't there. Ben wanted to talk about how the Halloween show would be laid out, but Bryn pointed out that the show was a staff meeting subject, not a pub subject.

"And I have a bone to pick with you, lad," he said to Ben in his rich sing-song Welsh accent. "What's this about you taking all my best students away from their work this morning?"

"Are you telling me," said Ben, who loved to dig a little at the old-fashioned but loveable art teacher, "that my magic students are in your painting class, too?" he used the term 'painting' rather than 'art' because he knew it wound Bryn up.

"Yes, and some of them are quite good, in spite of your influence, boyo," he said. He hardly ever said 'boyo', unless he had taken the bait. "That Grice girl is particularly good."

He pronounced every syllable of the word 'particularly'. That meant that, although he'd had a bit to drink, he was feeling intense about his subject. Ben had too much respect for the Welshman to keep needling him now.

"Pamela?" he said. Then he had a thought. "Seriously, do you do sculpture in your class, too?"

"You, serious?" said Bryn. "Don't make me laugh. What are you going to have a go at now?"

"No, I mean it."

"We do any kind of art they want to. We do painting the most because that's what most people are expecting. But we *can* do sculpture. So, what is your punch line, then?"

"No punch line, honest. Pamela Grice is good with some pretty complex sleight of hand. She's a short, stubby girl, no offence intended, but her hands are different. She's really clever with them. Try her at sculpture, or anything that makes use of those talented hands of hers."

"Brain surgery," said Emily, who'd had enough of serious talk. "We could ask the professor to include brain surgery classes."

"That would be good for the Halloween show," suggested Ben.

"We're getting together with Mrs Cleese's class to do a couple of pieces from Rocky Horror," said Emily. "Do you want some mood pieces for your presentation, Ben? Some of the kids from your class are quite excited about what you are going to do."

"Here we go again," said Bryn, who could only offer a couple of spooky paintings for the show, "talking shop."

"We weren't talking shop when we were talking about *your* class?" said Emily.

"Devil woman?" suggested Ben. "Although, I imagine it probably won't be a woman doing the presentation on the night."

"You could always dress John Stockton up in a dress," suggested Emily.

"That's not the first time that's crossed my mind."

"We're learning new things about you all the time," said Bryn, happy to get his own dig in for a change.

On Saturday, Ben went to the hospice. He had only just started the habit of visiting on Wednesdays, but he had been so worried about Harrison that he felt he just had to go. He woke up in the early hours of Saturday morning and could not go back to sleep for thinking about it. He wanted to meet Harrison's parents, too. They would probably be there today. He got up and paced the floor until it was a reasonable time to go, then he got caught up in farm traffic, so he didn't get to the hospice until after half past ten anyway.

The Saturday morning event was a board games competition. Ben was surprised at how many different board games there were. There were a number of fairly conventional games, as he might have expected, but quite a few he had never seen before.

The pile of boxes on the table in the centre of the room included Snakes and Ladders, Ludo and one or two others he had played when he was younger, but the children had left them on the table and were all playing more modern and unusual games.

There were 'buying and selling', where the players simply used cards representing money and resources to buy further cards which were the resources needed to build a large kingdom, or farm goods, or whatever the game was about. Some children were playing a game with a big map of railway lines where the children had to claim routes. A couple of the older boys were playing a game with painted plastic soldiers that looked like Vikings, modern soldiers, flying creatures and science-fiction robots, each able to do different things in the game, doing battle over a modular landscape made of large hexagonal plastic tiles.

Sally, who was dressed in her usual uniform, met Ben with her customary warm greeting.

"How is Harrison this morning?" Ben asked her, even before saying 'hello' to her.

"And I thought you were here to see me," she joked.

"It's always a pleasure to see you, Sally," he responded. "How's Harrison?"

"He's had a couple of really bad days," said Sally, "but he's a lot better this morning. His mother came up on Thursday and stayed overnight. She left for home yesterday. She's got this arrangement with where she works that, in an emergency, she can drop everything at a moment's notice and come to visit Harrison if it was necessary."

Sally looked up into Ben's eyes. "It's good to have someone who would drop everything for you," she said.

Ben looked around him to see if he could find Harrison playing anywhere.

"I'm not sure he's up to playing at the moment," Sally said. "He'll be in his room."

Ben started to make for his room, when Harrison came out to meet them. He looked a little tired, but his general appearance was a lot better than Wednesday. He wore his dressing gown and slippers. He smiled a greeting at Ben, and nodded to the cat who looked as if he had not left his position on guard for days. At the nod from Harrison, however, Seefer trotted off down the hallway to find one of the other children to care about.

"I thought I would come out and see what was going on," he said. He walked slowly, as if moving any faster would use up too much energy. He sat and watched the models game, and Ben stood behind him.

At lunchtime, Sally set things in motion and then excused herself to go and meet another guest. Ben sat at the table with Harrison, who ate his small portion of salad slowly.

One or two of the children came up to Ben and asked him for one of his 'silly stories'. He tried to put them off, but a couple more came by and asked. He told them he had only come to see how Harrison was, not for a story, not today. It wasn't long before he had an audience of ten or more, two of the younger girls sitting on his lap.

"I think you should," said Harrison, who was being snuggled up to by a couple of the younger children himself.

"There was once a man," he started, "who lived all on his own at the top of a hill, in a great big house. One day, when it was time for bed, he went up the first flight of stairs, tripping on the second step from the bottom, but he didn't hurt himself; along the corridor, up the second flight of stairs, along the corridor, and into his bedroom. There was a knock on the door."

Ben freed one of his arms from the child on his knee, and knocked the table next to him.

"So he left his room, went along the corridor, down the second flight of stairs, along the corridor, down the first flight of stairs, tripping on the second step from the bottom, but he didn't hurt himself. He opened the door, and there, standing in front of him, was a gorgeous blonde woman.

"'My car has broken down at the bottom of your hill,' she said. 'Can I borrow your telephone?'

"'I haven't got a telephone,' he answered. 'But you can stay for the night, and we'll see what we can do to help you in the morning.' So he made her a drink, then took her up the first flight of stairs, tripping on the second step from the bottom, but he didn't hurt himself; along the corridor, up the second flight of stairs, and showed her to her room. Then he went along the corridor, and into his own bedroom. Then there was a knock on the door."

He knocked the table again.

"So he left his room, went along the corridor, past the blonde's room, down the second flight of stairs, along the corridor, down the first flight of stairs, tripping on the second step from the bottom, but he didn't hurt himself. He opened the door, and there, standing in front of him, was a beautiful red-headed woman.

"'My car has broken down half way up your hill,' she said. 'Can I borrow your telephone?'

"'I haven't got a telephone,' he answered. 'But you can stay for the night, and we'll see what we can do to help you in the morning.' So he made her a drink, then took her up the first flight of stairs, tripping on the second step from the bottom, but he didn't hurt himself; along the corridor, and showed her to her room. Then he went up the second flight of stairs, past the blonde's room, along the corridor, and into his own bedroom. Then there was a knock on the door."

He made the knocking sound again, and when he took his hand back, the little girl wrapped herself around it again.

"So he left his room, went along the corridor, past the blonde's room, down the second flight of stairs, past the red-head's room, along the corridor, down the first flight of stairs, tripping on the second step from the bottom, but he didn't hurt himself. He opened the door, and there, standing in front of him, was a lovely brunette."

"Like Sally," said one of the girls.

"If you like," said Ben. "Like Sally.

"'My car has broken down at the top of your hill,' she said. 'Can I borrow your telephone?'

"'I haven't got a telephone,' he answered. 'But you can stay for the night, and we'll see what we can do to help you in the morning.' So he made her a drink, and then he took her up the first flight of stairs, tripping on the second step from the bottom, but he didn't hurt himself; and showed her to her room. Then he went along the corridor, past the red-head's room, up the second flight of stairs, past the blonde's room, along the corridor, and into his own bedroom.

"In the morning he got up. He went along the corridor, past the blonde's room, down the second flight of stairs, past the red-head's room, along the corridor, past the brunette's room, down the first flight of stairs, tripping on the second step from the bottom, but he didn't hurt himself.

"He was making breakfast in the kitchen when the blonde girl came in.

"'What would you like for breakfast?' he asked. 'You can have toast, bacon and egg or cornflakes.'

"'I would like cornflakes,' she said, and he got her breakfast ready. Then the red-head came in.

"'What would you like for breakfast?' he asked. 'You can have toast, bacon and egg or cornflakes.'

"'I would like bacon and eggs,' she said, so he started to cook her breakfast. Then the brunette came in.

"'What would you like for breakfast?' he asked. 'You can have toast, bacon and egg or cornflakes.'

"'I'll have cornflakes,' said the brunette.

"Which just goes to show – two out of three people have cornflakes for breakfast."

He stopped, and waited for a reaction.

Nothing.

He looked around at Harrison, who was smiling the biggest smile he had seen on him since he first saw the lad. Ben wasn't sure whether he liked the joke or he was just delighted that it had fallen so flat. A couple of the older children, eventually, groaned, and then a little giggle rippled around his audience. But that was the most he got for that one. Gradually, they drifted off to other things.

"Do you really come here just for me?" Harrison asked, when they were on their own a little later on.

"Yes," said Ben.

"Why?"

That question stumped Ben. "I don't know. I've signed up for the St Mark's Hospice visiting scheme, and you're the person I visit."

"In spite of the fact that I don't like magic?"

"Possibly I saw it as a challenge," said Ben.

"Sally would like to think you come here for her," said Harrison. "She likes you."

"She's a very nice person," said Ben. "She likes everybody."

"That's not what I meant. She doesn't know about you and Emily."

"I'm sure she met Emily a few weeks ago," said Ben. Or did Emily visit when she wasn't there?

"I mean, you and Emily being *together*," said Harrison.

"She doesn't need to know everything about me," said Ben, who didn't understand the average teenage boy's thinking. In fact, he wasn't even sure that 'teenage boy' and 'thinking' fitted into the same sentence.

"I think she might need to know *this*," said Harrison.

"Why would she be interested in my private life?" he asked. "I'm sure she has enough on her plate looking after you lot."

"I get tired but I can't sleep," said Harrison as if he was suddenly changing the subject. "If I think too much, I get depressed. I would like to watch a video, but I don't like to watch one on my own. Would you watch a film with me?"

"Yes, certainly. Do you have 'The Fifth Element'?"

"No, I don't think so," said Harrison. "I was thinking of 'The Lord of the Rings'."

"Which one?" asked Ben.

"All of them," Harrison replied. "The extended versions. All night long."

"Today?"

"Tonight."

After lunch Harrison went for a rest, and Sally came and met with Ben again. She had someone she wanted him to meet. He was an older man, slightly taller than the diminutive Sally, but not by much. He had thick dark brown hair the same colour as Sally's and a face full of care-lines. He wore smart casual clothes and a clerical collar.

"This is my father, Donald Hinton," said Sally.

"Hello, Father Donald."

Sally giggled. “No, he’s not Father Donald. He’s a Church of England vicar. St Mark’s Church. He’s *my* father.”

“Just Donald will do,” said the vicar. He had a rich, fruity voice full of warmth and humour. “Sally’s told me lots about you. She says you have tamed young Harrison.”

“I didn’t know he was wild,” said Ben, and Donald’s laughter was gentle and polite.

“I think he is more depressed than wild,” said Donald. “But he was like that *all the time*. Since he’s met you, he has taken an interest in what’s going on around him a little more.”

“I didn’t think I’d done very much, really,” said Ben.

“Perhaps you are more magic than you thought,” said the vicar, “which was why I wanted to meet you.”

“You want a magic show?”

“Not exactly,” said the vicar. “I want to learn magic. Without having to enrol in your college, that is.”

“There’s a good magic club in the town. They are really nice people. They might be able to help.”

“This is something specific,” said Donald. “I have seen a Christian magician perform, using magic tricks to get a message across. He was really good. Sally tells me you have done a message trick like that.”

Ben cast his mind back to the one and only show of his that Sally had seen. He had done the flower trick, where he encouraged his audience to care for each other and help each other’s “flowers” grow. He rather hoped she hadn’t told him about the Sally’s bottom trick, too.

“It wasn’t exactly a *religious* message,” said Ben.

“I think I am alright with the religious message part,” said the vicar. “It was the magic part I wanted you to help me with.”

“I might be free tomorrow,” said Ben.

“I won’t be free then, being a Sunday,” said the vicar. “I have three services and an afternoon snooze to occupy me. Don’t tell my parishioners about the snooze part.”

“Next weekend we have a big show at the college. Perhaps you can let me have your phone number and we can sort something out next time I’m in Stevenbridge. I’ll show you the magic shop.”

“There’s a magic shop in town?”

“Not a lot of people know that,” said Ben.

They exchanged telephone numbers and the vicar left Ben with Sally.

"Can I stay the night?" Ben asked her.

"I thought you'd never ask," she answered.

"What?"

"Watching 'Lord of the Rings' with Harrison?" she said.

"That's right," said Ben. "Tonight, he says."

"It's his favourite set of films, but he likes company. I'll let the night staff know. Oh, I must warn you, he cries at the final song, but pretend you don't notice."

"I cry at the bit where the newly crowned king bows down to the hobbits," said Ben.

"If he wants to watch it now, it means he's getting better," she told him. He stayed for the afternoon, getting to know the children and growing to love the hospice itself and the work that they did there. Sally went home at five o'clock, and the night staff took over. Mrs Engles left a short while later, having introduced Ben to Georgia, an older lady who referred to him as 'Sally's Ben'.

Ben and Harrison watched the films together in Ben's room. They turned the sound down low enough so as not to disturb the other residents, but loud enough to enjoy in comfort. Seefer spent the entire night with them on Harrison's bed, but spent more time looking up at Harrison than at the film. Ben was fascinated in the cat's purpose here at the hospice – he seemed to be there for the comfort and support of the residents. But it was almost as if he *knew* that was what he was there for.

Ben enjoyed the films, but he was struggling to keep his eyes open by the end. He didn't look at Harrison during the last song. A few minutes after the final credits, which were about twenty minutes long and Harrison played right to the end, the young lad settled himself down. It was about six o'clock in the morning and Ben crept out of his room. Making sure the staff knew he was leaving, he went out to his car and drove home.

He remembered that he had intended to buy a Dictaphone voice recorder for Martin this weekend, but it was too late now. Or too early. Perhaps he would be able to go and get one next week.

When he finally got home to his apartment, he realised how tired he was. He went straight to bed and did not wake up until Monday morning.

10.

The last week of October would be the half-term holidays in school time, but there was no such break in Lockley College of the Arts. All of the actual lessons, however, were suspended, and every day this week became like the average college Friday, in that the whole day was given over to practice, preparation and rehearsal. Bryn Jones said it was a shame that every day wasn't like Fridays in other ways, too, then the staff would spend each evening at the Tin Whistle.

Normally, the Halloween show would be on the Friday to round off the week, but the village hall management group had requested a Saturday night show, partly because they could get a bigger audience, and partly so that they did not have to move a Young Farmers group which met on the Friday evening. Although this gave them an extra day's preparation time, nobody was going to take advantage of it and the rush and panic of it all would still set in on Saturday afternoon.

Poor weather meant that, when Professor Kennington wanted a word with Ben, it had to be indoors. He chose the staff room rather than his cramped office, and he chose the time on Monday morning when the other tutors would be in their lessons, except for Bryn, who was also present.

When Ben got there, the professor handed him a sheet of stiff paper, with sticky tack on the back of it.

"I found this tacked to the door of my office this morning," he said. Ben took a look at it. It was neatly printed in the same style as the notices that had appeared on his cellar door. It read, "Professor Dumbledore's office."

"A compliment of the highest order, I think," Ben said, desperately trying to hold back his laughter.

"Not one of yours?" said the professor.

"Not one of my own," said Ben, "but one of my students'. I've had some similar signs put on my door."

"Yes, I know," said the professor, who seemed to know more or less everything that went on in the college. "Any idea who is doing it?"

"No," said Ben. "I was thinking of sleeping down there in the cellar one night to see if I could catch them in the act."

"Or you could enlist the help of one of our security guards," mused the professor, "unless you have already enlisted them for some other task?"

"Gordon reports to you?" said Ben, very much aware of what the professor was talking about.

"I would let the students enjoy the joke if I were you, Ben," said the professor, obviously not willing at the moment to discuss any more serious subject. "If they start putting rude or unpleasant things up, we'll start calling in the troops. Until then, this is a college of creativity, and the signage is an expression of that creativity. As long as they don't start calling me Gandalf, I'll be happy."

Bryn had listened to the exchange between the other two without comment. But now, Professor Kennington got down to business.

"With the college getting bigger, I thought it was time to create a bigger management team. I wondered if I could ask you, Bryn, to become my deputy head teacher, effective immediately, and for Ben here to become the official pastoral officer."

"I would be delighted, Professor," said Bryn.

"Deputy head teacher, though?" questioned Ben. "I mean, you aren't known as a head teacher, more as 'the principal.' Perhaps Bryn should be deputy principal. Or vice-principal."

"I don't want any title with the word 'vice' in it," said Bryn, "especially in a college full of such, eh, *creative* students. And particularly if you and the bodyguard team think there might be drugs on the premises."

"The students might think they have to come to you for their supplies," said Ben. The professor frowned. He tolerated rather than appreciated Ben's humour, but that might well have been out of order, so he smiled an apology at the principal. Then he realised, as the professor could not read body language very well, he might not have picked up on it.

"Whatever the title," Bryn said, his sharp, musical Welsh accent coming through strongly, "I am accepting the post. Thank you, Michael."

"Good, good. Ben?"

"We've talked about the need for a pastoral position before, haven't we, Professor?" Ben asked.

"Yes, about a year ago. But then it was an unofficial position. Now we have a larger number of students here, and you have shown that level of pastoral care in the way you deal with the young people here."

"I have no experience or training."

"You can go on any training courses you feel may help, but I would disagree about your experience."

"We should give it a proper title," said Bryn, displaying the sense of humour Ben always thought he hid so well. "The Vicar, perhaps? Reverend Ben April."

Ben accepted the position, if only to shut Bryn up. It was afterwards, as he wandered the college grounds, that he considered what it might mean. Last year he ended up with only seven students in his class and he felt like a mother to them all. When they performed well, he felt proud of them; when things went wrong for them, he felt bad. Perhaps Bryn might start calling him "Mother Inferior". He got involved with the community life of the college and, if that was what a pastor was supposed to do, then the role suited him.

However, if it was now to be made official, how would that change things? Would people at the college no longer come to him because they would see him as some kind of agony aunt? How did professional pastors normally deal with their day-to-day caring? For that matter, who did he know who was a professional pastor to ask? He could think of only one person – Sally's father, Rev Donald Hinton, who he had only just met. Perhaps he should speak to him about it.

At the front of the main college building, Ben saw Shelley and Xander, together as usual. On the front lawn, right next to the main driveway that ran the length of the converted Georgian mansion, there was a huge old tree. It was at least three metres thick at the base, and grew almost as tall as the three-storey house. It was losing some of its leaves as autumn set in, and the branches were dripping from the morning's rain. Xander and Shelley were standing at the base of the great tree, looking up as if they had lost a kite or something in the higher branches. Ben approached them, and overheard them talking about climbing up there.

"I'm sure you're not *really* planning to climb the old tree," he said to them as he got closer. "It's one of the biggest no-no rules of the college."

"It's completely theoretical," said Xander. "And no, of course we wouldn't climb it. This tree is the village's pride and joy. We were just…"

"Theorising," finished Shelley.

"There looks like a natural shelf about halfway up," said Xander. "if you could get up there, you might be able to see into some of the girls' rooms."

"And you want to do that, do you, Xander?"

"Me? Certainly not! But somebody might. I was thinking of protecting the girls' privacy, that's all."

"Honest," said Shelley, in spite of the fact that she did not sound that honest. "Have a look for yourself."

Ben stood close to the tree and looked up. There was, sure enough, a little shelf-like ledge some way up, and it looked like it might be possible to climb up there, as the gnarly old tree had branches and bumps that might provide foot-holds all the way up. Ben leaned against the tree and spread his arms out to see if he could climb it at all. The bark was wet from the earlier rain. If it had been dry, it might have been possible to climb. Then he stopped, and turned to look at Shelley and Xander, who, in turn, were watching him.

"Are you trying to get me expelled?" he said.

"Tutors can't get expelled," Shelley laughed.

Ben reminded them that the professor was serious about the no-climbing rule and warned them not to attempt to climb the tree. Then he made his way to the cellar to make a telephone call. He was vaguely aware for a moment that he was being watched. He looked around and saw Gordon in the main entrance doorway, who had been watching the exchange between him and the two students. He nodded to the security guard, who acknowledged him politely and continued on his rounds.

Back in his classroom, he made a call to Rev Donald Hinton.

"Donald Hinton," said the rich voice on his telephone.

"Hello, Reverend Hinton," he said. "Did you have a good snooze?"

"I'm sorry?"

"Sorry, it's Ben April here. The magic man."

"Hello, magic man. Have you got your diary handy to work out some dates?"

"Actually, that's not why I phoned. I wanted to ask you about pastoral care."

"Certainly. You can come and see me any time."

"I thought you might be able to give me a booklet," said Ben.

"People normally visit me in person," said the vicar.

"Do you get a lot of people asking about pastoral care, then?"

"It's my job."

"I didn't know. You train people?"

"Train people?"

"You said it was your job."

"Pastoral care," clarified the vicar, "not training people. Why are you asking about training?"

"That's why I phoned. To ask you to teach me something about pastoral care."

"Oh," said the vicar, the laughter in his voice sounding through the telephone line. "I thought you wanted some pastoral care yourself. I thought you wanted to unwind to me, about Harrison or something."

"No, my boss has just asked me to be the pastoral carer at the college," explained Ben. "And I don't know anything about it. I thought perhaps we could do a swap. I'll teach you some magic, and you can teach me about pastoral care."

"I think you're wrong," said the vicar. "Sally's told me about you at the hospice. She thinks you're a natural carer. Nevertheless, I'd be happy to 'do a swap', as you call it, but to be honest, all you have to do is be yourself and listen to people."

"Both at the same time?" asked Ben.

They set a date to meet for their exchange of expertise and Ben started getting a few things ready for this week's preparation. His class had, with a small amount of help from his knowledge of magic and, in particular, his specialised equipment, prepared their part of the performance already. They would practise it a few times and tweak the script, but from their point of view most of the work for the magic trick was done. The class members had plenty to do in other classes and there was a lot of transporting and backstage work to be done for the weekend. The college would hire three minibuses to move props and equipment to the village hall, and students would be working hard on the Saturday to make everything ready. The differences between London and country students had been put aside, and the young people began working as a team to make the show a success.

By Friday night, everything that should have been done had been done, and there was only the actual physical preparation of the hall left to do. The staff met, as usual, for their Friday night social. This time, everyone was at the Tin Whistle, even Professor Kennington, who usually left the tutors to their own social time. Bryn and Ben's respective 'promotions' were among the discussion topics that night.

"If Bryn doesn't want to be called the vice principal, what *do* we call him?" asked Ben.

"Sir," suggested Jim Hunter.

"Your majesty," said Emily.

"You can call me anything you like..." started Bryn.

"...As long as you don't call me too late for tea," finished Ben and Emily together.

"Sorry I am so predictable," said Bryn. "We can't all be live-wires, like you two, can we?"

"Lieutenant," suggested Ben. "If we can't have name with vice in it, perhaps something military?"

"Captain?" someone suggested.

"Wouldn't I be the captain?" asked the professor.

"You would be the admiral," said Emily.

"I always imagined that the admiral stayed at home and sent the crew out to war," said the professor, "I always see myself as someone who is leading at the front line, so to speak."

"Front line is about right," said Bryn. "Sometimes I feel like I'm going to war rather than teaching a class."

"If the professor is the Captain," said Ben, "perhaps Bryn is the cabin boy."

"Is that an official title?" asked Emily.

"I think second-in-command of a college is hardly an unusual position," said Bryn, wanting to redirect the subject before it got to where Ben and Emily obviously wanted it to go. "Pastoral carer, though, that's another thing. What do you think Ben should be called?"

"You can call me Ben," he replied.

"Oh, no, you're not getting off that lightly," said Bryn, and from the torrent of vicar jokes that followed, Ben could see that the rest of the staff agreed.

Eventually, Ben suggested they were getting pastor point of no return, and Emily said perhaps he should be known as Pastor Parcel from now on. They finally decided on Pastor Sauce.

During the evening, nobody talked about their class's part in the show or work worries. That night was a time to unwind together with a laugh – the calm before the storm, as it were.

The following morning, the atmosphere was very different. There was a certain industriousness, an intensity to everything everyone was doing. People were beginning to realise what had not been prepared that should have, one or two of the students were getting nervous about their performances, and Ben's limited pastoral skills were seriously needed. Xander Herron, who suffered from serious stage fright, was also a great help to some of the other students, particularly the ones that had never done a show before. Xander was not actually performing in that evening's show, but he was one of the main backstage helpers, so part of his job was to see that everyone was ready when the time came. He paid particular attention to Pamela, who was part of the welcome team for the audience, doing a few card tricks for groups as they arrived.

"I think I'm getting ill," said Martin. "I've got a touch of Alice."

"Alice?" said Ben.

"Yes," said Martin. "It's an illness. Christopher Robin went down with it."

Rich Collier swaggered about the place but did not do very much to help people, although Ben noticed that John Stockton put some effort into helping get ready, include mundane lifting and carrying. Ben's opinion of him was beginning to change.

Rich, however, was noisy and hampering to the others. He gave contrary instructions and treated nobody and nothing with respect. He did not seem to be all that steady on his feet, either, occasionally bumping into things and people. It was as if he was drunk.

All three of Gordon Franklin's security team were on duty during the day, two at the village hall and one at the college. Gordon himself watched Rich, and asked Ben if Rich was supposed to be performing that night. Ben confirmed that he was to take part in the magic performance. Gordon suggested that perhaps he might have taken something to bolster his courage, and that they should probably find a replacement for him in the show. Ben watched Rich for a while, but had to agree when the lad threw up into the bushy plants behind the village hall. Gordon escorted him back to the college, where he would stay for the duration of the show. A lad called Tim Yard, a student from Ben's class, was prepared to perform in his place. Tim was nervous at the sudden fame coming his way, but an encouraging word from Juliette, who had performed at the previous year's Halloween show, soon helped.

Most of the village turned up for the show. There was a great deal of support for the college in the village. A number of villagers worked there as members of the cooking team or ground staff. Some sent their children there, and, of course, the Tyler family were well known and loved in the village, and Ben's work with Mark was much appreciated.

Pamela and Xander, with help from other students, did a good job of welcoming people into the hall, which was very nearly full before the show started. There were paintings from the art class which decorated the little entrance way and the main hall, and the college's lighting and sound engineer students were all ready to do their part. Singers, dancers, readers and dramatists all played their parts in entertaining the village people in a spooky, atmospheric show.

When it was the magicians' turn, two small tables were placed on the stage, like coffee tables, but higher. They were placed either side of where Tim would stand in the centre of the stage. Six clear glass sherry schooners were placed separately on thick wooden place markers, carefully placed on the table with much show and fuss by one of Ben's students. Each schooner held some clear liquid. They were handled with great care, as if spilling any would be extremely costly. The wooden coasters were marked with numbers one to six, and at the other table six small dishes with square, green oases were also placed. The team were dressed in black, and moved slowly and carefully about the stage in a ghostly and sombre manner. This was one of those times where setting up the equipment was part of the performance.

Then the stage was clear of everyone except Tim.

"Who would dare to challenge the gods?" he said. "Who is holy and righteous, and can stand before your maker and say, 'I am good'? I have six potions here to test the strength of anyone's resolve. All I need is a volunteer from the audience, someone with the courage to come up and help me."

They found someone fairly quickly, a girl of about 11 from the village school, who was instructed to throw a dice on the table where the oases were, and to call out the number she threw in a loud, clear, voice. Tim explained that she would eliminate, by her dice rolling, all of the glasses with poison in, and leave him to drink the one that was safe. Then he paused as he was explaining himself.

"You have been a good girl, haven't you?" he said, "because this only works if you are good. If you have been bad, the consequences could be serious. For me."

She giggled. Someone in the audience, probably the girl's parents, made a comment that made their nearest neighbours laugh. The little girl rolled the dice as instructed, and called out the first number.

"Five."

Tim picked up the glass on the base numbered five, and carried it carefully and reverently over to the first oasis. He poured it over the green block, which immediately began to dissolve with much spitting and crackling.

"I'm glad that wasn't me," said Tim, and the girl (whose name he had forgotten to ask, Ben noted) began to realise that this trick was serious. When she called out the next numbers, her voice began to sound a little shaky and nervous. She was the perfect choice of helper, Ben thought, as she was confident, but only up to a certain point. The nerves showing in her voice enhanced the atmosphere of the performance.

She called out several more numbers, and Tim asked her to roll again when they were duplicates of numbers already rolled. The contents of four more glasses were poured over the oases, dissolving them dramatically, until only one glass and one oasis remained untouched. Tim thanked the girl for her help, and asked her to return to her seat. The applause for her was muted, because Tim had expertly created an atmosphere of fear and tension which the audience found it difficult to break.

"It was not whether *you* were good or bad, of course," said Tim after the unnamed girl had sat down. "It was me. Have I been good? Have I done anything to displease the fates? Will they punish me?"

He picked up the final glass, and held it in front of his lips.

"Let he who is without sin drink the first glass."

He drank half of the glass, and paused in front of the audience for a while, his face pale and serious. Then he smiled, and took the glass to the last oasis, and poured the other half of its contents over it. The water soaked in to the green block without damaging it, as water should.

Tim took his bows and the show continued.

Afterwards, Tim received many compliments about his performance. Even John Stockton said that it was better that Rich's performance would have been. There was a lot of tidying up to be done afterwards, so most of them were extremely late getting back to the college. Possibly because of tiredness, or maybe because Rich was not around or all three security members were patrolling, but the celebrations later that night were much less like a wild party than they had been on recent Friday and Saturday nights.

11.

"May I come in?" said Ben in a quiet voice as he poked his head around the door of Emily's classroom. It was early, and the classes had not started yet, so Emily was in the room on her own.

"Of course," said Emily, the inquisitive look on her face displaying the obvious curiosity she felt about what Ben was up to. He sneaked in, closed the door quietly behind him, and made for the windows. Standing by the large windows in such a way that he would probably not be seen, he peered outside. The windows had net curtains, but the sunlight outside made it possible to see the front driveway and out across the front lawn, as far to the left as the large tree, but not quite far enough to see the side garden. There was nobody out the front of the great house, not even an early morning jogger.

"I can't see the side garden from here," he said.

"Would you like me to ask the professor to get builders in to move the room?" suggested Emily.

Ben looked at her as if to say, 'you're being silly.' And she looked back at him as if to say, '*I'm* being silly? You're the one who has chosen a room to spy from, then complained because it is in the wrong place'.

"I want to see what Shelley and Xander are up to," he explained. Emily joined him at the window and stood right up close to him in such a way that he was distracted and wanted to abandon his mission.

"What are Shelley and Xander up to?" asked Emily, her voice as quiet and conspiratorial as Ben's.

"I don't know. That's why I'm in here. They were looking at the big tree last week as if they planned to climb it. Now they are in the side garden.

"What about your cellar?" suggested Emily. "You can see the side garden from there."

Ben's classroom was mostly below ground, at least from the front of the house. The land sloped downwards towards the lake at the back, which provided an outside entrance for Ben's cellar room. Inside the room, the only windows were high slits at the top of the walls, which, if you could climb up to them, would provide limited views of the side garden in question.

"I was there a short while ago, and I saw some movement out there. When I looked, I caught a glimpse of Xander, but I couldn't see that much from there. I sneaked round the back of the house, and saw them preparing something. It looked like they have some kind of video camera from Shelley's media studies class."

"Do you think they were looking at setting up a camera from the tree?"

"They were in the garden."

"I mean last week, when you caught them looking at the tree."

"Oh, yes, possibly."

"What for?"

"I have no idea," said Ben. Emily looked out over the front lawn to the trees that lined the top of the slope that took the grounds out of sight down to the stream. She peered closely. Ben followed her gaze out towards the row of trees. He bent his head down close to hers, and could not see what she was looking at.

"There's someone in the trees at the back," she whispered.

"Nope," he said, not able to see what she saw.

"Between the third and fourth tree."

Ben looked carefully, trying not to be further distracted by how close Emily was standing to him, and following the line of her arm as she pointed to the trees. Yes, she was right. There was someone there, someone who had obviously found a better vantage point from which to watch the two students than he had. It was somebody who was better equipped, too. Whoever it was seemed to have a pair of binoculars. Ben looked to see if he could see the man more clearly.

"I think I should tell Gordon about this," he said.

"I think he already knows," said Emily. "That *is* Gordon."

Ben looked again. It was indeed Gordon. He could just about tell from his posture and build.

"I'd better warn him off."

"Warn him off?" said Emily.

"I don't want Xander and Shelley to get into trouble. Gordon and his mob might think they are spies, or something."

"I imagine Gordon and his, er, mob, are a little better informed than that," said Emily. "I'm sure I've seen him saying 'hello' to Shelley."

"Still," said Ben, "I get on quite well with Gordon. I should go and talk with him."

"Right now?" she asked, leaning her body a little closer to his. "Right now, while he is out there 'on duty', so to speak. You'll walk across the lawn in full view of Shelley and Xander, and talk to a security guard while he's hiding in his little cubby-hole doing his job."

"Maybe you're right," said Ben, who did not really want to move from this position next to Emily anyway. Unfortunately, lessons would be starting soon and he would have to leave her to her work. He would speak to Gordon later, perhaps in the canteen before lunch. Gordon and his team did not visit the staff room a great deal, but one of them was usually around the dining room for a coffee before the students finished their last morning class.

Sure enough, Gordon was there.

"I saw you watching Shelley and Xander earlier," said Ben as they sat down together with their late morning drinks. The smell of Gordon's coffee was particularly strong, and almost put Ben off his weak tea. Whenever Ben had seen Gordon drinking anything, which was not very often, it had always been extremely strong coffee. In fact, even when he joined them at the pub, he didn't remember Gordon drinking alcohol.

"And I thought you went in to Miss Darkchilde's classroom for other reasons," said the bodyguard.

"You knew I was there? I went up the back stairs."

"I'm good at my job."

"What other reasons?"

"Never mind. About Shelley and Xander?"

"I imagine they sneaked off together to get a bit of privacy," Ben suggested, hoping he could gently put Gordon off investigating them. "You know they're, you know, together."

"No, I didn't know that," said Gordon. He looked straight at Ben for a while, as if he was assessing the teacher, wondering if he should let the magician in on what was going on. Eventually he decided that he should. "But it wasn't for 'privacy', as you put it. That's not why they were there this morning. They were working for me."

"What?"

"I noticed that they've been concerned with what's going on with the student parties, same as you, so I thought I would enlist them to help me find out what's going on."

"Enlisting students?"

"I think they would have done something anyway. I thought it would be better to work *with* them than to let them get into trouble on their own. So they do their thing with the camera, and I watch out for them."

"And what is their thing with the camera?"

"Last week one of my men found one of the places where the lads are keeping their stash of party tablets. It's at the bottom of the sand bucket in the side garden. Nobody goes there normally – there's not enough sand in it either to put out a fire or to throw over the driveway when it snows. It's quite a clever place to store drugs. But we don't know who is storing them there. What we need to do now is catch whichever student is using them."

"Presumably Rich Collier."

"More than likely, but we don't want to jump to conclusions. We have done a covert search of his room, but we didn't find anything. The thing is, a handful of tablets is easy to hide, and given who his father is, we don't want to make a big fuss, or challenge him publicly."

"Given who his father is?"

"He's the head of an influential government department. I thought you might know that. Anyway, me and my team are here to protect the students here against a possible terrorist attack on the children of government officials. We're not here to stop petty crime."

"And what are Shelley and Xander doing?"

"They are trying to set up a camera for when Collier, or whoever it is, goes to collect their stash from the sand bucket. They are hoping to catch them in the act."

"And what will happen then?"

"It's up to Professor Kennington. But I think you probably know what will happen."

"It's in the rules for the college, and the professor won't back down," said Ben, remembering the professor's opening speech on the first day of term and the small rules book given to every student and tutor in the college. "If they are drinking, it's a warning. If it's a banned substance, they are expelled and the police are brought in."

Gordon nodded. Ben realised how much this would hurt the professor, and wondered if it might be time to warn Rich about where this was going to end up if he didn't change. But was it his place to interfere? After all, he had just been made pastoral carer for the students in the college. Perhaps this was one of those pastoral duties. Perhaps he would ask Rev Hinton about it this afternoon when he went to visit him in Stevenbridge. Gordon seemed to be able to read his thought processes by studying his face.

"I'm telling you this in confidence, Ben," he said, with a little warning tone to his voice. "You know that."

"I was just wondering what I should do."

"You were just wondering if you could persuade Rich Collier to give it all up before it all turns bad."

"You *are* good at your job, aren't you?"

"Xander and Shelley have already tried. They have been both friendly and nasty. He's told them in no uncertain terms to mind their own business. This outcome, the thing with the camera, is their idea, their solution. They haven't reached that decision lightly. I think you should leave it to them."

Ben knew that Gordon was right, in spite of his feelings.

"You know, I don't care that much for Rich Collier," he said. "But I do care a lot about the professor. He's put his heart and soul into this college, and I think it would break his heart to have to expel anyone."

"He's stronger than you think," said Gordon. "In fact, he's stronger than *he* thinks."

In the few minutes that were left before lunch, Ben decided he would visit some of the different classrooms and see what was going on. He was often aware that he felt shut away in his little cellar and he thought that, in his capacity as the pastoral care person (he really must get a proper title), he should get out and about and meet more of the students who weren't actually in his magic class. The classes, however, would soon be coming to an end, so he only had time to pop in to one of them before they finished for the morning.

Hard though it was, he managed to build up the strength not to go and visit Emily's class, but rather he went upstairs to one of the large converted dormitory rooms where Bryn Jones held his art class.

All of the students were busy concentrating on their painting this morning and Bryn was walking among them offering encouragement and advice as they worked. Ben was surprised at how few students the Welshman had in his class. There were twelve young people there. Bryn actually ran three separate classes so that he could look after fewer students at a time, enabling him to give more attention to each individual. In fact, Ben found out later that this was the largest of his classes. The other thing that surprised Ben was how untidy the room was. He had always imagined that Bryn would be spotlessly clean and tidy and that the class would be silent and regimented. In fact, the room was beautifully messy, even down to each student having a different sized canvas and painting different subjects.

Bryn greeted Ben cheerfully, showing him around the room and pointing out particular pieces he thought the magician might appreciate. Down at the Tin Whistle, there was a lot of banter between them which almost bordered on rudeness, and they would tease each other relentlessly, but in front of the students there was a great deal more respect between them. Although Ben represented everything unconventional about the college as opposed to Bryn being conventional and traditional, it was Ben's classroom that actually looked like a proper classroom and Bryn's upstairs converted dormitory seemed to have nothing of the standard classroom about it at all.

Bryn pointed out Pamela's work to Ben in particular, partly because he was proud of his talented young student and partly because he knew that she was also in Ben's class.

She looked quite comical at her work, because she was the shortest person in the class, but she had the largest canvas. She worked with six different sized paint brushes, the smallest being so small Ben imagined her threading a needle with it and the largest was a decorator's brush he might have used to paint the woodwork at home. She had to stand on tiptoe in order to reach the top of the canvas. She was painting a countryside scene, but from her imagination rather than from real life or a picture. Her style had a cartoonish quality about it but the picture, while not containing any actual detailed parts, gave the impression of being full of content and features. Her short arms swept across her imagined landscape as she coloured the different greens and browns of summer becoming autumn and she told her story on the canvas.

Ben had not thought of the creation of a painting as being like telling a story before today. The start of one of his crazy ideas came into his head. He did not have time to discuss it straight away with Bryn or Pamela, because the lesson was coming to an end. He would be eating quickly in the dining room, then off for the afternoon to Stevenbridge to visit the vicar of St Mark's. But he would hold that thought in his head, and start plotting with Bryn and Pamela as soon as he could work out the logistics of his plan.

St Mark's vicarage was in the middle of Stevenbridge, but although it was in the town, it was placed in a quiet road and felt quite secluded. The large house was surrounded by a high wall with lots of climbing plants adorning it. Ben parked his car at the side of the wide driveway and admired the garden for a moment before knocking at the door. He was no gardener himself; in fact, he often referred to himself as being harvest-time's grim reaper. However, he did appreciate a good-looking garden, and even in the middle of a dull autumn day, this garden was beautiful.

He knocked on the door, and was greeted by Mrs Hinton, a short, round-faced woman who looked quite similar to her daughter Sally. She led him in to the vicar's study. The office was like a lounge, with comfortable chairs, and a tidy desk and computer in the corner. Ben was there to teach Donald Hinton a few magic tricks, and then they had a cup of tea and some excellent cakes provided by his wife before they would talk for a while about being a pastor. The tricks that Ben taught were basic magic, a little of the easier sleight of hand and one or two simple card tricks. Donald commented that he was looking for something he could use to illustrate a Christian message, with something disappearing and then coming back, perhaps.

Donald Hinton had been searching the Internet for various resources, too, and had come across Christian Magicians UK, an organisation set up to support the ministry of Christians who were also magicians, particularly where they wanted to use their magical skills to illustrate a message. Donald had been inspired by this organisation, as well as the Christian entertainer he had seen, to have a look at what he could do with Ben's help to enhance his preaching skills. Ben had not come across Christian Magicians UK before, but was interested in that particular application of his art.

When Mrs Hinton came in with the drinks, she took a long look at Ben, as if she was trying to see something there. Sally had probably talked about him, and she was trying to see something her daughter had seen in him. Looking back at her Ben could certainly see where the young carer got her big brown eyes from.

"I think the word 'pastor' is putting you off," said Donald when they got down to talking about Ben's new role. "From what you've told me, your principal chose you for the role because of what you are already doing. You just need to carry on doing the same thing."

Ben laughed. "I've just spent an hour teaching you some of the secrets of magic. You've got to spend an hour teaching me the secrets of *your* trade."

"That's fair enough. But I have a secret that it's not too easy to pass on."

"Try me," said Ben.

"I have a basic belief that God loves me, and that He is with me in what I do, especially when I go about the business of serving Him. I am successful in what I do, but not because I am any good. Rather, I believe that all my success is down to Him."

"So I don't stand a chance, then," said Ben.

"Sorry?"

Ben got a little embarrassed, getting himself in a position where he was about to own up to a vicar that he wasn't sure that he believed in God. In fact, thinking about it, it wasn't that he actually believed there was *no* God; it was just that he had never really given it much thought.

"I don't really have your faith," he said.

"And yet there is something about you that makes your boss think you'll be good at this."

"Are you saying that it's something that 'God' put there?" asked Ben.

"Well, actually, no, that's not what I was suggesting, but it's not a bad idea. The point is – some of us are naturally good at stuff. You may have a God-given gift that your professor has seen. Me, I put it down to God because I know I'm not that good. But I'm not sure that I can help you learn the techniques of pastoring because I never actually learned them myself."

"Presumably you went to a theological college or something."

"Oh, yes," said Donald. "I did really well there. I learned a lot of theology, church history, how the Church of England works, but very little about pastoral visiting."

"So how do you do it?" asked Ben.

"What *I* do is pray about things and expect God to be there. You'd be amazed at how often He comes in and helps people when there is nothing *I* can do."

"What happens to people when God helps them? Do they suddenly get converted and become all religious?"

Donald laughed. "Most of them don't. Sometimes very practical and ordinary things happen in ordinary ways that only seem like a miracle because they happen at the right time. Some people might just say they are happy coincidences, not miracles at all."

"And *are* they happy coincidences?"

"That depends on whether you have 'my faith', as you put it. I really believe it is God at work. It can't be just me. Like I said, I'm just not that good."

"Is that why people think they need your help? Because you've got God on your side?"

"Possibly," said Donald. "It's hard to explain."

"Try me."

The vicar thought about it for a moment.

"I believe that mankind was meant to be with God. If God's the boss and everyone is obedient to His way of doing things, then the world works properly and nothing ever goes wrong. If that happened, we wouldn't be having this conversation – nobody would need our help. But we, that's people in general, ignore God, reject Him, if you like, and we want the world to work our way, not His. But it doesn't.

"I believe that we need to get back to God and start doing things His way again. That's why God sent His son Jesus to come to earth and live here among us and then to die for us. To bridge the gap between heaven and earth and to give us the chance to be where we should be again. My job in pastoral care is to bring God with me into people's troubled lives."

"And what is *my* job?" asked Ben.

"That's a difficult one," said Donald. "I'm not trying to tell you what you should believe, but the only kind of pastoral care I can help you with is one with God in it."

"So I can just pray and go up to God and say 'hello'," said Ben, hoping he didn't sound sarcastic.

"I'm afraid not," said the vicar. "You're doomed."

"What?"

"Not just you, you might be pleased to know. Imagine a perfect God in a perfect place. There's nothing bad about him. Then you turn up. You're not a bad bloke, but 'not bad' isn't good enough. You're not perfect. Neither am I. Nobody's perfect, after all."

"That's for sure," agreed Ben.

"So how can you stand in front of a perfect God?" Donald continued. "Darkness can't survive in the presence of pure light. Surely, if God is so holy, you'd be blasted to bits just trying to enter His presence. Now I can tell you, God doesn't want that to happen, so what He needs to do is devise a way to let us in."

"If we're dark, to use your analogy, He would have to make us light," said Ben. "My mother has been trying to make herself lighter for years. She just can't find the right diet."

"If we're doomed to be destroyed, perhaps He could send someone to be destroyed instead of me?" suggested Donald. "That's what Jesus did when He came to earth. He went through the torture of a Roman crucifixion, pure light taking on the darkness, so that I could take on His light and stand before God."

Donald stopped talking, and Ben could not think of a comeback. He just nodded politely and tried to get his head around Jesus deliberately getting sent to the cross, not by the Roman authorities, but by God himself. He stretched his mind to start thinking about God seriously, possibly for the first time. However, it made his brain hurt, and his mind came up with too many questions.

"But surely," he said eventually, "if there was a God, he wouldn't let all those kids you've got in your hospice be ill."

"He wouldn't *want* them to be ill. But how can we kick God out of our lives and then blame Him when things go wrong? With the hospice, I feel it is part of our way of showing His love in the world. It's not about solving problems; it's about being compassionate on His behalf."

Ben nodded. "You can feel the compassion there, alright. Your daughter in particular, she's just a whirlwind of…" he risked saying the word, "of *love* there."

"I'm very proud of her," said Donald. "All the staff members there are brilliant. Which is more than I have been this afternoon. It's getting late, and I'm afraid I haven't helped you with your quest to become a pastoral carer, or whatever your job title will eventually be."

"I think you *have* helped. Without any training, you're a successful pastor because of what you believe. Well, I believe in my students. I also believe in the professor, and if he has the faith in me to do the job, then he must be right because he's a genius. It may not be as great a belief as yours, but it will help me to do my job to the best of my ability anyway."

When he drove home, he took a long route so that he could think things through. Emily had told him that when she had something on her mind, or if something was winding her up, she would take a longer route home to give her thinking or unwinding time. While he was out on the country roads, driving in the dark because of the late November afternoon, he mulled over what they had spoken about, and what he had failed to ask Donald. He had forgotten to ask about what he should do about Rich Collier, whether he should warn him about Xander and Shelley's plan. However, although he had not mentioned it, he had found the answer. He said he believed in his students, so he should allow them to solve the problem in the way they felt was right, and he should not interfere. He also said he believed in the professor. Yes, he would be hurt if he had to expel one of the students, but, as Gordon had reminded him, the old man was strong. Perhaps, this time, being a pastoral carer did not mean interfering, but rather letting it happen and being there to pick up the pieces afterwards.

When he finally pulled up outside his apartment, he realised that he had once again forgotten to buy Martin a voice recorder.

12.

Emily's sing-song laughter caught Ben's attention as he prepared a newspaper for a magic trick in his next class. She had come to visit him, and was laughing at the new sign someone had posted on the door: "Warning: may cause drowsiness".

"Hello, Ben. Have you found out who's doing this to you, yet?" she indicated the sign.

"No," said Ben. "But I have a few suspects."

"A few?"

"About nineteen. That's my whole class. Plus possibly half the staff. I don't think it's the professor, and I get here before Bryn in the morning, so it's probably not him. Then there's you."

"It's not me. I'm not that clever."

"You *are* that clever, but you don't laugh at your own jokes, so you're off the hook."

"It's good to know that you have faith in me, and that you will believe anything I say," said Emily with the most insincere smile she could muster.

"I didn't say I would believe everything you say."

"Is it done in the morning, then?" she said quickly, obviously trying to get Ben to suspect her.

"Usually," Ben said, ignoring her baiting, "between when I leave in the evening and when I get here the following day. And it's changed on lesson days – it stays the same until Wednesday mornings, and then changes on Thursdays and sometime Fridays as well. That's why I think it is someone from my class. One of the boarders, probably, because the one- or two-day students leave before I do and I usually get here early."

"You've really got the detective thing going, haven't you? Since you and Gordon have been plotting."

He smiled at her. Yes, he thought, I have got the 'detective thing' going, as you put it. But you don't know just what I have planned to find your real surname.

In fact, Ben had been planning for a while. He had made excuses on at least two occasions in the last week to go up to the office and visit the professor's secretary there, the lady from the village who came in on one or two days each week to keep the books and the paperwork in order. While he had been there, he had taken a good look at the office and, in particular, the door. He had made a note of the type of lock and done a little research on how to pick it.

He had picked up a set of lock-picks a couple of years ago having attended a lecture on escapology, although he had not given much time to actually learning how to get into a door lock. It was not too difficult to get out of the old-style police handcuffs, and the more serious escapology took years of hard work and practice, so he had decided he would not study that particular discipline in too much detail. The lock on the office door, being an internal door and not needing much security, was a basic 2-lever mortise lock, so he hoped that, when the time came, it would not provide him with too much trouble.

With all the cloak and dagger stuff going on with Shelley and Xander's efforts to stop Rich, it had got Ben in the mood for carrying on with his plans to find out Emily's real name.

"I wanted to ask you something," said Ben.

"How romantic," said Emily.

"It's the hospice I visit."

"Yes?" said Emily, warily.

"They're always looking for new entertainers on Saturday mornings. I know you're busy then, but I wondered if you could spare a morning and come and sing to them."

"I'm not exactly a children's entertainer," she said. "and I'm not sure a night-club singer is what they are looking for."

"Your voice would enchant anyone of any age," said Ben.

"You charmer," she said. "But actually, I'd rather not." There was something in her voice that made him wonder if there was a particular reason why not. He did not ask her; he didn't feel he needed to. He just looked at her for a moment. She looked back at him with some emotion in her face.

"My mother died of cancer," she said. "She had been ill for a while, but didn't make a fuss about it. When Dad finally persuaded her to go and see a doctor, it was quite advanced. She deteriorated and died over the next year. It's what made Dad go all sensible after a pretty wild life. I was ten years old when she died. When you said you were going to be visiting Harrison at the hospice I thought, that's great, but please don't get me involved."

"I'm sorry."

"When are you going there next?"

"This afternoon. Well, this evening, after their story time."

She had to think carefully for a moment, mulling over in her mind whether she should really say what she was about to say. Then she asked, "Can I come with you?"

"Are you sure?"

"No, not really. But I think I should. Just to say 'hello'. Dad nursed Mum for the last year himself. There was some support available, but he felt it was too late for him, and he should see it through to the end alone. He's never loved another woman, not before or since, and it was hard for him at the end. I would like to see more of this place that offers the kind of help that we didn't have."

Emily had to leave to prepare her own lesson and when he was sure she had gone, Ben stood on a chair and looked out of one of the high windows. He saw a number of students moving about, going to their lessons. His own students would not be with him until later that morning. However, with so many people about, his master plan would have to wait.

He had been fascinated by how Gordon's security team were both discreet and effective. Gordon had known that he had sneaked into Emily's classroom, and yet he hardly ever saw them about the college. He did not even know which one of them was on duty. It would be interesting to see if he, a magician, could do the same sort of thing. His intention was to find out what Emily's real surname was by breaking in to the office and looking at the files. He would then find a way to drop it into the conversation at some perfectly timed moment for the greatest effect. All he had to do was take a look at the staff files without anybody knowing.

The subject in his lesson today was children's magic. There had been a time, back in Birmingham, when at least half of Ben's magic was performed to children. These days he did a lot more for adults at places like the Shining Star nightclub, usually as a supporting act to Emily, but when he was at teacher training college, a lot of his money had come from children's parties.

Children's magic, he told his class, was not necessarily less sophisticated than performing for adults. It certainly wasn't an easy option. He personally preferred the colourful props which made the job of entertaining children easier, rather than clever sleight of hand or the more close-up style of magic which is more popular these days. However, the real skill of children's magic was in keeping their attention for more than a few minutes. Television seemed to have trained children to pay attention for only small amounts of time, and when you have to do a half-hour show for them that includes them having to actually sit still, this creates a challenge for even the most skilled of entertainers.

The class brainstormed types of tricks they had learned already that might fit into a show for children, and how they might adapt the presentation of a trick they would use on adults to make it suitable for a younger audience. Martin pointed out that brightly coloured little boxes that did marvellous things would be suitable for adults, too, and went about creating comedy routines that had the students giggling. Mark didn't understand the difference between making a child laugh and making an adult laugh. Rich tried to 'help' him understand by telling a rude joke. This helped Ben to start a secondary discussion about how a good performer never needs to resort to bad language or smutty jokes, but he was countered by members of his class naming a few top-class comedians who did virtually nothing but smutty or bad-taste jokes.

At the end of the lesson they had aired a lot of opinions and learned no new magic tricks. The amount of actual magic they were learning in this group was considerably less than Ben would have liked. They had some fantastic discussions, but that was not the point of the class – not entirely, anyway. He promised to correct that by concentrating on some of his collection of children's props in Thursday's lesson.

Ben managed to sit with Emily for lunch again, which always helped his day go well, but he did not find an opportunity to sneak to the office before leaving for Stevenbridge in the afternoon. Emily had accompanied him to the hospice once before, just for a few minutes on the way back from her father's birthday party, but had only stayed around the entrance hall. She had not actually visited the children there. It hadn't crossed his mind that it might make her feel uneasy.

"Remind me to buy a Dictaphone voice recorder in Stevenbridge," he said to her on the journey.

"Why do you need a Dictaphone?"

"Not for me – Martin Kent needs one to make notes in his cases. He can't read, and I said I would get him one."

"It's nearly Christmas. When did you say you'd get him one?" asked Emily. Ben had an idea that she already knew the answer.

"Weeks ago," he admitted. "But I keep forgetting."

"You're not likely to get one today, either," she said. "It's already after five and we'll be going straight to the hospice. The shops will be shut."

"Oh, well," he said. "Saturday, then."

Sally Hinton, with her hair down and more casual clothes on today, met them in the entranceway. She looked as if she was about to give Ben a greeting hug, but she took a glance at Emily, and for some reason decided to hold back.

"This is Emily Darkchilde," Ben introduced them.

"Emily," said Sally, and something in her voice suggested to Ben that she was beginning to work out their relationship. Ben was not sure whether to introduce Emily as his girlfriend, as he thought the word 'girlfriend' was rather a teenage thing to say. But he did not like the idea of the word 'partner', either, because that was *too* deep a word. As much as he wanted to, saying 'this is the woman I love' was definitely out of the question. It didn't matter, because he was sure Sally would know they were together.

"Darkchilde?" said Sally, as she shook her hand in greeting. It was as if something just clicked, like she was remembering something. "Like the 80's rock band?"

"You know about Darkchilde?" said Ben.

"Oh, yes. One of my dad's favourite groups when he was, well, before he became a vicar, I think."

"My father was lead guitarist for Darkchilde," said Emily, warming to this young woman. "And a singer in the group, too. He called himself Johnny Darkchilde, and I took on his surname as my own stage name." She touched her tanned face. "I *am* a dark child, after all."

"Are you two…?" Sally started to ask Emily.

"Yes," said Emily, without giving Sally the need to finish the sentence.

"Oh," Sally replied, her shoulders slumping a little as if she was disappointed. "Oh, well. I wish you well, and all that." She turned her lovely brown eyes to him, but carried on talking to Emily. "I think I would make a play for him myself, if he was free."

"He probably wouldn't notice," said Emily, and Ben didn't know what she meant by that. He was sure that Sally had not been serious about making a play for him, as she had put it. She was just nice to everybody.

Sally took Emily on a little tour of the hospice, while Ben visited Harrison. The teenager was quite well today, out of bed and dressed and looking fairly healthy, except, as usual, for his dark, sunken eyes, which always displayed a worn-out look.

"So, when are you going to tell all the kids another of your cornflake stories?" asked Harrison.

"There's a story I shouldn't tell the younger ones, even though it starts 'Once upon a time'," said Ben.

"Not suitable for children?" said Harrison.

"Definitely not."

"Well, you can tell me, then," said Harrison. "Just me."

"Once upon a time," Ben said, "there was a little green man, and he lived in a little green house in a little green town. One day, he went up his little green stairs into his little green bathroom and turned on his little green tap. When his little green bath was full, he took off his little green clothes and got in to the water. Then there was a knock at his little green door. He got out of his little green bath and put on his little green towel. He went down his little green stairs and answered his little green door. Standing there was a little green woman. He was so shocked to see a little green woman, that he accidentally dropped his little green towel. The little green woman screamed, and turned and ran across the road, where she was run over by a big red bus.

"Which just goes to show – you shouldn't run across the road while the green man's flashing."

Harrison almost laughed out loud, which was quite something for him. "You're right," he said. "You shouldn't tell the others."

Ben was pleasantly surprised at Harrison's state of health. This was the best he had seen him. He was more cheerful than usual, too. They chatted about all sorts of things, including Ben's attempts to teach the vicar some magic.

"I like Donald," said Harrison. "I think it was him who set up this place."

"And he lets you call him Donald," Ben said.

"Like you let me call you Ben."

"But I'm only a few years older than you. He's *really* old. And he's a vicar." Ben had an old-fashioned idea that you shouldn't call a vicar by his Christian name. When he thought about it, he realised that was a silly notion. It was called a 'Christian' name, after all.

"Yes," said Harrison. "I think I remember that vicars aren't allowed to have first names. But if it makes you feel any better, I'll let you call me 'Mr Bell' from now on."

Ben was surprised at how light the conversation had become. Perhaps this was one of the little miracles that Donald had talked about. The quiet and morose Harrison Bell was being flippant and jokey. Maybe Ben's silly story had set up the mood, and possibly, Ben hoped, his visits were really making a difference after all.

"Mr Bell," confirmed Ben. "Right. I'll have to give you a ring sometime."

"Do you know, Ben, I'm sure that's not the first time I've heard that one."

They chatted for a while, until Ben realised that Harrison was getting tired, so he made his excuses and went to find Emily and Sally. They were sitting on the hospice's cushioned chairs, and Emily was stroking Seefer, who was sitting on her lap and purring loudly. Well, Ben thought, I would be purring loudly if I was there. The two ladies were getting on really well, laughing and joking together, although Ben could not help feeling they were laughing at him. Dismissing it as him being neurotic, he joined them. They stopped laughing, immediately adding to his neurosis.

"I must be the luckiest man alive," he said in his most charming voice (he hoped that's what it sounded like, anyway). "Here I am, in the same room as the two most beautiful women in the world."

"First and second most beautiful?" said Emily.

"No," said Sally, turning to look at Emily. "He wouldn't put you in second place, surely."

"And what about Juliette?" said Emily.

"He's got another one?" asked Sally, mock shocked.

"I don't think anyone's *got* Juliette," said Emily.

"I don't think I ever said Juliette was beautiful," said Ben.

"You don't think she's beautiful?" said Emily. "She'll be gutted when I tell her that."

"No, I mean, when we were talking with Juliette, it was about the Fifth Element. The word wasn't beautiful, it was perfect."

"So you and I are only beautiful, Sally," said Emily, "and Juliette's perfect."

"Yes," said Ben. "No. Look, do you want a lift home tonight, or are you walking?"

"Beaten," laughed Sally, "so he resorts to threats."

"Get two girls like you together and there's sure to be trouble. I should have known I wouldn't stand a chance."

"Look, before you go," said Sally, looking at her watch and going all serious, "there's something I want to ask you. Both of you, if possible. We have a big Christmas dinner here on Christmas Day. I wondered if you would come and join us. If you could do a bit of magic, Ben, and Emily could sing for us?"

"That would be a lot better than me doing magic and Ben singing, believe me," said Emily.

"I'd be happy to," said Ben. "Magic, I mean, not singing. But Emily?"

"Yes, me too," she said. Whatever had happened between Emily and Sally had obviously calmed her fears and won her over, and it was arranged for them both to join the festivities. Ben didn't make Emily walk the five miles or so back to her home, but decided he would give her a lift after all. She invited him in to her cottage in the country, and had a late-night glass of wine, and they talked until after midnight.

Ben did not want to talk to his mother about not going home for Christmas Day, but it had been a couple of weeks since they last had a chat, so it was about time. He arrived before Mark on Thursday morning, and went down to the cellar before the lesson to make the call.

The phantom door labeller (there had to be a better title for him than that) had put a new notice on the door: "Specially formulated for Children." Ben thought, as children's magic was the subject they were covering right now, that narrowed down the suspects to members of his class.

He turned on his mobile and dialled the number. His mother answered quite quickly.

"Hello Mum," he said.

"Ben dear! It's good to hear your voice. I'm glad you finally got your telephone fixed."

"It wasn't broken."

"It must have been, otherwise you would have called me before now. I tried to phone you twice last week, but your phone was turned off."

"Sorry. I turn it off to work, and then I forget to turn it back on again."

"You never have your phone on," she said. "How can I get in touch with you if your phone isn't on? I could die, and you wouldn't know."

"If you died, I don't think you'd phone and tell me anyway."

"I would, you know," she said, and Ben heard the humour in her voice. "How's that lovely Emily Darkwoman?"

"Childe."

"Surely not. I thought she was a teacher."

"Very funny. You set that up beautifully. You're getting quite good at the jokes, aren't you?"

"It's hereditary. I get it from you."

"Well, she's fine. I imagine she would probably send her love if she knew I was talking to you."

"So when is she coming to visit us? Will you be able to bring her for Christmas?"

"I haven't asked her, but I wonder if we could make that Boxing Day? The people at the hospice have asked me to do Christmas dinner there."

"The hospice," said his mother, almost without hesitation. Ben realised that this would be the first Christmas he would not be spending with his family, and he would be disappointing his mother by not being there. But she would not let that show in her voice, of course. "That's a great idea. You must be a real blessing to those children there. Yes, Boxing Day, that would be fine."

His mother was a great, supportive lady, in spite of the way he disappointed her so often. She was proud of him as a teacher at the college, as someone who worked with disadvantaged or disabled young people, but he still thought she would prefer it if he lived a little closer to his family home in Birmingham.

The morning's lesson was a success, and, although one or two of the students felt that children's magic was beneath them, in general they all had a lot of fun with some of the more comical props.

Ben hung around for the afternoon, spending a lot of time with Mark, and then he planned to stay at the college for the evening meal after all of the day students had gone home. Mark and he normally shared some tricks from 'the good old days' or worked on some of the old classic comedy routines. Mark was trying to master making cards appear from the air, but he struggled to hold his hands in the right position. He normally put his difficulties down to the natural difficulties people with Asperger's Syndrome had with complex motor skills. Today, in fact, he just seemed distracted and not his normal self.

"Everything alright?" Ben.

"Mmm," responded Mark, which was not his normal answer. Actually, it was his normal answer to most people, but not to Ben.

"Is anyone getting at you?"

"No, it's fine. Honest."

"John Stockton alright with you?"

"Yes, he's okay, now, really."

Mark put a bit more effort into his magic, but Ben was sure that something was distracting him. The problem was that once he decided not to talk about it, there was nothing Ben could do.

At the end of the day Mark left promptly. Ben went upstairs, more or less following him out of the building. He saw Mark's mother in the car park, come to pick him up. She gave him a lift to and from the college on most days, but stayed with the car so as not to embarrass him. Ben was a distance away, but thought he heard her say something like, 'have you told him?' as Mark got into the car.

No, thought Ben, he hasn't. But he probably will soon. Right now, Ben himself had some plotting of his own to do.

In the evening, a lot of the boarding students went to their rooms or the common room, or played on the snooker, air hockey and football tables in the games room. The classroom area, and, in particular, the corridor to the office, would be deserted. He made his way up the stairs to where he hoped there would be no students or staff.

The old building had some very large doorways, inset quite deeply into the thick internal walls of the house. This was good for Ben, because he could hide himself in the recesses that this architecture created, listening carefully for any signs of movement before sneaking on to the next part of his journey.

Ben found that the 'Mission Impossible' theme tune was playing in his head as he sneaked along the upstairs corridor towards the professor's office. At the door, he looked around nervously, bent down and pulled out his lock-picking set. He was aware of every creak and bump in the building as he pushed the forcing bar into the keyhole to see if he could connect with the bolt. He fancied he could even hear the noises from the kitchen on the opposite side of the building.

As he fiddled with the forcing bar, a small, hard piece of metal used to engage the main bolt while the thinner pick was used to raise the levers, Ben realised that something was wrong. The bolt was in the wrong place. The door was already unlocked.

He stood up straight, putting the lock picks away quickly. Then he tried the door. It opened easily and quietly, as if it had just been oiled. In fact, he even imagined he could smell the oil. Inside, the professor looked up at him from his office seat. He had a small brown folder in his hand.

"Professor Kennington," he said, his voice cracking a little. "I didn't expect you here."

"Then why would you come up here?"

"I thought, well…" Ben's mind could not provide him with an answer fast enough.

"You see," said the professor quickly, possibly to save Ben further embarrassment, "when you made two or three visits up here in the last week or so, I started wondering why. I thought, at first, it might be something to do with this conspiracy of yours to work with Gordon Franklin and his team to catch these students with the 'happy tablets'. Miss Darkchilde suggested that you might be trying to find out what her real surname is. After I had a word with Gordon, I thought she was probably right, and you had to find a good time to come up here when you thought nobody would be here. The best time this week would be after college on Thursday."

The professor's face looked serious. Ben had probably been just about to commit a sacking offence.

"I have here," said Professor Kennington, "Miss Darkchilde's file, the one you might be wanting to look at. Obviously, it's confidential so I won't allow you to look at it. However, I can tell you the surname on it."

"You can?" asked Ben. His throat felt dry. He had not worked out yet whether he was in trouble or the butt of a joke. In fact, he was not sure which one he wanted to be right now.

"Yes. It's Darkchilde."

"That's her real surname," said Ben. "The one she was given at birth?"

"No," said the professor. "It is her professional name, the one she uses at work. Her real name is not on her paperwork, so if you had done something really stupid and broken in to my office, it would have been for nothing."

"Then you don't know her real name either."

"Actually, I do."

"How?" asked Ben.

"When I asked her to join the team last year, I also asked her for her name. She told me, but she also said she wanted to be known as Darkchilde. This is, as I have said before, a creative college, so I respected her wishes."

"What is it?" asked Ben. "Her real name."

Professor Kennington could not keep a straight face any longer, and he laughed. He laughed like Ben had never seen him laugh before. He had been stressed by the possibility of the students using drugs and the tense relationship between the Londoners and the locals, and this little diversion gave him the tension break he needed. He laughed a lot more than he needed to. His eyes watered up with laughter tears and his cheeks went red, and it took him a minute or two to recover. Then he put his serious face back on.

"I'm sorry, Ben. When I said I respect her wishes, that includes her wish that you don't find out what her real name is."

"Do I need to apologise to you?" said Ben, changing the subject for a moment.

"For this?" said the professor. "No. I haven't enjoyed myself so much in years. And I am sure that she will tell you her birth name eventually. If you ask her the right question."

13.

Ben arranged for the class to use the downstairs theatre for one of his lessons. Of the two theatres available to the group, the one downstairs had a higher ceiling, which was going to be important for this session. It was raining lightly outside with a chilly sort of rain, so the group would be held indoors today.

When his class had filled the front row of the audience seats facing the stage, Ben announced his guest. Stephen Goss, a professional clown, entered the stage from the small cramped area out of sight of the audience which the college amusingly referred to as 'backstage'. Stephen was an old friend of Ben's from his days as a performing magician in Birmingham. Ben had taken up doing magic shows to help pay his way through teacher training, and then he found he preferred magic to teaching. Steve Goss had befriended him and helped him join a magic club where he could learn more skills. Steve did some magic himself in his children's entertainment, but did not consider himself to be a magician. He was an older man, about retiring age, but he was strong and healthy-looking, which he put down to the constant exercise of clowning. Today he was there to help introduce the students to juggling, which was why Ben had booked the room with the higher ceiling.

He entered the performance area already juggling. He held two black rubber-sheathed control sticks in his hands, and he was throwing and catching a brightly coloured flower stick from one to the other. He was dressed, to a certain extent, in one of his clown costumes, in that it was colourful and brightly-patterned. He was not wearing any silly gimmicks or clown makeup, however.

He did a few tricks and stunts with the flower stick, spinning it around the control stick, throwing it into the air and catching it and creating a helicopter-like effect using both controllers, then he moved on to something else. In just a few minutes, he showed the class plate spinning, diablo, poi, scarves and even spent a moment or two juggling balls.

The plates were plastic plates specially made for spinning, and he threw them from one stick to another, passed them onto his fingers and held four and once. He made the diablo walk up the string, jump so high it nearly hit the ceiling,and bounce on the tightened string over his head. The scarves increased in number as he started with two, and then kept taking additional ones from pockets all over his bright jacket and trousers until he had six on the go.

When he stopped, he took a little bow and came down from the stage and closer to his audience. He had them move their chairs around him so he could chat with them in a more casual way.

He opened his mouth to speak and then looked at Mark and changed what he was going to say.

"Hello, Mark. It's good to see you."

Mark was delighted that he had remembered his name. He had visited to do a session last year and met the young lad then. Steve looked at him for a moment or two as if he was trying to work something out about the young lad. Then he continued with his talk.

"I'm sure Ben has taught you all about magic. I thought I would I would teach you some *real* skills."

"The skill of throwing things about," said Ben. "You don't need an expert for that. You just need to get married."

"Magic is easy," quipped the clown, "I went to the supermarket last week and made loads of money disappear."

"Clowning is easy," said Ben. "Especially for you. You just stand about being your normal self and people laugh at you."

They bantered for a while. They couldn't help it. Every time they met they would have a go at each other, and today, even with Steve being Ben's guest, was no exception.

"Ben's mother was surprised when he was born. She was expecting a baby."

"I wouldn't say that Steve was stupid, but he thought Sherlock Holmes was a block of flats."

"And Ben thought Manual Labour was a man from Spain."

"When God made Steve, He was only kidding."

When the class settled down, Steve got on to the business of juggling. He talked for a short while about the different items. Some of the class were fascinated to learn that the ancient Chinese used the diablo as a weapon to throw at the enemy. They would have been made of clay, and sometimes filled with burning oil. Some of them might have had holes in to make screeching sounds as they flew through the air, to strike terror into the hearts of their enemies.

He also told them about how learning to juggle builds confidence and fitness, without the boring business of going to the gym. Then he and Ben took them in groups to teach them how to use the different pieces of equipment. Ben was not an expert juggler but he had learned enough from his old friend to help the students to learn the basics.

He had imagined that the dextrous Pamela Grice would learn quickly but, in fact, she struggled. Steve pointed out later on in the session that her skill was in her fingers, which would be great for art and card manipulation, but it was a co-ordination of the arms and palms of your hands which were needed with juggling.

He pulled out a toothbrush from his bag of supplies, and balanced it carefully on one of the control sticks for his flower sticks. He gently started it spinning around the stick, until it built up quite a momentum. Pamela had a go, and was not too bad at it, but she was better without the control stick, just spinning it around her fingers.

At the end of the session, everyone had enjoyed themselves, and one or two had decided that they would look into juggling a bit more. Ben called Pamela, who seemed to be feeling a bit down about her failure to progress much with the juggling, to hang around a bit at the end.

"I've had an idea," he said to her.

"Say no," said Steve, who was starting to pack his equipment away within earshot of Ben and Pamela. "Ben has these ideas. Whenever he says 'I've had an idea', grown men shrivel into nervous wrecks, great nations crumble and big companies go out of business." He shrugged his shoulders. "Just warning you, that's all."

"It's about performing on stage at the Christmas show," said Ben. "Hear me out."

He told Pamela his plan, which involved gaining the co-operation of a number of the different classes, and Steve listened in.

When he had finished outlining his scheme, the clown laughed out loud.

"Say yes," he said and Pamela did, with enthusiasm. They chatted a little further about the work involved in carrying out Ben's idea, but it was soon time for lunch.

In the dining room, Ben introduced Steve to Martin.

"I thought you two should meet," Ben said. "Martin is a bit of a clown, too."

"Not in the sense that *you* are," he said to the guest. "I'm more of a comedian. I don't think I would be so good at the silent comedy bit."

"You play with words like I play with actions," said Steve.

"That's right."

"Talking of words," said Steve, "did you know that if you say the word 'apple' over and over again really fast, it sounds like the word 'gullible'?" Martin, of course, did not fall for it.

"So when you perform a trick, you explain everything?" Steve continued.

"Not everything," said Martin. "But I like to support my performance with a bit of witty banter."

"Not much you can learn in Ben's class then."

"Ho, flippin' ho," said Ben with every bit of sarcasm he could muster.

"Sometimes, actions speak louder than words," said Steve. "The look on your face when you make something disappear, as if it was a surprise to you, or *showing* your hands to be empty instead of *telling* people they are empty."

"That faltering move I make when I lunge towards the woman in the bra trick," Ben said, getting into the conversation and supporting Steve instead of joking at him.

"You still do the bra trick?" said Steve to Ben.

"Do you do that as well?" Martin asked Steve.

"Me? No. I work mostly with children. I know some children's magicians who do it anyway, but I like to keep my children's magic on the right age level. That trick would go down well with people your age, but my image is the nice old grandfather figure, so it doesn't suit my stage persona. But I saw Ben do it once at a big business reception."

"The one at the car factory," Ben said, remembering that performance with some amusement.

"That old lady you picked was a gem."

"She didn't know what was going to happen to her, but she went along with it beautifully."

"Everyone thought you had really taken her bra off."

"And she didn't tell them otherwise."

"Then you found out she was the boss's wife!"

"Should I leave you to your 'good old days'?" asked Martin.

"Ah," said Steve. "Nostalgia isn't what it used to be."

They were interrupted by Emily, who knew Steve was going to be visiting that morning and was looking forward to seeing him again. They had met last year when he visited the college, and Ben had taken her to see him during the summer holidays.

"Emily Darkchilde!" said the old clown. "Will you marry me?" He stood up and she gave him a greeting hug.

"In the absence of any other offers, I certainly will," she replied.

"Do you think he'll get the hint?" said Steve.

"Not in a million years," she replied with a laugh.

Xander and Shelley, who had been in Ben's class when Steve had visited last year, also came to say 'hello'. Shelley wanted a word with Ben in private, so he left Xander and Emily with Martin and Steve and took in to a more private corner of the dining room.

"Everything alright?" said Ben,

"I just wondered if you had anything more on Rich Collier?" she asked. "Gordon, Mr Franklin I mean, said you knew about what we were doing."

"With the camera? How is that going?"

"Not too well. It has a limited battery life and we haven't got any film of Rich doing anything yet. We have to work out when the best time is to turn it on."

"Perhaps it isn't him," suggested Ben. "Or maybe he hasn't gone out to his secret stash?"

"Mr Franklin says that the bucket was definitely disturbed last weekend – probably on Saturday sometime, maybe after dark. Someone went there, but we didn't pick it up on the camera."

"It is possible that Rich, or whoever it is, has found out about the camera?"

"I thought that. But Gordon says that some of the tablets are still there. They would have sneaked them away or sabotaged the camera if they knew."

"Then it's just a case of trying different times until it works," said Ben.

Shelley paused and looked up at him. She was trying to work out how to ask the next question. They had been talking quietly so as not to be overheard but the next thing she said was quieter still.

"Are we doing the right thing?"

"What do you mean?" he said, matching the volume of her voice.

"Are we stirring up what doesn't need stirring up? Are we causing trouble when what we should be doing is keeping the peace?"

Ben wanted to give a reassuring answer but he was having some doubts himself.

"I don't know," he said eventually. "I think you are doing what you *think* is the right thing, and with good intentions."

"You mean, the kind of intentions that the road to hell is paved with?" said Shelley.

"I'm not sure I believe that saying," said Ben. "I think if your heart intends to do good, then some good will come of it."

Some particularly loud laughter came from Steve's table. Emily, in fact, was laughing louder than the others, so Ben immediately drew the conclusion that they were laughing about him.

"Excuse me," he said to Shelley. "I must remove any trace of Steve Goss from this college before he tells them anything about my past life that he will regret."

"Don't you mean that *you* will regret?" said Shelley.

"No. Believe me, it will be him that regrets it!"

In the afternoon, Ben took Steve to the hospice. He had arranged for the clown to do a little act for the children there instead of their usual story time. On the way they chatted about the college and his work there.

"It's a very different group from last year," Steve noted.

"It's bigger, to start with. Nineteen. It was a bit of a struggle giving them all some time while they were learning the juggling."

"Well, they weren't really *learning*, were they? It was more like they were playing, fiddling with the equipment. Perhaps one or two of them will pick it up a bit. Some of the smarter-looking ones thought it was beneath them."

"They are from VIP families in the City."

"Have you told them that the Magic Circle includes a member of the Royal family?"

"They would all queue up to join."

"Martin, now. He has some learning difficulties, doesn't he?"

"How did you know that?" asked Ben. "You were only with him for a few minutes."

"I'm a genius," said Steve. "And I make a point of observing people. I think clowns should study psychology even more than you magicians do. And what's with Mark?"

"He was bullied a bit at the beginning of term, but he is alright now. Well, something's going on, but he won't tell me."

"It's not bullying," said Steve. "He's feeling guilty about something."

"Guilty?"

"Or bothered. He doesn't want to tell you because I think he thinks it will change things. Or that he will let you down somehow. And that young lady, the short girl, Pamela. She's a bit smart. But she doesn't know it, does she?"

"She has some confidence issues. That's why she wants to learn how to perform. You should see her with a pack of cards."

"You can't *perform* with a pack of cards. You can only do tricks," said Steve, and although he could not see the clown's face because he was concentrating on driving, he just knew there was a twinkle in his eye. Steve was no fan of card magic, and if he and Ben ever got together for more than a few minutes, they would revive this old argument.

"Of course you can. Some card magic is more highly skilled than anything you do."

"I'm not saying it's not skilled, I'm just saying you can't *perform* it."

"It's as much a performance skill as you tripping over your oversized feet. How can you say you can't perform with cards, when you make even falling over into a performance?"

They laughed as they dragged up old arguments, with Ben defending card magic in spite of not actually being a great fan of the discipline himself. They got to the hospice in plenty of time for Steve to get into costume for his little show.

He did half an hour of slapstick and juggling, making the children laugh with his clowning and astounding them with his skills. Afterwards, they ate together with the children in the hospice dining room.

Sally, dressed with her uniform fully buttoned up and with her hair back in its formal setting, greeted them in order to say thanks to Steve for his work. She had with her a pretty little five-year-old girl who was holding on to her hand, all wide eyes and fascinated by the events of the afternoon.

"This is Cherry," said Sally. "She is visiting for the afternoon. She wanted to meet the clown."

"You're not afraid of clowns, then?" said Ben. "A lot of little girls are." And he whispered to Steve, "You frighten the life out of me."

"I'm not a little girl," said Cherry, who was all eyes and rosy cheeks. She had a crown of light brown hair which was thick, but fairly short. "Mummy says I'm a big girl."

"You are a big girl," said Steve, "Ben here is not very good at guessing how big people are."

Cherry turned her adorable face on Ben.

"You're Ben," she said, "the magic man."

"Hello, Cherry," said Ben. "Yes, I'm Ben, the magic man. It's nice to meet you." He took a sip of his tea.

"Sally has told me about you. I like Sally. She's nice. People here say she is in love with you."

Ben nearly choked on his tea, and Steve laughed until the tears ran down his face.

"Why are you laughing?" said Cherry, who was not lacking in childish confidence.

"Clowns are supposed to laugh," said Steve, barely controlling himself. "It's good practice."

Later on, Sally, who had not appeared to respond in any way to Cherry's comment about her and Ben, told them that Cherry was a day visitor, but she was deteriorating, and a difficult home situation along with declining health meant that she would soon be a resident here at the hospice. Steve found that difficult to take in. He kept shaking his head. Ben looked at him, and thought he had actually started to look old.

Ben had noticed that Harrison had not been present for Steve's show. He asked Sally if the young lad was alright. Sally explained that he had told them he didn't like clowns.

"I must take Steve to meet him, then," said Ben with a cheeky grin.

While Steve was wearing some clown-style clothes, he had not put on the full makeup. This was partly because he was making the long journey home tonight, and partly because, knowing that there were going to be younger children there, some of whom really might not like clowns, he only dressed the part and left his 'face' off, as he put it. After all, he said, if they had not worked out that he was a clown from his antics, he was never going to convince them with makeup.

Ben knocked on Harrison's door and went in, followed by Steve, who had heard Sally say that he didn't like clowns.

"Hello, Harrison," said Ben, who was reading. "This is Steve. He's a…"

"Visitor," said Steve quickly.

"Clown," said Ben, annunciating carefully.

"Hello, Steve," said Harrison. "Sorry I missed your show."

"Sally told me you don't like clowns," said Steve. "Ben thought he might inflict me on you anyway."

"Oh, it's not that," said Harrison. "I thought it would be kid's stuff." He put his book down and took a good long look at Steve. "No offence intended."

"None taken," said Steve. "Ben's been insulting me all day. I thought he brought me in here because the two of you could gang up on me."

"I wouldn't do that," said Harrison, then he smiled. "*We* could gang up on *him*, though."

"You're supposed to be on my side," said Ben.

"You know, Ben is a good person, really," said Steve. "He was a very good boy at school. He was the best-behaved person in his class. When his teacher said they should all go out in single file, he was the only one that did."

"Well, *I* heard that his teacher fancied him," said Harrison. "She kept putting kisses at the bottom of his work."

"Well, *I* heard," said Steve, "that his parents kept on playing practical jokes on him. He got home from school one day and they'd moved house."

"He went to a good school. It was approved."

"His first job after he left school was as a bouncer at Mothercare."

"He wanted a career as a window cleaner, but didn't want to start at the bottom of the ladder."

"He is different from everyone else I know. His nose runs and his feet smell."

This went on for a few minutes. Ben couldn't feel got at by the banter, because he had never seen Harrison so animated and enjoying himself. Steve had done in two minutes what he had wanted to do for the last two months. Unfortunately, he could see that Harrison was tiring, so he had to cut the visit short.

They said goodbye, and Harrison asked if he would come back some time.

"If you do, I promise I will actually watch your show next time."

Ben told him after they left his room how unusual that exchange was for Harrison.

"I must say thank you for bringing me here to see this part of your life," said Steve as they walked together back out to the car park. "I don't think I could do what you do."

"I noticed how that little girl, Cherry, affected you," said Ben. Steve was being serious, and Ben felt it appropriate not to joke right now. "But what you did for Harrison was unbelievable. He is so much, well, less depressed than when I first met him."

"That wasn't me, that was you," said Steve. "It's okay doing a show, but I wouldn't want to visit the children regularly like you do, and get close to them. It would break my heart."

Then he took a long look at Ben. "It will break yours, too."

14.

Ben bought a Dictaphone Voice Recorder from an office supplies company in Stevenbridge. He thought, rather than going straight to the hospice on that Saturday morning, he would go into town first and actually get the device that he had promised to get for Martin. He knew that, if he did not make this his first task, something would be sure to distract him and he would end up going home without buying it yet again. He left his home in Lockley early in case it took a while to find the one he wanted, but he managed to find the perfect item almost immediately. It came with a separate battery which he pocketed, intending to put it in later when he got home. After taking so long to buy it he realised, walking out of the shop, that he could have bought one online weeks ago.

After that, he visited his friend from the magic club who owned 'The Glass Slipper' which was a theatrical and party costume shop with a magic shop section at the back. He asked about printed silks.

"We have lots of printed silks," his friend told him.

"Yes, I know," said Ben. "But if I wanted a silk printed specially, could you get one organised for me?"

"Yes, but it would be expensive. They are made by a company in America."

"So you couldn't get one by Christmas?"

"No, sorry. Wait a minute. Words or Pictures?"

"Just words," said Ben.

"Does it have to be on a silk? What about a thin cloth?"

"That would be fine."

"I can get iron-on letters, and there's someone I know who could put them on to a cloth for me."

"Can you make them big?"

"Any size you want."

"For Christmas?"

"No trouble."

Ben placed his order. Then he went on to the hospice to say a quick 'hello' to Sally and Harrison. He had not known that Sally had taken a shine to him until she had told Emily during her visit a couple of weeks ago. In fact, even now he wasn't sure that it wasn't one of their jokes. They seemed to get on rather well, and he was a little bothered by the way they seemed to like a giggle at his expense. Never mind, he thought, Emily wasn't with him today.

When he got to St Mark's hospice, he was pleasantly surprised to hear from Sally that Harrison's parents were there. He had managed to miss them on a number of occasions, so it was good that they could finally meet.

Mr Bell was a tall man, probably in his late thirties or early forties, with prematurely greying hair and thick glasses that made his eyes seem unnaturally big. He wore a light jacket, which, although it was smart, he managed to make look untidy. He had a quiet voice, but he spoke with calm and confidence. Mrs Bell was a little shorter, fairly wide-shouldered with dark eyes and lots of worry lines in her face. Sally arranged for them to meet with him away from Harrison's room. They had spent an hour or so with their son that morning when they arrived, but he needed a little snooze at the end of their time together so they were free.

"We're glad to meet you at last," Mrs Bell said, "Harrison has told us about you."

"Something about you being a history teacher," said Mr Bell, shaking Ben's hand with a gentle and friendly handshake.

"I'm a teacher," said Ben, "but not history."

"Oh, sorry," said Mr Bell. "It thought he said you told him something about Alexander the Great."

"Oh, yes. I take it he didn't tell you all the details?"

"No, just that you like military history, or something."

"And green issues," said Ben. "But I was just making conversation to see if I could find some common ground with him."

"We appreciate what you're doing for him," said Mrs Bell. "He's been struggling to come to terms with his illness. We think you are helping him in a big way."

"That's very kind of you," said Ben, "But sometimes I wonder what I can do in a couple of hours a week."

"He has started to live a little since you started visiting," said Mrs Bell. "Sally tells me you even spent a whole night watching The Lord of the Rings with him."

"I like The Lord of the Rings," said Ben. "Still, as you're here I suppose I had better not hang around and make Harrison any more tired. I'll be on my way."

"Oh, no, don't go on our account" said Mrs Bell. "Geoff and I are going out to have a bite to eat while Harrison's sleeping. We'll be half an hour or so. I'm sure Harrison would be delighted to know you are here. If he wakes up." She faltered a little, and corrected herself. "I mean, if he wakes up before we get back."

While his parents were gone, Ben quietly walked into Harrison's room and sat by his bed for a while. He looked quite peaceful there, and his eyes did not look as dark and sunken as they usually were. The expression on his face was one of calm.

After twenty minutes or so, he opened his eyes.

"Hello, Ben," he said sleepily, almost as if he was expecting to see him. "I was just dreaming about heaven."

"And then you wake up and see me. That must be frightening."

Harrison smiled sleepily, not moving his head from what was obviously a comfortable place on his pillow.

"It was good," said Harrison.

"What, seeing me?"

"Heaven. It was, well, it was hard to describe. I was there, and Jesus was there to welcome me. There wasn't any pain or discomfort. I can't remember whether I felt tired or not, but I don't think I did. Everything bad in the world had gone away."

Harrison blinked and began to wake up properly. He sat up in the bed and looked at Ben. "What was I saying?" he said.

"About heaven," said Ben.

"Oh," said Harrison, and the darkness began to return to his eyes. "It was just a dream."

"It doesn't sound like a bad dream, though," said Ben. "There's something good in it that might be worth holding on to when things feel grim."

"Things do feel grim sometimes," the young lad admitted.

"I know."

"Are you a believer, too, then?" said Harrison. "Like Sally and Donald?"

"Yes. No. I don't know, really. I've never given it much thought."

"*You've* got plenty of time," said Harrison. Ben knew what he meant when he emphasised the first word. Harrison himself would not have that long to sort out what he believed. They fell into silence, not knowing how to continue this particular conversation.

Ben tried to change the subject, but he could not get much more out of the lad, and his parents came back a short while later, so Ben said his goodbyes and returned to his apartment in Lockley. He had let his house get a little untidy, and he had promised to keep it in a good condition, so he set about tidying it up a bit. He started on the kitchen, which, as small as it was, needed the most work. After an hour or so, he was satisfied that it looked acceptable, but he didn't feel like doing the rest of the house so he sat down and fiddled with the Dictaphone he had got for Martin. He needed one of those tiny screwdrivers to unscrew the battery compartment, so he went out to his car to get one, then came back into the house and sat on his bed to install the batteries and test the device. It was easy to operate; when you put your finger on the button, it recorded. When you took it off, it stopped.

"There once was a white woolly sheep," he said into the machine, "who ran up a hill rather steep; for all that it mattered, he was feeling quite shattered, and spent the next three days asleep."

He played it back, and was particularly pleased with its clarity and volume, considering he had not held it too close to his mouth. He put it in his jacket's left pocket to take to Martin, when there was a knock on the door. It was Emily.

"I'm glad you're in," she said. Her voice was stressed and urgent-sounding. Her face was lined with concern, as if there was some sort of emergency going on. "We thought you might be at the hospice. We've been trying to get hold of you, but your phone isn't switched on."

"What's up?"

"Rich Collier has been taken to hospital, and the police are ready to arrest him for possession of class B drugs."

“What?” said Ben, standing in the doorway of his granny flat like bowling pin waiting for impact. Emily did not repeat herself, but waited for a moment for his brain to engage. This news was not really a surprise, after all.

“Your car?” he said after a second or two. She nodded. It would be easier for her to bring him back here later and drop him off on her way home. In the six-minute journey to the college, she tried to tell him everything she knew about the incident.

She normally went home each night to her cottage which was a little less than a half-hour drive away. On Friday nights, however, she went to the Tin Whistle with the other staff members, so reserved a little room at the college so that she could have a drink did not have to drive all the way home to Newbridge afterwards. She had stayed overnight at the college yesterday, so that she would be there in the morning for her singing class, and the student party had been quite raucous. She had tried to intervene to calm things down and one the lads had been rude and threatening to her. Susannah, the woman from Gordon’s bodyguard team, saw what was happening and whisked the lad away to have a quiet word with him. She actually pinned him against a wall and whispered in his ear. Emily did not know what she said to him, but he looked pale and terrified afterwards. The party was dissolved immediately with lots of threats made by the three tutors who were on site, supported by the houseparent staff from the village. Rich had not been directly involved with the incident, but he had gone off in a sulk because it was his party that was being disbanded, and he then left the building in the middle of the cold, November night so that nobody knew where he was.

In the morning, the security team asked Shelley and Xander to recover their camera and see if he had appeared on it. Sure enough, he had been caught going for his drugs in the sand bucket, so the police were called in. Rich was not well-hidden at this point, having taken more of the tablets than he should have in his sulking fit. They found him lying unconscious among the trees, and the top end of the front playing field, freezing cold and looking quite ill. An ambulance was called and he had been taken to Stevenbridge hospital later that morning. Emily’s class finished early, and she had been trying to call Ben since. She knew his habit of keeping his telephone turned off, so she eventually called the hospice. He had left before she called. A little later, she decided to go out to his apartment and get him.

When they got to the college, Ben went straight to see Professor Kennington. This was where he thought he would be needed the most – not as a pastoral carer for the students, but for the professor himself.

"How is Rich Collier now?" Ben asked as he entered the staff room. Bryn was already there. He was actually kneeling at the feet of the professor, holding a mug of tea for him. The professor was sitting in an armchair, looking fairly calm, but pale.

"The hospital called a short while ago. Young Rich is recovering. He will be alright."

"And he will stay alright," said Bryn, "unless he comes within a mile of me." There was a fury in his voice that Ben did not think he had witnessed before. Bryn loved the college almost as much as the professor did and he saw this as an attack on their work here.

"What will happen, now?"

"We will not be seeing young Rich Collier again," said the professor. "He will not be coming within a mile of Bryn, you might be pleased to know. The police are currently upstairs, doing a search of all of the students' rooms. The students, in the meantime, have been cleared out of all upstairs locations and are waiting in any available downstairs room. The dining room staff are working overtime, too." The professor looked directly at Ben. "The students will be a little confused and stressed themselves, I imagine."

Ben, who was not always as quick on the uptake as he should be, did not have any problem seeing what Professor Kennington was getting at this time. Bryn was looking after the old man, so Ben excused himself and made his way to the main downstairs theatre, where many of the students were milling around speculating about what the police might find. All of the staff and students had been banned from going upstairs while the police were carrying out their search. Emily, meanwhile, was talking to the people in the dining room.

Xander and Shelley were in different rooms, too. For some reason, they felt that Xander was the best person to calm the girls (aided by Emily) in the dining room, while Shelley was working with the lads in the theatre and games room. When Ben came in a number of the lads were standing in a circle, or in what Ben, on another day, might have light-heartedly called a 'thicket'. The circle opened to accept him. John Stockton was there in the centre, and Ben could not work out from his expression whether he was angry or depressed.

"John," said Ben by way of a greeting. "I'm sorry to hear the news."

"Is Rich okay? I heard he had hypothermia."

"He's fine."

"Until his dad gets hold of him," said Charles.

"I think his dad might be a better option that Bryn Jones right now," said Ben. Two of the young people chuckled weakly, and then they stopped because they saw that John wasn't laughing.

"Look," said Ben, looking directly at John. "I want to be of some help and support here. I'm sorry if I've criticised you in the past, but I want to be on your side now."

"Even if I'm going to be kicked out of the college, too?" said John.

"Will the police find anything in your room?"

"No," said John. "I was always against Rich's party tablets. But I have taken them once or twice, in the past."

"In the past," said Ben, half question, half statement.

"Never here at the college. I hated Shelley here for interfering, but she was right, wasn't she?"

"She usually is."

"We're on the same side now," said Shelley. "I told you, Ben is the kind of person you can go to."

"What's going to happen now?" John asked Ben.

"I don't know. I don't imagine the professor has worked it all out, yet. I would say the next few days won't be easy. We'll try for business as usual; normal lessons on Monday, I imagine. Your parents will all be informed."

John let out a swear word, but Ben did not reprimand him.

"Scary, is he, your dad?" said Ben. Emily and a couple of the girls from her class came in with a tray of drinks and cakes. Ben used the rush for the food to take John aside.

"I hope you don't have to leave us," Ben said.

"Me, too."

"You can talk to me any time. I know we haven't hit it off, but it's a serious offer." John was polite in his response to Ben's serious offer, but it was more likely he would confide in Shelley than in his tutor.

It was several hours before the police had finished their search, and as the students returned to their rooms, there was much complaining about the mess that they had left behind them. Ben found that students complaining about untidiness had a funny side to it, but he was run ragged giving assistance here and there about the place, so he didn't really have time to turn it into a joke.

He no longer had a room at the college, so he could not stay the night there as he would have wanted to.

"I think I should be around tonight," he told Emily in the few minutes that they happened to be in the same place at the same time.

"You can use my room," she said.

"Emily Jane Darkchilde!" he said, mock shocked. "What are you suggesting?"

"I'm suggesting you use my room while I go to my home and sleep in my nice, comfortable bed."

"And that's all you were suggesting?" said Ben.

"Yes, that's all."

"Oh, well," said Ben with a shrug of his shoulders, and he accepted her offer.

"And my middle name isn't Jane."

Here we go again, thought Ben.

The night shift turned out to be easy. The students were in no mood for partying and small groups met in the different meeting rooms and in the corridors and on the stairwells, all still speculating as to what kind of trouble they were in and what would happen if this got to their families. The police had not found any further drugs, except in Rich Collier's room sticky-taped to the underside of his bed. The professor had decided he would not investigate further or hold any of the other students responsible for Rich's actions or the wildness of their parties. He was going to write a letter to the parents of all the students informing them of what had happened, but he was a genius with words, and would find a way of putting it so that the parents would not have any heavy concerns about the incident. Rich would not be named in the letter, of course, but the fact that he ('one of the students') had been expelled and placed in police custody would be explained.

On Sunday, after lunch, Professor Kennington received a visit from Rich Collier's father, the Right Honourable Dr James Collier, with lots of letters Ben couldn't remember after his name. Professor Kennington asked Ben to join them in the staff room, which was otherwise deserted. Bryn had gone home and not felt it necessary to return today, being Sunday.

James Collier with lots of letters was a big man in British politics. That is to say, he was a big man. The fat, or muscle, or whatever it was on him was spread out evenly over his body, so his fingers were podgy even though his stomach was not as huge as the impression he gave when he walked into the room. He had an angry expression on his face, and Ben did not know whether that was there all the time, or if he had put it there especially for this meeting. He was bald but for wisps of dark hair over his large ears. Ben wondered if the tall, skinny Rich was going to turn out like this. It seemed unlikely.

Ben was not normally a prejudiced man, but he decided very quickly that he did not like Collier senior. Ben stood while the professor and the politician sat facing each other.

"I'll come straight to the point," said Collier. "I want you to drop all charges against my son."

"No problem," said the professor with a smile. He had been talking to Gordon Franklin, who had briefed him about Collier and told him what to expect. Ben, however, did not expect his quiet, amiable reply to Collier's angry statement.

"The college has not charged your son with any crime," continued the professor. "The police, however, have, and I have no intention of obstructing them."

"So what you are saying is that, when the police free my son, you will have him back."

"Certainly not," said the professor, still seeming relaxed, still smiling amiably. Ben watched carefully as the tension built up in the room. He had the distinct impression he was about to witness a battle of giants. He put his hands in his jacket pockets. His left hand rested on the Dictaphone he had not yet got around to giving to Martin. He held the device lightly in his hand while it was still in his pocket and squeezed down on what he hoped was the 'record' button.

"Your son broke the rules," the professor continued, "and we have acted in accordance with the agreement which he signed at the beginning of term. If the police let him go, then he will still not be allowed back onto the premises."

"Even if the police drop all charges."

"That seems extremely unlikely after what they told me yesterday."

"But it's different today, now that I have had a word with them," said the big man, leaning towards the professor in a manner that Ben thought was an attempt to be intimidating. He hoped that the Dictaphone was getting all this through the lining of his pocket.

"You have instructed the police not to ahead with the charges?" said the Professor.

"As I am instructing you to take Richard back, and treat him with a little more respect."

"Respect?" said Ben angrily, almost letting go of the record button. Professor Kennington held up his hand and Ben shut up.

"No," he said to the big man.

"I could make life difficult for you," said Collier, the volume of his voice turned up a notch.

"I have had a difficult life, Mr Collier," said the professor. "I don't need you to help make it more difficult. As Mr April here was no doubt about to say, young Rich has shown no respect himself despite our efforts, and he has expelled himself by using drugs and attempting to persuade other students to use them. I have no intention of allowing him to come back and do it again."

"I will have this place closed down," said Collier, his voice booming in his anger, "and neither of you will ever work in education again."

"I'm sorry," said Ben, trying not to laugh, "I didn't quite catch that?"

"I don't think this is a laughing matter," Collier bellowed, turning in his chair to face Ben. "People like you don't come up against someone like me and get away with it. I am in a position of great influence and I can see to it that you never work again."

"Great influence," said the professor, "earned by your honesty and integrity, no doubt."

"Don't play games with me."

"I think you're mistaken," said Ben. "It's me who plays games. The professor is always straightforward. I think, at this stage, threatening him is only going to make him dig his heels in further."

"Money, then," said the big man, his antagonism turning into scheming. "Is that it? I can put quite a lot of good money your way if you would take Rich back, and stand by me when I talk to the police about dropping the charges."

Ben could see that the professor was about to object most strongly, but he wanted Collier to say more into his Dictaphone before this conversation was over, so he interrupted again.

"So you haven't yet spoken to the police? You gave us the impression that they were ready to let him go on your instructions. And now you are talking about using this college's past financial troubles against us as well, are you?"

"I can put one million pounds your way if you simply keep this incident a secret."

The professor almost exploded. He had a sense of legality and fairness that made this play by Dr Collier completely unacceptable. He also had no idea that Ben was recording what the politician said, or that he was deliberately goading him into saying something even more incriminating.

"How dare you threaten me and try to bribe me. I think this conversation is over, Dr Collier. I must ask you to leave this minute!"

"Before you go," said Ben with a much more amiable smile and a gentler tone, standing as close to Collier as possible without giving the game away. "Is there anything you would like to say as a parting shot? More threats? Increase the bribe? Perhaps you'd like to tell us how you intend to persuade or instruct the police to drop the charges?"

Collier grumbled and spat out a few obscenities before leaving. Outside, Gordon watched his chauffeur drive him away from the college before he joined Ben and the professor in the staff room. Ben beckoned the security officer in when he knocked lightly on the door. Michael Kennington said nothing. His face was red with anger.

"Gordon," said Ben as the security man entered the room. "I have a question for you."

"Go on," said Gordon.

"What is the legal status of this?" he asked as he took the Dictaphone out of his pocket and laid it on the table. He rewound it to the beginning. The professor's furious attitude changed completely. He looked as wide-eyed as a child at Christmas as he worked out what Ben had done. Gordon smiled.

"You taped the conversation?" asked the professor.

"Yes," said Ben.

"Did he threaten you?" asked Gordon.

"And tried to bribe us," said Ben with a smile. "He also swore and blustered a lot."

"A secret recording of your conversation with Dr Collier wouldn't stand up in a court of law, if that's what you are thinking," said Gordon.

"I expect it would stand up quite well in a national newspaper," said Ben.

"I will not resort to that sort of tactic," said the professor.

"Perhaps just letting the police hear it will help them change their minds about dropping the charges?" suggested Ben. "Seeing as Mr Collier has not got as far as convincing them, just yet."

"What made you think of bringing a recorder in to the staff room?" Gordon asked.

"I'm a magician," said Ben, simply, not wanting to admit that, if he had not got such a bad memory, he would not have had the device with him. He had just been lucky. He was eager that Gordon heard the conversation. He pressed 'play' and sat back in triumph, arms folded. His own voice sounded from the machine.

"There once was a white woolly sheep, who ran up a hill rather steep; for all that it mattered, he was feeling quite shattered, and spent the next three days asleep."

15.

The heavy dark clouds which seemed to hang over the college on Monday morning reflected the depressing mood which had caught hold of people there. Ben had his work cut out for him getting around as many of the students as possible and keeping them informed about what was going on with Rich. He tried to play the part of the 'morale officer', as some of the Star Trek geeks among them called him, attempting to keep people as positive as possible. However, it was going to be a struggle.

Professor Kennington had given Ben permission to tell them everything except the incident with Rich's father, but somehow that part of the story was getting around anyway. They asked about whether Rich might go to prison for drug dealing, which Ben thought was unlikely because the number of tablets he peddled was quite small. He told them that it was more likely that he would get a reprimand, and that he probably had more to fear from his parents than from the police. One or two of the students from politicians' families, who had met Dr Collier, agreed with Ben about that.

However, the police had been very unhappy when they heard the recording of the conversation which Ben had showed them. At Gordon's suggestion, they made some copies of the tape. Ben was relieved that the recording device had worked, and had recorded the full conversation with Dr Collier in addition to his own piece of rather embarrassing poetry.

Gordon had suggested that they play the recording to Dr Collier, and politely request that he gets in touch to apologise.

"Are you suggesting we blackmail him?" The professor had said.

"Certainly not," said Gordon. "He is in an emotional state right now. I just think it would be good to ask him to apologise. Having a copy of the tape will just show him how unreasonable he has been in the heat of the moment. I am sure he will regret it in the morning."

The professor was not stupid, but he accepted this reasoning anyway. Ben himself really wanted to blackmail this objectionable man even though it went against his principles (or his principal), so he had been willing to accept Gordon's reasoning just so that this incident could be brought to a satisfactory conclusion. He did at least part of what Gordon suggested and had copies made; then he went to the police to tell them about the meeting.

It turned out that the police had not actually dropped the charges, but had handed the recovering Rich Collier back to his father awaiting a decision from the Director of Public Prosecutions. The police were interested in their copy of the tape, from which the white woolly sheep poem had been erased, and were unhappy that this politician felt he could 'instruct the police' to get his son's charges dropped.

Now, for Ben at least, it was more about the students than the problem that Dr Collier had created. Professor Kennington would mull over the advice he had been given by Gordon and, later, Bryn and he would no doubt make the wisest decision. Right now, with morale in the college seriously low and fears of an uncertain future, Ben had to deal with a number of questions from the young people.

Ben saw Emily only briefly, as she was looking after the girls' questions and concerns, mostly from the safety of her classroom. Juliette was as supportive as ever, but Shelley did not seem to be around. In fact, Ben could not recall seeing her since they were both in the theatre on Saturday afternoon.

"So, what happened with Rich's dad coming around yesterday?" asked Xander at lunchtime. Ben had decided to eat before the lessons ended, then sit around in the dining room and wait for the flood of questions. Xander was one of the first, this time without Shelley by his side.

"He came to talk to the professor about Rich's situation," Ben said with some caution.

"And there was an argument," said Xander in eager anticipation of a juicy story.

"I would say it was more like a discussion," said Ben, not actually denying that Xander's description might have been more accurate.

"Yes, but what happened? People are saying he threatened to beat Kennington up."

"Xander."

"*Professor* Kennington, sorry."

"He did *not* threaten to beat Professor Kennington up," said Ben, being honest, but obeying the professor's instructions to keep the details confidential. "Tell 'people' that."

"So, what *did* he threaten?" said Xander, who was far too clever to let it go.

"He asked for Rich to be allowed back in the college."

"You're not going to let him back, are you?" said Xander, some distress in his voice at the idea.

"No, we are not," confirmed Ben.

"Some of the London people, the ones connected to politics in particular, are saying that this incident will see the end of the college."

"Last year, there were rumours about the end of the college, too. I think, possibly, we'll be around for a while yet."

"Have a word with John," said Xander, as if he knew something that Ben didn't.

It was later in the afternoon when Ben found John. The young politician was sitting in the cold on the low side garden wall, staring out over the field. He was looking at the trees where the barely-conscious Rich had been found on Saturday morning. He looked a little lost and alone.

"Mind if I join you?" asked Ben and John barely nodded his head in response.

"They say snow is on its way," said Ben, making conversation rather badly.

"In a week or two," said John. "Something about pressure changes in Greenland, or something."

"I imagine your parents don't know about the situation with Rich yet? Or do they know his father?"

"Everybody knows his father," said John in a completely fed-up voice. Obviously, Dr Collier had been shouting about the incident to every parent of the college students that he knew.

"How are things between you and them? Your parents, I mean."

"They called me, and we had a long talk."

"Bad?"

"I'm not sure. They will support Dr Collier, even though they don't like him. We'll all be taken out of the college. So, yes, that's bad. But not as bad as it's going to be for you."

"Me?"

"The college."

"Because of the revenue we would lose if you and the others leave?"

"More than that."

"Did they tell you that Dr Collier intended to do more than persuade them to remove you from the college?"

"He's starting some campaign against you. Or at least, against the professor. Something about him not being fit for work."

"Dr Collier isn't fit to run the country, but that's not stopping him," said Ben.

John shrugged.

"I said I believed in our political system," he said. "I do, honestly. But sometimes, some people abuse their power. If they have enough supporters, they think they can control everything."

"You're not 'in power' to exercise that power for your own benefit. You're in it to serve."

"That's right."

"I think I should warn the professor. Is that alright with you?" asked Ben, not really needing his permission.

"I think he has some friends in high places, too," said John.

"Juliette's father thinks favourably of us, and *he* has the ear of the Prime Minister, I think. But I don't think Professor Kennington will resort to calling in the big guns unless there was nothing else he could do."

"There are other guns, just as big, that the professor might be prepared to bring in. I hope so." Once again, John seemed to know something that Ben didn't. Perhaps he just spent too much time hiding away in his cellar. John was well-connected, so he probably made it his business to know what was going on. He may even know Emily Darkchilde's real surname. Ben refrained from asking him.

"Let me know what happens," John said. "Please."

"It seems you know more about what is happening than I do," replied Ben, "but yes, I will keep you informed as much as I can."

The professor was in the staff room, and so was Bryn and Emily and one or two of the other teachers.

"Have you told Dr Collier about the recording yet?" Ben asked as he walked in, nodding to his colleagues in lieu of a greeting.

"No," said the professor. "I needed time to think about it."

"Well, he's making good his threat. He's getting all the parents he knows, all the ones with money and influence, and putting them against the college."

"I know," said the professor, and his voice sounded even, not distressed in any way. "I have been on the telephone to some of them in the last hour or so. I had to tell them what he said to us."

"He will just deny it."

"I told them we recorded it."

"You told *them*, but not *him*?"

"Yes," said the professor, and his shoulders slumped a bit. "I also hinted that the recording might be handed over to a national newspaper fairly soon."

"But Dr Collier himself doesn't know this."

"I have told three sets of parents so far. I imagine he will know about it fairly soon. That's why I came down here. I needed to be away from the phone. Becky is in the office, and will send for me when he calls."

"And I expect she'll probably not be able to find you."

"Oh, she knows where I am," he smiled, "but it might take a while for me to get to the phone."

"You're playing games," said Ben. "You don't play games."

"I don't *like* playing games," said the professor, "but I *will* play if I have to. I didn't start this game, but I will play it to the end."

"Can I come with you?" asked Ben. "When you go to the office to take his call? I know I won't hear his voice or see the expression on his face, but just hearing your side of the conversation will feed my imagination sufficiently."

"It might not go well."

"I know."

"I suppose," said Bryn, "seeing as you made the recording, you should have the privilege of going to the office with the professor. But I am the deputy head, second in command, lieutenant or whatever you want to call me. I think the professor needs me by his side."

"I think he doesn't need a second in command right now," grinned Ben. "He needs a pastoral carer."

"He needs the one person in the college who has been his friend for the longest time."

The banter between the two of them successfully showed the professor that he had the support of his staff, and even seemed to lighten his load a little. He agreed for both Bryn and Ben ('the flowerpot men', as Emily called them) to accompany him when Dr Collier called, which was just a few minutes later. They followed the principal up the wide staircase to his office, where they listened in silence, hoping to work out everything that the big man said to the professor from the one half of the conversation.

"Hello, Doctor Collier, I hope I didn't keep you *too* long… Yes, that's right… No, I was unaware of the recording, too, until after you left… No, I have not reprimanded him; neither do I know how many copies he made... I think the word 'illegal' is a little strong. I am sure we have plenty of signs around the college saying that we are a performing arts college and we use recording equipment. Perhaps you didn't notice them – after all, you were quite angry yesterday when you visited. And I feel that offering me a bribe is a little bit more illegal than us recording you offering it, so it might be worth consulting your solicitor on that one… hello?

"Oh dear," the professor said, putting the telephone down. "He seems to have hung up on me."

"He is not backing down, then?" said Bryn.

"I think he may need legal advice, first," said the professor.

"He might have better solicitors than we have. It could get nasty."

The professor sat down in his chair. He looked sad and tired, but not angry or worried. He smiled up at Bryn and Ben.

"He *does not* have better solicitors than us," he said, looking at Ben, because Bryn already knew. "If he does his research, he will know that quite soon, and it might make a difference in our favour."

"Something I don't know?" said Ben.

"I love it when I know something you don't," said Bryn. "I don't know whether you know *this*, Ben, but I am the longest serving member of staff here. I think I am the only teacher here who has been here before Michael came. When he changed the place into what it is today, he had a great deal of support, including a very good friend of his – someone who is regarded as this country's top lawyer. He is probably the reason why this place has stayed open through troubled times."

"And I need to have a talk with Sir Gerald fairly soon, I think," said the professor. "But it might be best if the two of you do not listen in on *this* conversation."

The two teachers left, and as they walked slowly down the wide stone stairway back to the staff room, Ben asked Bryn for more information.

"Sir Gerald. I have it in my head that I've heard that name before."

"He might have visited this college since you have started, although you might not have known who he was. He thinks very highly of you," said Bryn, getting as much mileage out of his 'secret' knowledge as he could. "You should meet him one day. But don't do any of your magic tricks; he wouldn't be impressed by them."

"Who is he?" asked Ben.

"Sir Gerald Hickman, a top lawyer, like the professor said. *The* top lawyer, probably."

"Hickman?" said Ben. "Shelley's father?"

"Grandfather," said Bryn. "Very nice man. Generous soul, like his granddaughter. You haven't seen the young lady around today, have you?"

"No," Ben replied, thoughtfully. "She's normally in the middle of everything. I don't know where she is now."

"She disappeared rather late yesterday afternoon," said Bryn, his smile almost reaching his ears. He was *really* loving this. "Nobody seems to have seen her since."

"Paying a visit to her grandfather?" suggested Ben, catching on at last.

"Off for a little break to his mansion in the Cotswolds, I should think," said Bryn. "They have a lot to talk about."

Ben wondered if the professor got as little sleep as he got over the next couple of days. Students and teachers alike had been worried about the future of the college and there was much unnecessary speculation about what might happen next. The professor spent a lot of Tuesday visiting all the classes and being as reassuring as possible. He continued to look sad and tired, but not worried. There was something about his attitude, even under these circumstances, that inspired hope. He never seemed to worry about things, but carried an attitude about him that said whatever happened, he would deal with it. If the college did close down and his dream came to an end, he would cope. It was as if he was able to shut his emotions down and just think.

Ben wished he had such a talent right now. Both his emotions and his brain were not doing what he wanted them to do. Lack of sleep meant that he felt like he could laugh or cry at any moment, and he felt strongly about every student's desire to stay here at the college and improve in the performance of their various skills and talents. He couldn't switch off his thinking, either, and his ideas for Pamela's Christmas performance buzzed through his head, mixing with what he would say the next time he saw Harrison or what it would be like out here in the wilds if the heavy snow that was forecast actually fell on Lockley. He knew that the kitchen was stocking up on food and supplies in case road communication got bad and they couldn't get their normal deliveries in.

He had noticed, over the next two days, that none of the students said that they were going to leave the college. In spite of the threats that Dr Collier might have made, and the reluctant support that John Stockton had suggested some of them gave to him, the parents seemed to be keen on keeping their offspring here at Lockley. Perhaps they had spoken to each other as well as to Dr Collier, or possibly they had been contacted by Sir Gerald Hickman, or Professor Kennington had persuaded them that his college was the best place for them to be. A little optimism was beginning to seep back into the place.

When Mark turned up on Wednesday morning, the first day of his half-week at the college, Ben realised that everything had happened since Mark had last left the premises. No doubt the entire village knew by now what had been going on over the last five days, but Mark's mother would not have burdened her son with it. He turned up as usual, having no clue as to what had been going on. Like many people with Asperger's Syndrome, he was unable to read body language or interpret the moods of people around him, so it would be difficult for him to be aware of the situation without being told in detail about it. Ben was already fed up of talking about it, and he thought he would do them both a favour and not mention it unless Mark asked. Anyway, Mark had something else on his mind.

He rushed down to Ben's classroom as soon as he got there. His face was screwed up with concentration and determination.

"Ben," he said almost before he was through the door. He looked around to make sure nobody else was there.

"Hello, Mark," said Ben.

"I need to t-talk to you."

"Certainly," said Ben. "What about?"

"I m-meant to s-say this b-before, b-but I d-didn't know how t-to t-tell you."

"This is the big secret that has been getting you down?" said Ben.

"I should have t-told you. It's b-bothered m-me ever s-since."

"Tell me now, Mark. I am sure it will be fine."

"I've b-been offered a j-job."

"That's fantastic," said Ben. Only about ten percent of people with Asperger's Syndrome hold down a job, and Ben knew that his mother was very concerned for his future. "How did that happen?"

"I have b-been t-talking to people on the Internet," said Mark. "There's a p-place in Stevenbridge that has seen what I d-do. With c-computers. They want me to work p-programming c-computers for them."

"That's fantastic," Ben said again, struggling for words. Then he had a thought. "But I thought you were unhappy about something."

"I am," said Mark. "I don't want the j-job."

"What?"

"I d-d-d…" he struggled with his words, and stopped, as Ben had told him in the past, and took a deep breath. "I don't think I c-could do it. It would m-mean leaving the c-college. Now, before the end of the year. And I w-would have to…"

"Have to?" Ben tried to encourage him.

"I just d-don't want to leave the c-college."

"You would have to what?" Ben persisted.

"I-I would have t-to m-meet n-new p-p-people."

"You're afraid," said Ben. Mark's head went down and he took on his customary pose examining the floor.

"Mark," Ben continued. "Most people are afraid to some extent when they start a new job. Don't worry about your feelings."

"Were you afraid?" said Mark. "When you c-came here?"

"No," said Ben, "I was really looking forward to it. It was when I met you that I started to be afraid."

Mark laughed. It was hit-and-miss as to whether Mark got Ben's jokes, but this one had broken the tension.

"This place that wants to employ you," asked Ben, "do they know about your Asperger's?"

"Yes."

"And they want you anyway?"

"They want m-me *b-because* of it."

"What?"

"P-people with Asp-perger's are often g-good with c-computers."

"Of course," said Ben. "I would accept. Take the job. You might not get another chance like this."

But Mark was still unsure. Ben realised that he was giving Mark the same advice that his mother would be giving him – sometimes he saw Ben as a surrogate father – but Mark was an adult now, and had to make his own mind up. However, Ben worried that he would make the wrong decision.

As Mark went about his own preparations for the lesson, Ben thought back about his own life decisions. When he was at teacher training college, he paid his way, at least to start with until he came into some money, by taking up magic and doing shows and parties. Then, when he qualified as a teacher, he decided he would rather be a performer instead, and disappointed his mother by leaving the teaching profession even before he started. He was hardly the best role-model for Mark.

Ben's mind also went back to when his old friend Steve Goss paid his visit, and how sharp the old clown's observations were, as always. Steve had noticed that there was something going on with Mark. He also remembered what he said on the way out of the hospice, how the place had affected him emotionally. He thought about John Stockton's efforts to improve in contrast to Rich Collier's lack of same, and he had another idea.

He hadn't really liked John from the beginning, probably because of his earlier attitude towards Mark. However, the lad's efforts were starting to win him over. Whatever he felt about Rich, John had stood by his friend, and even now he was actively encouraging people not to say bad things about him. Now it was time, thought Ben, to build some bridges and possibly give the young Londoner an experience he might not have had before. He invited John to join him on his Wednesday afternoon trip to the hospice.

John was reluctant at first. It was not because he did not want to visit the hospice, but rather because he thought that Ben wanted to give him a lecture on behaviour and attitude while they made the journey there. Ben told him that it was about giving him an experience outside of the college and he finally agreed to go. There were no lectures on the way.

When they got there, earlier in the afternoon than Ben normally arrived on his Wednesday visits, Sally greeted them both, and took John for a guided tour of the place while Ben went to see Harrison. Sally flirted with John in the light-hearted way she had originally flirted with Ben, and John obviously enjoyed the attention she gave him. Her father, Donald, was there, and was able to share with John a little of his vision for doing some good in the community which, Ben hoped, would appeal to the young lad's political mind. Donald also explained the financial stresses that St Mark's hospice was always under, getting no direct support from the government and constantly having to fill in reams of paperwork in their applications for grants and aid.

Ben knocked on Harrison's door. The lad was out of bed and dressed, which was a good sign. In his current tired and emotional state, Ben would not have coped well if Harrison was ill.

"Hello, Harrison," he said. "You know, I had a terrible experience the other day. I just went in to a pub out in the country, on the road to Newbridge."

"Newbridge?" said Harrison. "That's not far from here, is it? Your Emily Darkchilde lives there."

Ben was astounded at Harrison's knowledge. "Yes, that's right. It's around five miles from here. Emily lives in a cottage in the country just outside the town. But how did you know?"

"I Googled Emily Darkchilde."

"It didn't tell you her real surname, did it?"

"No," said Harrison. "What is her real surname?"

"No idea," said Ben.

"Anyway," said Harrison. "This pub."

"Yes," continued Ben. "It was deserted. I mean, the door was open and everything, but there didn't seem to be anyone around. Then I heard a voice."

Ben put on a silly, high-pitched voice. "'Hello there', it said. 'It's good to see you. It is always good to have such a fine-looking gentleman as yourself in our establishment.'

"Well, I looked around to find out where the voice was coming from, but it looked like the little bowl of peanuts on the bar was actually speaking. I bent down to take a closer look.

"'Hello?' I said, and they replied to me. I was amazed. The peanuts were really talking. They said all sorts of nice things about me. I was stunned. In my shock, I took a couple of steps back, and I bumped into the cola machine.

"'Oi!' it said. 'Watch where you're walking, you clumsy old fool. I don't know, we really get some idiots in here sometimes.'

"Well, at that point the bartender walked in from out the back. 'Hello,' he said. 'Welcome to our pub. Just so you know, the peanuts are complementary, but the cola machine is out of order."

Harrison laughed. He actually laughed, out loud, a proper laugh, the first time he had laughed that way in all the time Ben had known him. Ben had been worn down by the events of the past five days, and was feeling more emotionally fragile than he normally would. Seeing Harrison laugh like this almost made him want to cry.

Then they chatted together for a little while, and the conversation came easier that it had in the past, which Ben saw as progress. Harrison talked about Christmas coming, and how he had made friends with the new little girl, Cherry, who would probably move in as a resident here sometime during December. Very soon, it was time for the Wednesday afternoon story before tea time.

Rev Donald Hinton told the story, which he introduced as a true story. He told about when the fishermen at the Sea of Galilee were in their boat and a storm blew up, but Jesus was sleeping. He made the children make storm sounds, rapidly tapping their legs for heavy rain and blowing for the wind. Ben noticed John was surrounded by younger children, including Cherry, who was visiting again today. There were two on his lap, which looked comical as John was a thin young man and didn't have that much room on his lap in the first place. Cherry sat on the floor clinging to his leg, and a fourth was standing next to where he was seated, leaning against him and wrapping her arms around his. They were all around six years old. He seemed to be loving it. Ben wondered if he was sorry they were too young to vote, then he silently told himself off for being negative about him.

Donald told them about Jesus standing up in the boat, which was in danger of capsizing in the terrible storm, and telling the wind to shut up, and telling the rain to stop. And it did! The fishermen all wondered who he was, that could do such things. Donald talked about what happens when our own lives feel stormy, and about finding someone we can turn to when we need some calm.

At tea time, the adults all sat on different tables. John ate with his entourage of six-year-olds, Ben ate with Harrison and a couple of the older lads, and Sally and her father joined the others. After tea, Donald approached Ben.

"Can I show you this?" he said, pulling out some playing cards. There were just six cards in his hands.

"Ooh, I'm not so sure," said Ben. "Playing cards are the 'Devil's Playthings', aren't they? I'm not sure a man of the cloth should be messing about with things like that."

"The Devil's Playthings? I like that. I'm not sure I have come across that phrase before."

"You've obviously led a sheltered life."

"I don't think so," said the vicar with a grim smile. "But I'd be grateful for your opinion of this trick anyway. I got it from someone on the Internet. I joined Christian Magicians UK, like we said, and they have been very helpful. I'd like to run this by you."

"That would be great," said Ben.

"I want to do the whole talk, not just show you a trick," he explained.

"That's what I am always telling my students," said Ben.

"Right," and he composed himself. "I want to teach you Magic Spelling. What you do is take one card from the top and put it on the bottom for each letter in the word. Like this."

He picked up one card form the top of the face down pack, and put it on the bottom, and said, "A." Then he did the same for "C," and "E," before turning over the next card and revealing an Ace of Spades. He put the revealed card down on the table next to them.

"Now it's your turn," he said, and handed the cards over to Ben. "I want you to find the two."

Ben copied Donald's actions. He had done a similar trick before, but he was not sure where this one was going.

"T, W, O," he spelled out, and then turned the next card over. It was not a two. It was the King of Hearts.

"Ah," said Donald, taking the five remaining cards, including the King of Hearts, back from Ben. "The King of Hearts. I am so glad you found that one. The King of Hearts is my favourite card in the pack. Do you know why? You see, thirty-eight years ago, when I was sixteen, I made Jesus the king of my heart. I suppose up to that point I always wanted to be my own boss, but I have found that, with Jesus as the king, things have gone the way they should. But what I wanted you to do was this. T, W, O."

He returned the King of Hearts face down on to the top of the deck and counted out the spelling. When he revealed the top card this time, it was the Two of spades, which he laid on the table next to the Ace.

"Have another go," he said. "See if you can find the three."

"T, H, R, E, E," spelled Ben, working through the deck as Donald had shown him. He turned over the King of Hearts again.

"Ah," said Donald. "Did you know, although I made Jesus the king of my heart, I haven't always acted as if He was king. Sometimes I've taken my life back; I've done things my way. This hasn't always been a good thing. Luckily, every time I have gone wrong, I have been able to go back and say sorry, and God has always forgiven me for the times when I've acted as though Jesus was not the king of my heart. But what I wanted you to do was this. T, H, R, E, E," and he spelled out the next card, revealing the Three of Spades at the end of it. Having placed the three with the first two, he handed the cards back to Ben and asked him to find the four. Ben, of course, found the King of Hearts again.

"Ah," said Donald. "The King of Hearts card reminds me that Jesus is always the King, even when we don't feel like he is. Sometimes, when things are really not well with my world, when I am feeling the pressure of things and everything is getting me down, I can talk to the King in my prayers, and I just know He is in control. But what I wanted you to do was this. F, O, U, R," and he revealed the four, and put it with the others.

He handed over the cards to Ben to have a go at finding the five.

"Seeing as there are only two cards left, it should be easy enough," he explained. Unsurprisingly, Ben found the King of Hearts again.

"This last appearance of the King of Hearts has reminded me to ask you to think about something. I've told you about who is King of my heart. What about you? Who have you made the King of *your* heart?"

Donald finished off by finding the Five of Spades, and laying the last card in his hand, the King of Hearts, on top of the others on the table.

"What do you think?" he asked.

"Brilliant," said Ben. "It's a great use of an ordinary card trick. And you had obviously practiced well."

"Two days," admitted Donald. "I practised every spare moment I could get. It nearly drove my wife mad."

Ben soon had to leave, so he detached John from his miniature fan club and took him back to the college before going back to his own apartment.

John didn't say a word for the whole journey home. Ben had hoped that the hospice's bright and positive atmosphere would be a benefit to him, but it seemed that the place had a very profound effect on him indeed.

Professor Kennington called Ben and Bryn into his office first thing on Thursday morning. Ben thought of them as Ben and Bryn now, rather than saying Bryn first in his head, because Emily's little title for them made him laugh, and the current crisis was the wrong place to laugh at 'flowerpot men' jokes.

"Dr Collier got in touch with me yesterday evening," said the professor. "It was fairly late, so I thought I would leave it until now to tell you. He was very polite. He apologised for causing us so much trouble and for his son's behaviour over the last few weeks. He also offered us a substantial compensation: twenty-five thousand pounds."

"We could convert that barn into classrooms for that," said Bryn.

"But we won't," said the professor. "I turned him down. I also promised, without his asking, that the recordings would be destroyed."

"All of them?" said Ben, already knowing what the professor would say.

"All of them," said the professor. "I gave my word."

"But twenty-five thousand pounds," said Bryn, and the sum of money sounded all the more special when he said it with that fabulous Welsh accent, Ben thought.

"...is nothing to him," said the professor.

"But to come to you humbly and apologise," said Ben, realising what the professor was getting at, "that would have cost him."

"That's why I thought an apology was all we needed," said the professor.

16.

Shelley Hickman returned to the college later on Thursday, and her return brought with it a return to normality for the staff and students. Word had got around that the professor had 'won', and that support for the college was stronger than ever. Even the phantom sign writer struck again. The sign on the door on Friday was 'Keep Alert. They make good pets.'

The magic lessons this week had not really sparkled, especially as it included talks and research on past masters and the history of modern performance magic. Mark was fascinated by magicians of past ages, but the class wanted to do magic tricks, so Ben had tried to reproduce some of their most famous performances.

He had gone home as early as possible on Thursday, almost as soon as Mark had left. He went to bed almost immediately, and slept soundly until morning. Now, on Friday, he was feeling a lot stronger, although he still took it easy watching the efforts of the small number of students who came down to the cellar to join him and Mark for their practise session.

Pamela popped by to say 'hello', but went away quickly, explaining that she was working on her Christmas show piece.

The morning went by slowly, probably because Ben was eager to meet up with Shelley and ask her a few questions.

Ben found Xander and Shelley sitting together at lunch. No surprise there, he thought. They were surrounded by the other students, all eager to know what Shelley knew. Ben had only just found out about Shelley's family's connection to the college, and was surprised that so many students already knew that she was the one to go to if you needed to know anything. Having said that, he thought, the two students were always what he called the founts of all student knowledge, so he should have expected the kind of crowd that they were generating.

He stood behind the crowd, waiting his turn. As soon as they noticed him there, they parted for him to join them, just like they had in the theatre on Monday. Someone gave up his seat for Ben to sit opposite Shelley. However, they did not leave him in peace. They crowded back around them and were extremely quiet, for a group of young people, eagerly waiting for the exchange between the two.

Ben leaned towards the young dancer and looked at her, and she looked back. He said nothing to start with, but looked as if he was about to. The other students seemed to move in closer.

"When I look into your eyes," he said in a mock romantic manner, "I see two beautiful reflections of me."

"I'll use that one," said Xander.

"Hello, Ben," said Shelley. "If you don't mind me being personal, you look tired."

"It's been an eventful few days. *You* took a holiday."

"Everybody knows," said Shelley. "Rich's dad tried to have a go at this place, and he lost. The only thing they didn't know was that Dr Collier offered money by way of an apology."

"The professor didn't accept it," Ben told her. "He might have seen it as some kind of bribe."

"The professor turning down Dr Collier's gift has created a problem," said Shelley. "He's got some money, thousands, I think, ready to donate, but the professor won't accept it."

"That's right," said Ben. "I think the professor thinks he's rubbing Collier's nose in it. He has accepted Collier's apology, and that's enough."

"Ben," said Xander in a reproachful way.

"What?" said Ben.

"*Doctor* Collier."

"Sorry," said Ben with a smile. It was only fair, as he had reprimanded Xander for not using the professor's title. But perhaps he felt that after Collier's behaviour, he did not deserve the respect of his title being used.

"How much?" said Xander.

"I'm *very* sorry," said Ben.

"No, I mean how much money did the professor turn down?"

"Twenty-five thousand," said Ben. Now, why did he tell them that? The professor probably would not want that kind of information to be passed around the college, and he had just said it in front of Xander, Shelley and a horde of students. He could hardly swear them to secrecy. Well, he could, but it wouldn't mean anything.

"And now he has all that money set aside," said Shelley, "and he can't do anything with it."

"I'd like to have so much money I didn't know what to do with it," said Ben. "Perhaps Dr Collier could put some my way."

There was not much new stuff to be said, and the gossip turned to light-hearted chatter. The tension among the students was beginning to dissipate. Xander and Shelley were good for this college, thought Ben. They were also good for each other. It was strange, how they were always together, but they weren't that affectionate. Perhaps Emily and Ben were role models for them. They, too, spent plenty of time together, but they had not become all that expressive in their affection.

Ben realised how much he had missed Emily in the last few days. She had always been someone he could talk to, unwind to when the pressure was on, but the busy-ness of the past few days had seen them both, although based in the same building, going in different directions. Right now, there was nothing he wanted more than some quality time with her. At the end of the school day, she was tidying up in her classroom.

Ben came in and looked around. There was nobody else there. He went over to the window and looked out over the field.

"What is it?" Emily asked, joining him at the window.

"Just making sure we are not being watched," he said, and he turned to her and took her in his arms and gave her a kiss. She responded, and an immeasurable amount of time went past quite quickly.

"Yes," said Emily in a soft voice when they finally, reluctantly parted an inch or two. "That was a long time coming. It's funny how we can be in the same building and not be together."

"I was thinking exactly the same thing," Ben said.

"I think I got that."

"It's been a hard week."

"But we are through it," Emily said. "You have been brilliant."

"I think everyone else has been brilliant, I only…" but Emily interrupted him.

"Don't argue with me," she said, and then she kept his mouth occupied so that he couldn't argue even if he wanted to.

That evening, in the Tin Whistle, all of the staff that could make it were there. Emily had taken to parking her car, when she was driving, by Ben's granny flat, and walking with him to the village pub. It was only five minutes or so away but if they walked *really* slowly, they could make it fifteen.

Bryn was fielding questions that night, and Ben realised how fed up he was becoming of the Rich Collier story. Perhaps 'fed up' was the wrong way of putting it, but he had definitely had enough. He and Emily left together early. They had both been in the centre of it enough, especially Ben, and it was Bryn's turn to have the limelight, as deputy head, lieutenant, or whatever his title might eventually be.

"I haven't had a drink tonight," said Ben. "I can give you a lift back to the college, if you like."

"I haven't had a drink, either," said Emily. "I am not going back to the college tonight. I cancelled my lesson with the children tomorrow. I'm going straight home, and I will sleep away the weekend."

"You have time to come in for a while first?"

"Of course," she said. They spent an hour or two in each other's company, pleased to be away from everything else, and delighted to be together. Staying awake for longer but with each other seemed to wash away the tiredness and stress of the last few days.

"You know," said Emily, nursing a mug of tea and looking completely relaxed in Ben's armchair, "although we've been apart doing our various different things, we have both been working together separately."

"You said you didn't have anything to drink," joked Ben.

"I mean, you and I have both been the pastoral carers while the whole college has been stressing about this Collier thing. Everyone comes to us, students *and* teachers."

"Yes, they do, do they?"

"Like I said, we make a good team," said Emily, "even when we are not in the same room."

Emily left for home eventually, and Ben finally made it to bed. On Saturday, rather late in the morning, he got up and made his way to the college. He arrived in time for lunch, which he made his breakfast. That was becoming a habit, but he was never reprimanded by the kitchen staff, who all treated him as if they were his mother.

In the afternoon, he walked around outside. It was very chilly. The sky was heavily clouded now, and the forecast snow seemed evident in the weak light. People had warm clothes on and some even wore coats, but they still did not stay indoors. John Stockton had some sheets of note paper in his hand when Ben met him on the front lawn.

They said 'hello' to each other and John showed him his notes. He had decided to have another go and producing a political-style leaflet. This time, however, rather than a 'vote for me' type of leaflet, he had decided to put Shelley up as a leader for a new student union. He told Ben that Shelley had sounded quite shocked at the idea, especially coming from him, because they had spent most of the term arguing. There was nothing they seemed to be able to agree on. Ben was interested to hear about his plans.

They went inside to get an afternoon coffee, but went back outside to chat, because that was where John thought he could find the people he wanted to talk to.

"It sounds very interesting," Ben told him as they sat down on the stone seat next to the reed pond at the front of the kitchen area. "This is a bit different from your earlier 'Vote for me' leaflet."

"The exercise early in the term was just that," said John, "an exercise in creative writing. It didn't mean anything then. But since this Collier incident people have been asking for a student union. Shelley has gone to the professor, and he seems to be in favour of it. I thought I would put together a more serious paper. Only this one is not for me. I thought I would put her up for president."

"You fancy her, don't you?" said Ben after some thought.

"I beg your pardon?" said John.

"You like Shelley."

"I *respect* her," John said. "We haven't always seen eye to eye, and I think what she did to Rich was horrible, but I can't deny that he deserved it and she was only acting in what she thought was the best interests of the college."

"And now you're giving her your support."

"And you have said yourself," he continued as if Ben had not said anything, "that if there was a student union, she should be the head of it."

"And you have just discovered that she is well-connected, too, which might in the future help your political career."

"Yes, of course," said John.

"Nope," said Ben. "If that was true, you would have denied it. You fancy her."

"I think you are living in a fantasy world," said John, who, for some reason, felt he had the right to talk to his teacher that way. I suppose he does, thought Ben, seeing as I have just challenged him on his feelings for Shelley. "It's not Shelley I fancy."

"I think some phrase about protesting too much comes to mind," said Ben. "But I wouldn't pin down hopes about winning the young lady's heart. You'd have to get past Xander first."

"He is quite protective of her, isn't he? They are good friends. But I'm sure if she was interested in… in anyone, he would not stand in her way."

"I think he might. Good friends?" started Ben, but he didn't get to finish his argument, as John saw the person he had been looking for. He excused himself and called over to Martin, who was running across the field.

"Hey, Martin!" he called. Ben remained by the pond, but he heard what happened next. Being a Saturday, Mark was not at the college to help John put his ideas into a design he could use on the computer, so he was looking for someone else who could help. He picked the wrong person if he thought that Martin could do it.

"You're good with words. And I've seen you work with Mark at the computers," John said, handing Martin his sheet of notes. "I don't suppose you could help with this? You could probably come up with something clever."

"No, I'm alright, thanks."

"Well, at least you could take a look at it," John insisted, thrusting the paper into his hands. Martin looked down at the sheet. Ben did not work out what was about to happen as he turned to walk down to his classroom, but something stopped him and made him listen in on the conversation from a distance.

"Look," the young comedian said, "I can't help you right at the moment."

John took a good look at Martin and the way he was holding the piece of paper. Clues from the past term must have slipped into John's mind. He remembered how Martin had behaved in class, especially when there was reading or written work to be done. He snatched his notes back from Martin.

"You can't read," he said. "You can't read, and you probably can't write."

Martin looked back at him, a mixture of emotions in his face.

"I could read and write even before I went to school," said John, not so much boastfully as incredulous at finding out that Martin couldn't.

"I suppose your mother wasn't in a drug rehab institution before you were three, either," Martin spat out and stormed back towards the house, brushing past Ben. Ben called out to him as he did.

"I'm in the cellar for an hour or two, Martin. I'll open up the classroom, but only for you."

John looked at Ben, almost as if he did not know what he had done.

"We must be a real disappointment to you," Ben said to him angrily as he walked across the front of the building towards the side of the house where his cellar was. He realised that he had just ruined what he had thought was becoming a good relationship. When he got to his classroom, he noted that the 'Lert' sign was still there. Nobody had changed it since yesterday, then.

He sat on one of the student's chairs in his room, wondering about Martin and John. In some sense, the two lads were representative of the different cultures in the college, but they had not actually been at each other's throats all the time. John had laughed, in the past, at Martin's jokes, and Martin had listened to John's opinions, even to some of his political arguments. Just now, John was prepared to ask for Martin's help. They had not actually been all that antagonistic towards each other, but they had never been friends.

Well, they certainly weren't friends now.

Martin came down to Ben's room a few minutes later. He glanced briefly at the 'Lert' sign on the way in. He looked a little down, and the sparkling personality and the comical remarks weren't there.

"Take a seat," said Ben.

"Now everyone will know," said Martin, slumping into the chair at head of the classroom, the chair Ben normally used.

"We could ask John to keep it confidential."

"Once one person knows anything in this place, nobody keeps it confidential," said Martin. He picked up a Chinese coin and fiddled with it. It was a large metal disc a little bigger than a £2 coin with a square hole in the centre. He walked it between his fingers.

"We did alright to keep it to just a few of us up to now," said Ben, "but I suppose it was always going to get out eventually."

"I suppose," said Martin. He relaxed a bit. There was nothing he could do about this situation, anyway.

"Can something be 'always eventually'?" said Ben.

"What?"

"Can it be always eventually going to get out?"

"I expect so."

"Your English is better than mine," said Ben. "You should know."

"It's like the letter to the zoo," said Martin, brightening up a bit.

"What letter?"

"When you don't know how to put something."

"What are you talking about?"

"A man wrote a letter to the zoo," said Martin, the humour coming back to his voice. "It said, Dear zoo, I'm thinking of starting a zoo myself. Can you send me two mongooseses? No, that's not right. Dear zoo, I'm thinking of starting a zoo myself. Can you send me two mongeeseries? No. Dear zoo, I'm thinking of starting a zoo myself. Can you send me two mongi? No, that's not right either. Dear zoo, I'm thinking of starting a zoo myself. Can you send me a mongoose? While you're at it, can you send me another one?"

Ben laughed, and then he had a thought.

"Why are you so good with words?" he said.

"I don't know."

"I mean, you can't read and write, but you're really clever with words. That's not right."

"You think I should be rubbish?" suggested Martin with a smile.

"I don't think anyone is ever rubbish. Being here has taught me that and I am sorry for every time I have ever looked at someone and thought they were no good. But you are *really* sharp with your words. You said as much to Steve Goss when he visited. Do you have dyslexia?"

"No, I was tested for that when I was at school."

"What is it, then? Why can you talk, but not read?"

Martin fell silent, and the spark of humour that was just beginning to resurface dulled again.

"Sorry," said Ben. "I didn't mean to pry."

"Bad upbringing," said Martin, shrugging his shoulders and hoping that was going to be enough of an explanation. "If ever I have children, I will make sure they are looked after in ways I wasn't."

There was a knock on the door of the classroom which sounded almost tentative. It was John. He spoke quickly before Ben could say anything.

"I've come to apologise," he said, "and to offer Martin any help he might want, any time he might want it."

Ben looked at Martin for his permission to let John in and Martin nodded. John came in and held out his hand for Martin to shake. The young comedian put down the Chinese coin and accepted his hand.

"I haven't, oh, how can I put it?" said John, unable to deliver the lines he wanted to use. "I haven't ever come across…"

"Clever people who can't do some ordinary things?" Ben suggested.

"Yeah," said John. "I thought Mark was stupid."

"But he's a genius," said Ben.

"Well, he's pretty clever," said John and Martin agreed.

"No," said Ben, "he's a genius. A real genius, I mean. He has an IQ of well over 150. He is in the top two percent of the country."

"I didn't know that."

"Some people think that Einstein had Asperger's Syndrome. They say he could unravel the secrets of the universe, but he couldn't boil an egg."

"His mind was a bit lop-sided, then?" said Martin.

"I think that might be the technical term for it, yes," said Ben. "A bit like you, Martin. You are really clever with words, but you can't read."

"So how do you survive in a world that likes everyone to be able to tick all the boxes?" asked John.

"I would survive by voting for a leader who will campaign for the rights of us lopsided people," said Martin.

"Which leader would that be?" said John with a cheeky grin.

"Someone who has seen some of the world out there," said Martin. "Someone who is not cocooned in their rich little world, with their rich little friends who don't understand what it's like to be passed between relatives because dad has run away and mum is locked up in an institution. Someone who believes that, just because you didn't stay in a school long enough to learn to read, it doesn't make you stupid."

"Someone," said Ben, "who has visited a place where children are looked after because they are terminally ill, and who, although he thinks that children's magic and balloon modelling and things like that are beneath him, he is still prepared to be surrounded by the little darlings and listen to their story."

John blushed and went all bashful, which was not something Ben ever expected to see.

"I..." John had to think carefully about what he was going to say next. "I *enjoyed* it. I don't understand what it did to me. Those kids might not be alive when I go to university next year, but they all, they all..." he couldn't say any more. His eyes went all watery and looked as if he was struggling to hold in his emotions. Martin was not sure exactly what was going on, but he must have worked out that something happened when Ben had taken John to the hospice earlier in the week – something life-changing.

"You want to do what I do," Martin advised the young politician. "When it all gets heavy, tell a joke."

"That's your natural defence mechanism?" said Ben.

"It got me through a pretty crappy life," said Martin.

"I've had a good life," said John. "I've got money, a good education, parents that care. I've been to America, Spain and Monaco. But I've never really seen the outside world."

"And then you come to a little corner of Norfolk," said Ben.

"But I want to be a leader in this country. I want to represent the majority, not just my rich mates. I want to stand for single-parent families, people who can't read, people who can't find a job..." Then he paused and thought about it, as if he had just worked it out for the first time, "...and disabled kids."

"I'll tell you what," said Ben, at last. "I'd vote for you."

17.

At the start of the last half-week in November the snow finally came. It started on the Sunday afternoon, and kept snowing heavily all night. In the morning, the ground was covered in a deep white blanket. Untouched snow in the countryside is a beautiful thing. This is especially so if you are looking at a photograph of it, or watching it on the television. Ben looked out of his windows on Monday morning, and, for several minutes, admired the beautiful scene. Then, when he worked out what he had to do next, his heart sank a little.

He was going to have to get in to work that morning and he was not going to be travelling by car. The college was just short of two miles away, a little less if you knew the short-cuts, which he didn't. He would probably get stranded there if he went, as more snow was forecast for later today. He did not have to ponder the problem for long to realise here would rather be stranded there in the college with all of its facilities (and stockpiled food) than here at the outskirts of the village. He put some overnight gear and a spare pair of shoes into a rucksack, dressed himself in his best walking shoes and warmest clothes, and started the journey as soon as possible.

As he left his house he met Bryn walking up the road from the village, where he lived. Bryn was dressed in equally weather-wise clothes, and also had a pack on his back.

"Decided to take the sensible option, have you, and leave your car behind?" said the Welshman.

"It would take longer to get all the snow off my car and start it than to walk," said Ben.

"And when you had started it, where would you go? You probably wouldn't even reach the road. Although, when I said the sensible option, I'm not sure that was the best thing to say. The real sensible option would be to stay in bed."

Bryn and Ben walked to the college together. It was a good bonding exercise, struggling through the snow and working together to negotiate obstacles as they crossed roads and fields painfully slowly on their journey. Bryn had lived in this part of the country for several years, and he often walked the area to take in its beauty. As an artist, not just an art *teacher*, he had displayed a number of his paintings, most of which were inspired by Norfolk countryside. However, everything was different when you wanted to get somewhere after a heavy fall of snow.

They finally got to the college in just short of two hours, and needed a serious break when they arrived. Ben had heard stories of people getting lost or stranded in English countryside, and he now understood how easily it could happen. It would not have been wise for Ben to have tried the journey on his own, without Bryn's knowledge of the journey to help him.

Hardly any of the teachers were able to make it in. There were one or two who lived on site, and the house parents, Tony and Becky, were there, of course, but they weren't teachers. The professor was there, which made Ben wonder, for the first time in over a year, where he lived. Emily also telephoned in saying she was stuck at home. Her cottage was a little isolated, and Ben realised it would have been impossible to travel anywhere along those country roads. He hoped that she was sufficiently stocked up to be safe there. He would call her as soon as he could. One of the cooks lived on site and the others had all been unable to come in, so the kitchen situation needed a serious rethink.

It was decided that the staff situation made it impossible for lessons to be held, although Bryn was more than willing to open up every facility for people to practice painting snow scenes. They gathered everyone together in the main hall to discuss what the professor called a 'survival plan' for the next few days. The atmosphere in the meeting was one of a sense of adventure, although if the snow persisted for many days it might turn a little more serious. Shelley was invited onto the stage with the staff. Although the student union was currently no more than an idea, it was thought that paying the young dancer this level of respect was a good way of showing appreciation for her part in the Collier incident (which was the name everybody now gave it), as well as giving her the respect she deserved in every way that she helped in the residential life of the students.

The first thing the professor pointed out was that the college was well-equipped for this kind of weather. The heating was working well and there were no fuel problems and a well-stocked kitchen. He also informed them that there was only one cook, who would have to work hard. Shelley indicated that she could put together a team of helpers from among the student to give the cook plenty of help. There was a large amount of vocal agreement from the students.

Ben and Bryn, along with Professor Kennington, suggested some kind of snowman competition. It was developed as they talked about it into a snow-sculpture competition. This idea was put to the students for open discussion from the floor.

"We could make an ig," said Martin.

"What's an ig?" asked Ben, knowing he was giving the young comedian a feed-line.

"It's an Eskimo's house without a loo."

The igloo-making idea was popular, and one or two teams of students made their plans. However, John Stockton had a better idea. With more than 100 students on site, and several acres of freshly fallen snow at their disposal, he thought it might be a good idea to have a go at a more ambitious project.

"What about a snow-castle?" he said. The size of the scheme appealed to everyone, and, with John, Bryn, and a couple of the art students as the architects, they set about create their masterpiece, filmed by Shelley and the media department. John gave instructions to everyone, including his teachers, and he made a good leader. He included all the different classes, getting the best out of their individual talents. Singers and dancers might still make good builders. He also mixed the different cultures, rich and poor, locals and Londoners, making sure everyone was catered for and nobody felt left out.

The small, rectangular rubbish-buckets that the college had in abundance were used to collect and compact the snow into bricks, which were then gathered together to start building the castle walls. The structure was built on the front garden, a little away from the main building. The first part of the castle to be built was a large archway which would be the main doorway. The blocks were graded so that the top of the two sides of the arch would meet and hold itself together. They decided there would be no other roof sections to the building, just walls, so there was no other delicate work to be done. The structure was made to a height of about two metres, so that it was as tall as the tallest person, but not so tall that people needed to stand on ladders or the like to build it. Pamela joked that if they had only made it half the height, it would still be bigger than her. The exception to the height rule was the archway front of the structure, which stood taller so that the opening would be high enough for everyone to walk through without stooping down.

Inside the square building, there were smaller rooms made, like little barracks. One or two of the students went off on their own to make snow-guardsmen and snow cannons. One particularly talented sculptor created a snow dog, howling at the moon, with incredible detail.

With more than a hundred people making the castle, the progress made in just a few hours was incredible. Several volunteers in the kitchen made an excellent stew for the evening meal, and the cook said she didn't have to do much more than give out instructions. During the afternoon, especially when it started to get dark, it started to snow again. The students wanted to stay out and work on the castle a bit more, but the weather was getting serious and the snow was heavy again, so they decided they should quit for the time being and see what they could do on the next day.

At the evening meal, which was quite early in the day, the staff that were at the college were persuaded to do a little show for the students, seeing as it was normally the other way around. An idea formed in Ben's mind about what he could do, especially as the majority of the staff here were not actually performers.

As they were getting ready for the 'late-night extravaganza', Emily called Ben on his telephone which he had, for once, left turned on for the day.

"I got through," she said, "I was wondering whether you would have your phone on today."

"I was worried about you."

"Oh, it's alright, Ben. I wouldn't even go so far as to get into the car on a day like this."

"That's not what I was worried about. You're stranded out in the country on your own."

"I've got my neighbours."

"There isn't another house for miles."

"There isn't another house for hundreds of metres. But the neighbours, three of them within half a mile of here, are very friendly and great support when it snows. Thanks for your concern, Ben love, but I'm well looked after. What about you?"

"I've got about 100 people looking after me. I'm at the college."

"Oh, dear," she said.

"We're doing a show tonight. The staff, I mean."

"That sounds like it's going to be fun."

"I just had a thought," said Ben.

"Just lie down for half an hour, it'll be alright."

"No, about you and the show. Have you got a camera on your computer?"

"Yes," said Emily. "Quite a good one. My dad gave it to me so we could have a chat every now and then."

"Excellent," he said, and he outlined his plan. The media department, led by Shelley, set up a link between Emily's computer and the big screen that was in the main theatre. When they did their show, Emily sang for them from home. She had her own backing tapes for shows she did when there was no live music available. She sang 'My heart will go on'.

The non-performing staff had a go at 'If I were not upon a stage', an old music hall piece with lots of arm and body movements which were co-ordinated so that the line of people performing narrowly escaped hitting each other. Ben did some magic, and the show lasted a little over half an hour. They all enjoyed it, and the students thought they might return the favour tomorrow.

Having had his chat to Emily, Ben turned off his phone and forgot, as usual, to turn it back on again.

That night, the snow froze, and then more snow fell, so that, in the morning, conditions were worse than ever. Some of the students were out early anyway, battling the awful conditions to make the castle look the way they had imagined it when they planned it. About mid-morning, the snow finally subsided and the students were able to finish the outer walls of the castle and work on some of the inner structure.

At lunchtime, thick, hot soup was served. As the dining room was not big enough for all the occupants at the college to eat there at the same time, they spread out into the games room and the nearby theatre. Ben managed to get a seat in the dining room, however, and some of his students joined him. Martin and John, who seemed to have started to become friends at last, were among them.

"You said if ever I needed to talk to you, you'd try to help," said John, sitting opposite Ben and leaning towards him as if to keep what he was saying confidential in this public place, his face an unreadable mixture of emotions.

"Yes," said Ben,

"Well, I wonder if you could answer a question for me."

"Anything," said Ben, fairly sure that this was not as serious as John was pretending.

"It's hard to put it in words."

"It's okay. Anything you want."

"What's a cornflake story?"

"What?"

"One of the children at the hospice – no, wait a minute, it was Sally. She said you told them cornflake stories. She said *she* didn't like them, they were silly, but the children loved them. So what are they?"

"Silly?" said Ben. "I'm gutted. They are serious stories."

"So, what are they?" John said again.

"Well," said Ben, as if he was deep in thought. "You know Jesus told parables, little stories with deep spiritual meanings?"

"Yes."

"Well they are nothing like that," said Ben. "They come from just after I left school. For one year, before I went to teacher training college, I was an industrial cornflake salesman."

"You sold industrial cornflakes?" said Martin, who was listening in.

"I sold cornflakes to industry and commerce. You know, those companies that stay open all night and feed their staff in the morning, care homes, hospitals, that kind of thing. In fact, there was one place I remember in particular. It was an agricultural college. I knocked on their door once and asked who would be the best person to talk to about cornflakes.

"'Oh, that'll be Jim," they answered,'" he said, putting on what he hoped was a country accent.

"'Well, can I talk to him, please?'

"'He's gone for cotton,' they said. So I went back the following week.

"'Where's Jim?' I asked. 'He's gone for cotton,' they said. So I went back the following Monday.

"'Where's Jim?' I asked. 'He's gone for cotton,' they said. So I went back the following Tuesday.

"'Where's Jim?' I asked. 'He's gone for cotton,' they said. So I went back the following Wednesday.

"'Where's Jim?' I asked. 'He's gone for cotton,' they said. So I went back the following Thursday.

"'Where's Jim?' I asked. 'He's gone for cotton,' they said. So I went back the following Friday.

"Well, eventually, I got to teacher training college, so I had to give up my job as an industrial cornflake salesman. A year or two later, I happened to be driving past that very same agricultural college, so I thought I would pop in and say hello.

"'Where's Jim?' I asked. 'He's dead,' they said. 'They buried him last week. They've just put up the gravestone. It's in the cemetery down the road, if you want to pay your respects.' So I went to the cemetery, and stood at his graveside for a few minutes. The gravestone read, 'Jim's gone, but not for cotton.'"

The castle having been finished, the students concentrated on their next task. They had decided to put on a show the following evening for the staff, returning the previous evening's favour.

Juliette sang 'Forever Autumn', which Ben realised she had chosen especially for him as she knew it was another one of his favourite songs. While she sang, photographs of the staff who weren't there because of the weather were flashed up on the screen behind her. Ben couldn't help feeling that the picture of Emily was up for longer than the others. He missed her, and the song made him miss her more. Juliette was really good, not just at singing, which was her top subject, but at controlling the mood of the audience.

Martin did a stand-up piece, and the others performed the kind of stuff you might get at a scout camp, but with the confidence, polish and style that they had been taught over the term by their performing arts teachers. Pamela had been asked to perform the piece that she was working on for the end of term show, but she said she was not ready yet, and she would prefer to wait until Christmas.

It snowed a bit more on Tuesday night. In the morning, the skies were a clear blue, and, after only a couple of hours more work from a hundred people, the castle looked magnificent. The film crew got busy filming the finished article and edited the film in order to send it to the local TV station, with which they had developed a good relationship. It was shown that night on the local news programme when they did an article about the weather and how it affected local communities. The film and media teacher had not been able to make it in, so he would be particularly proud of them when saw what they had done.

On Wednesday at lunchtime, Bryn met with the professor and Ben in the staff room. A couple of other staff members were there, too, although nearly everyone was helping in the kitchen. They talked about how they had coped with the snow, and the staffing problems that it had created.

"Oh, yes," said Bryn. "Mrs Tyler from the village telephoned in. She said that young Mark wanted to come in today, and was ready to walk in on his own if need be."

"I hope that you persuaded him not to," said Ben. "He would never make it."

"I told her to let him know that the magic session was cancelled for today, so there was no point in him being here. I think she was happy about that."

"There aren't many teachers who have a problem with their students enjoying the lessons so much that they have to put them off if they can," commented the professor.

"The weather forecast for the next few days is heavy rain," said Ben. "It will clear the snow quite quickly, I imagine."

"I think so," said Bryn. "I think it has been a good few days. This snow has brought out the best in our young people."

"Considering that we have recently seen the worst in some of them," said the professor, "that can only be a good thing."

Ben went down to the cellar. The activities of the last few days, or possibly the fact that there was no magic lesson today, meant that the sign had not been changed. In the privacy of the cellar, he made a phone call to Sally at the hospice. He had hoped that the snow would clear so that he could visit Harrison, but there was no chance of that. If the weather forecast was right, he would probably be able to go in on Saturday.

"Hello, Sally," he said.

"Hi, Ben. I take it the reason you have called me is to tell me you are snowed in."

"Yes. Sorry."

"It will break my heart not having you here by my side, but I think I can handle it. I'll tell Harrison."

"Thanks," said Ben. She still flirted with him, even though she had become friends with Emily. He hoped that what they said about her liking him was not serious. She was nice, but…

"I tried to phone you, but you had your phone turned off."

"Sorry," said Ben. "Habit." He really must get a land-line, he thought. Either that, or actually remember to turn his mobile on sometimes. Anyway, while he was trapped at the college, a land-line at home would not have been much use.

"Harrison will be disappointed," said Sally. "He said he wanted to tell the story this week. But I think he wanted you to be there. I'll let him do it next week instead."

"That would be good," said Ben. "There's supposed to be a big thaw this weekend. It should be okay by next Wednesday."

Harrison wants to tell the story, thought Ben. He has come on a long way.

"Can you pass on a message for me?" asked Sally.

"Yes, certainly."

"To that young man you brought to visit last week, John. Can you say 'thank you from us?"

"Okay," said Ben. "What for?"

"Oh, he probably didn't mention it. He arranged for one of his friends in London to send a very generous donation to us."

"Really? I remember your father telling him about your financial worries."

"Yes, well this will help a lot."
"Mind if I ask how much?"
"Twenty-five thousand pounds," she said.

18.

"There was once a monastery with a vow of silence," said Harrison. A small crowd of children sat round in a circle to listen to his story in the story area of the hospice.

"None of the monks in the monastery were allowed to talk," Harrison continued, feeling he had to explain what a vow of silence meant, "except on New Years' Eve, when just one person was chosen to say something. One particular year, it was Brother Andrew's turn to speak. He stood up in front of all the other monks and said, 'I don't like the food here.'

"Then he sat down again and all the other monks remained silent. The long, cold winter passed and the spring came. Then spring turned to summer, summer turned to winter and the New Year came again. It was Brother Simon's turn to speak. He stood up in front of all the other monks and said, "I *like* the food here."

"Then he sat down again and all the other monks remained silent. The long, cold winter passed and the spring came. Then spring turned to summer, summer turned to winter and the New Year came again. It was Brother John's turn to speak. He stood up in front of all the other monks, and said, "I like the food here, but the custard is always lumpy."

"Then he sat down again and all the other monks remained silent. The long, cold winter passed and the spring came. Then spring turned to summer, summer turned to winter and the New Year came again. It was Brother Stephen's turn to speak. He stood up in front of all the other monks and said, "I am the cook, and I don't like people criticising my food."

"Then he sat down again and all the other monks remained silent. The long, cold winter passed and the spring came. Then spring turned to summer, summer turned to winter and the New Year came again. It was Brother Edmund's turn to speak. He stood up in front of all the other monks and said, "I think we should use more fresh vegetables in the food instead of this frozen stuff."

"Then he sat down again and all the other monks remained silent. The long, cold winter passed and the spring came. Then spring turned to summer, summer turned to winter, and the New Year came again. It was Brother Derek's turn to speak. He stood up in front of all the other monks and said, "I'm leaving this monastery. I am fed up with the constant bickering."

The older children laughed long and hard, and everyone gave Harrison a great round of applause for his story. Ben had not heard that one before,so he made a mental note to add it to his list. He also gave Harrison a clap. The young lad talked to him afterwards.

"I didn't realise how tiring it is standing up in front of lots of people," he said. He looked a little worn out and beads of sweat were beginning to form on his face and forehead. When Harrison had discovered that Ben was going to pay a visit on Saturday to make up for not being able to make Wednesday, he asked Sally if he could perform his story then instead of waiting. Sally had no problem agreeing.

The rains on Thursday and Friday had melted most of the snows in the Stevenbridge area. Huge chunks of ruined castle still littered the front lawn at the college like dirty white relics from the dark ages, but the country roads were driveable again. Harrison's parents, however, had not been rained-on so profusely, so they were still stuck at home and not able to visit. That was one of the reasons that Ben felt a visit on the weekend would be useful.

Harrison soon had to make his excuses, however, as exhaustion was beginning to set in and he felt he should try and sleep for a while. Sally got a bit of time alone with Ben, so she was able to give him some news.

"I wanted to say how grateful I am for the work you've done with him," she said, sidling up close to him in order to speak so that only he could hear. "He's changed, for the better. He doesn't have as many bad days, either, which is good, especially with what the doctors are saying."

"What are the doctors saying?" asked Ben. He always liked the attention she gave him, even the flirting, but her leaning against him like Emily did was making him feel a little uncomfortable. She was not trying to 'make a play' for him, as she said she might, surely?

"He's getting worse. He should be ill more than he is. They think his current state of mind is down to you."

"He could get better?" said Ben, not understanding what she was trying to tell him.

"No," said Sally, snuggling closer still. Ben put his arm around her. This was not flirting; this was a distressed friend needing comfort. She responded, her arm around him, her big eyes displaying her emotions as she struggled to say what she needed to. "He won't recover, he is too ill. His parents know that, and they are looking at taking extended leave from their jobs to spend as much time as possible down here as soon as the snows clear where they are. But he needs a friend like you, too, right now."

She let go of him and stood back, looking up into his face.

"Sorry," she said, and Ben didn't know if she was apologising for getting close or expressing her sorrow at Harrison's current state of health.

Up to when Sally said that, Ben had felt that it had been a good few days. His class at the college was coming together now, with John having made peace with Martin and Mark, and with the crisis of the heavy snow unifying the different cultures among the students and beginning to make them into a team. The signs on his door continued to be good-natured, with the latest being 'Ben 4 Emily'. Emily had come back to the college on Friday for the free study time, but nobody seemed to have got much work done. She and Ben had arranged to meet this afternoon, and catch up on some missed 'together' time at her house. He got there early, because he did not want to hang around at the hospice while Harrison slept.

She was delighted to see him earlier than they had arranged, and gave him the usual affectionate greeting. She could tell he was not completely at ease, and drew him in to her warm, cosy living room, out of the chilly December air. She sat him on her two-seater sofa and got him a hot drink. He just sat, and she served him his tea and sat at his feet, and allowed him to sit in silence.

Ben wondered if she should be a doctor, rather than a singer. She sat there doing nothing, just being, and he felt better. He wondered if he should mention Sally's hug, or whatever it was, and decided that he had to.

"Sally gave me a hug today," he said. He had not said anything for several minutes, and then the first thing he said was that. The image of that deep pit he so often dug for himself once again came into his mind. However, Emily was more gracious than he had given her credit for, and did not make a joke about it.

"She cares about you," she said, simply. "What happened?"

"Harrison's getting worse," he told her, and she went quiet. She just sat up on the sofa with him, and wrapped her arms around him.

"Why aren't you still there now?" she said eventually. "I would have understood – you know that."

"He's sleeping. I might go back later and visit when he wakes up this afternoon."

"Was it nice?" Emily said as his emotional phase was beginning to lift.

"What?"

"Sally hugging you."

"Yes. No," said Ben.

"Thank you for being so specific," said Emily.

"It was good of her, but it wasn't *nice.* Nice would mean everything was okay. I think it was two friends knowing we both needed a bit of comfort."

"I understand. But you better watch out."

"There's nothing going on," said Ben.

"That's not what I meant," said Emily. "I mean you might have a rival for her affections."

"She has a boyfriend?"

"Not yet," said Emily.

"Who?" said Ben.

"Did you spend a lot of time with your students yesterday?" said Emily, seeming to change the subject.

"Yes," he said. "That is, I spent all day with Mark, as usual, and the others came by. Pamela's getting really good, but she spends more time in Bryn's class than mine, right now."

"Yes, so does Ginny. She's the girl that's singing for Pamela in the Christmas show. She can only do it up in Bryn's art room because *you* made it into a secret."

"It'll do Pamela good, having a secret. She needs her confidence building."

"She'll have her doubts before the performance."

"Of course she will; everyone does. But *after* the show, she'll be the tallest girl in the class." Ben chuckled at the irony of his own remark, considering that Pamela was probably the shortest person in every class she attended.

"What about John Stockton?" asked Emily.

"He's not in her performance."

"I mean yesterday. Did you see much of him?"

"I think he came down to say hello at the beginning of the day. I thought he wanted to talk to me about something, but there were too many people about. He went away. I thought he would find me later if he needed anything."

"And did he?"

"No. I had forgotten about it."

"He came to me instead. He spent a little time in my classroom. It seems with the thing about Rich, a number of students see me as part of the pastoral team as well as you."

"A sort of wise old woman?"

"Well, I'm not so sure about the 'old' part, but, mostly, yes. John came up before our first break. He listened to us sing for a while. He was a good audience. When he said anything, it was always a polite, carefully chosen encouragement."

"That's the politician in him."

"And when the girls went for their break – I always make them drink something – he hung around to talk."

"Is it confidential, or can I know what you talked about."

"It *is* confidential, but I asked his permission to tell you, and he said yes, as long as I make you promise not to laugh."

"I promise."

"He fancies your Sally."

Ben laughed.

"You promised," said Emily. Ben stopped laughing and took it seriously.

"He told you that?"

"He didn't say 'fancied', that was my word. He actually said he thought he was in love with her."

"And he is okay me knowing about it?"

"You are the only one who can do anything about it."

"Wait a minute," said Ben sitting upright, then immediately regretting untangling from Emily. "I'm not doing anything about it."

"You want Sally for yourself?" said Emily.

"No!" Ben protested, then he realised that she was controlling the conversation.

"Well," he said, "I suppose it would be good to have her on hand in case I ever get fed up with you."

Emily picked up one of her pretty cushions, caressing it in her hands and stroking the soft fabric gently, before hitting him hard over the head with it.

"All right," he said, surrendering far too quickly. "I'll put a word in. But I make it a personal policy not to get involved with student romances."

"Since when?"

"I just made that up."

Later that afternoon, before five o'clock when Sally would go home, he returned to the hospice. The journey was not long enough to dwell on how to put the situation to Sally. He thought of a number of clever things to say, but all of them clashed with all of the others. Would he tell her outright? Would he beat about the bush? Would she laugh in his face? How could he put John's case to her so that she *wouldn't* laugh? He had never considered, when he said 'yes' to Professor Kennington's invitation to become the 'pastor' for the college, that it would include matchmaking.

He was still mulling over different combinations and eventualities when he got to the hospice. In fact, he was so preoccupied with what he just knew would be an embarrassing situation, that he did not see the cat, Seefer, running across the car park to get out of the rain. Ben had his head down, and full of half-ideas of how to put John's feelings across to Sally. He pushed open the door and let it close itself behind him as he entered the building. Then there was an almighty 'thump' as Seefer hit the closed door.

Ben turned around and saw a dazed-looking cat on the other side of the glass-panelled door. He let him in, and Seefer glared angrily at him, shaking the rain out of his fur over Ben's legs. Mrs Engles laughed, and told Ben that the cat often ran into that door.

Harrison had slept a little, and he was in his room reading. Before Ben went in to see him, he had a little word with Sally. He made her stop working and actually sit down for a moment, and asked one of the other helpers to get her a cup of coffee.

"Do you like it strong?" he asked.

"Fairly."

"You're going to need it *very* strong for this one. You know John Stockton, the lad I brought to visit you?"

"Yes," said Sally. "Lovely young man. He was very generous."

"He thought highly of you, too," said Ben. All of a sudden, all of the clever words that had come into his mind on the short journey from Emily's house in Newbridge to here were no longer there. He searched his mind, but they were nowhere to be found. He had no idea why he was speaking for John, who was, after all, a confident young man who was quite capable of speaking for himself. A lot more capable than Ben felt right now, in fact.

"It wasn't his money," he said. Now, that was stupid, he thought. I want to build him up, not belittle him.

"He stole it?" said Sally, beginning to sound a little distressed. "I really do need a strong coffee."

"No, it's good money. He knew someone who wanted to make a donation. He directed it here because his visit here affected him strongly."

"It's a good thing my dad was here. He obviously made a good impression on John."

"That's what I thought," said Ben. "But it turns out that someone else made an even bigger impression."

"Little Cherry?"

"You."

"Oh," said Sally, "that's nice." Ben thought he saw her colour up a little. Perhaps she felt something for him, too.

"So, what about little Cherry?" said Ben, in the absence of any idea as to what he might say next. "Is she coming to stay, soon?"

"Next week, I think, or maybe the week after. Before Christmas, anyway." But Sally did not want to leave the subject of John. "Will John be visiting again, soon?"

"I think so," said Ben. "I think we're a bit busy getting ready for things at the college, so I don't know when he might be down. I might be able to bring him tomorrow."

"You're coming back tomorrow?"

"I wasn't." said Ben. "But I could."

"You'd do that for me?" Sally said.

"I think John would like to visit. But you'd miss him. You don't work Sundays."

"I could tomorrow," she said with an unusual eagerness in her voice. Now that was an interesting response, thought Ben, and he decided that, if both of them were interested in each other, he probably didn't have to get any more involved. Anyway, he was here to see Harrison, so he left her to the rest of her coffee and went to the young lad's room.

He was looking at a book, but not reading it, and was delighted to put it down and welcome Ben in. He called his little room his 'kingdom' or his 'domain', and had recently started to welcome his visitors in as if he was entertaining guests in his private mansion.

"Thanks for coming back," he said. "I enjoyed telling that story this morning, but it was really tiring."

"I know what you mean," said Ben. "Sometimes, when I do Saturday night shows at the Shining Star, I sleep until Monday morning."

"I'd like to see one of your shows some time. I mean the ones at the Shining Star."

"It's a nightclub."

"I know," said Harrison.

"It's for over 18's. Or over 21's or something."

"Do you do rude stuff?"

"What?"

"If it's for over 21's, do you do rude stuff? Are there strippers and that?"

"No."

"Well, maybe I don't want to go there after all," he grinned.

"Anyway, you don't like magic."

"I would go to enjoy the ambience," said Harrison, "for the experience of going to a night club."

"And to look at the girls."

"Yeah, that too." Harrison sounded a little wistful, as if his illness was going to prevent him from doing something he really wanted to do.

"If I bring a night club singer in here, would that do as an alternative?" Ben suggested.

"The Darkchilde lady? Sally's told us she's coming to sing at our Christmas dinner. Have you proposed to her yet?"

"I'll stop talking to you if you keep saying that," said Ben. He wondered if he should tell Harrison his plans.

"Can you get her to come sooner?" said Harrison, interrupting Ben's train of thought. "I might not last till Christmas."

"What?"

"I said I don't think I can wait till Christmas. It's three weeks away."

Ben went home via Emily's house, but, somehow, forgot to bring up what Harrison had said about him proposing to her. On Sunday at lunchtime, Ben managed to see John. He mentioned that he was going to the hospice that afternoon, just to pop in for an hour, and wondered if John would like to come along. He said that Emily had told him about Sally, and that he knew she would be there this afternoon although she didn't normally work Sundays. He tried to sound optimistic about John's chances, but he was also reluctant to get involved any more than this. Although, he did suggest that he might want to invite her to the Christmas show. It was normally family members only, because the hall would not be big enough for a large audience, but he was sure that, if Sally was interested, they could make an exception.

"That would be great," said John, with the biggest smile on his face that Ben had seen. He had just made the young, love-struck lad very happy.

Although John, like a number of the students, had a car on the premises, they made the journey in Ben's car. They chatted a little on the way.

"You didn't make fun of me about Sally," said John. "I appreciate that."

"Liking a girl isn't a joke."

"But I asked for help asking her out. I'm not supposed to do that."

"I must say I always thought you were the 'seize the day' type. Anything you wanted, you would just reach out and grasp it."

"That's true," John said with a laugh, but then his voice went quiet. Ben was driving, but he was aware that John couldn't bring himself to look at him when he spoke. "Except with girls. I could never, I mean, normally, I'm fine, but when there is one I really like, I go to pieces. Not like you."

"Me?" said Ben. "I'm probably worse than you are."

"But you've got Miss Darkchilde. That's like hitting the jackpot."

Ben smiled to himself. John was absolutely right, and he had often wondered why the God he wasn't even sure he believed in treated him so well as to give him Emily. But Ben had done nothing to 'get' her. It had just, sort-of, happened.

"I think you just make friends. Thinking about it, all of the girls I've known well were my friends. I don't think I ever thought of going out with any of them. I didn't even know Emily and I would be together until…" then he shut up.

"Until?" said John.

"Look, you're confiding in me, not the other way 'round, alright?"

The rain started to fall again when they got to St Mark's Hospice and Ben looked around for Seefer when he got out of the car, but all was quiet. He opened the main entrance door for John to walk through, carefully closing it behind him.

Sally greeted them both, paying lots of attention to John. Ben slipped away to speak to Harrison. He *really* didn't understand love, he thought. He did not know why he got on so well with Emily, how he had 'hit the jackpot', as John had put it. He didn't understand why this hospice, so full of a different kind of love, was so special, and he certainly didn't see what Sally would see in John.

He knocked on the door.

Harrison smiled at him, and cheerfully welcomed Ben 'into his domain'. Seefer was curled up asleep on his bed, and he was sitting in the chair next to it, his arm idly reached out to the cat and stroking its head. Ben noted how much more positive his attitude was lately. He noted that Sally's observations were right, and he felt that he possibly had done some good, after all. They chatted lightly for a while.

"The cat has paid a visit," said Ben. "You are privileged."

"He sat guard outside my room when I was ill," said Harrison. "Sally says he has done that every time I've had a bad day. But he doesn't often come in."

Ben looked at him. His face was still dark and sunken like it often was, but he was not as sickly and exhausted-looking as he had often been. Perhaps the doctors were wrong, and there was still a chance for him. Perhaps one of the vicar's miracles was happening right here in the hospice, and nobody knew it.

19.

On Wednesday, the sign on the classroom door was "Don't read this".

Mark turned up just after Ben and smiled at the sign as if he had to be polite to it. He was a little happier than he had been recently.

"Have you made a decision about the job?" asked Ben.

"Yes," said Mark, then he explained what he really meant. "I v-visited the p-place on Saturday. I was going to go b-before, but the snow stopped me. Mum t-took me. They were brilliant, ever s-so help-f-ful. They s-said I d-didn't have t-to s-stop c-coming to the c-college. I c-could work for them on M-Mondays and T-Tuesdays to s-start with. Then we would t-talk it over in J-June, about d-doing longer hours."

"That's fantastic," said Ben. "What about the journey? Will you find it hard to get to Stevenbridge, or will your mother take you? The buses from the village aren't very good, are they?"

"N-no," agreed Mark. "B-but they are happy with me working f-from home and sending it in. They say my c-computer is b-better than theirs, anyway!" Mark was beaming.

"The one you built yourself?"

"Yes."

Ben and Mark were still laughing and celebrating the news when the class started to arrive. John was very pleased to hear about Mark's job, and made a big fuss about congratulating him. Ben was amazed at how much the love of a good woman could change the young man. At least, that was what he imagined it was.

Ben avoided talking to the class about what they would do for the Christmas show in two weeks' time, as he was already involved with Pamela's and Martin's different performances. It was time for some light-heartedness in the class, so he introduced a couple of puppets. Sometime in the next year, he was due to bring in a ventriloquist to teach them for a couple of sessions. He thought Martin might go for ventriloquism in spite of the difficulty he had keeping his mouth shut.

In the meantime, although he had himself given puppetry a go and had not been very good at it, he thought he would at least give them a chance at handling puppets and see what came of it. He had two large people puppets and a monkey, and he knew something about the basics of controlling a puppet. Martin, as he had guessed, took to it straight away. Some of the others struggled to get the mouth synchronised with the words they were saying, and one of two of them seemed to make the puppets look up at the ceiling all the time.

The puppets were large devices with outsized fabric heads and wide slits for mouths. There were wooden blocks inside the heads to enable thumb control of the mouths. Ben had never bought a traditional ventriloquist figure (ventriloquists did not like to call them 'dummies') because he was no good at the skill, and they were quite expensive items.

Martin turned the puppets he was wearing to face himself, and said in a silly voice, without trying to keep his lips still, "Is that your head or was someone sick on your shoulders?"

Charles had a go at the same kind of thing, and said, "That's a nice nose you've got there, did you pick it yourself?"

Ben stayed around for a short while after his lesson, but he wanted to go and visit Harrison in the afternoon, so he set off soon after lunch. He'd had an odd dream about the lad last night, and he had woken up at about three in the morning feeling strange. He had no proper recollection of the dream, but Harrison had been on his mind ever since, hanging around in the background of his thoughts.

He drove down in the overcast weather. The skies were already beginning to darken at three in the afternoon when he pulled up at the hospice car park. It could have been the dark cloud that made the darkness come early as much as the time of year. It had not rained today, but the past few days had seen enough rain to last the rest of the year anyway. Seefer was sitting in the front doorway, blocking his path as if he did not want Ben to enter. He stepped over the cat and walked in.

Mrs Engles was not at the desk, so Ben went straight on through to Harrison's room without being signed in. He knocked on the door, and there was no answer. He pushed at the door, and it opened slightly.

"Ben," he heard Sally's voice calling loudly from the other end of the corridor, but she was too late. He had already seen inside the room. The bed had been stripped, and there were no books on shelves or the little table in the room. Everything had been cleared out. Ben did not know why, and was slow to work out what this meant. Sally ran towards him.

"Ben," she shouted again, not quite as loudly as she was getting nearer to him. She stopped at the door, next to him.

"I'm sorry," she said, her voice full of distress, more so than he had heard it before. "We tried to call you, but your phone was turned off."

"What happened?" he asked and his voice cracked a little.

"Harrison died last night," Sally said. "About three o'clock in the morning." She started to say something else, but nothing came out. Ben felt his legs go weak. He backed away from the door across the corridor and just about managed to sit down in the chair. Sally stood and looked at him, lost as to what to do or say. Someone called to her, but she did not want to answer.

Ben swore at himself for his stupid habit of keeping his telephone switched off. He probably could not have been here at the end anyway, but he would have known sooner, instead of coming in and finding Harrison's room empty and cleaned out.

"Harrison's parents are here," said Sally. "Do you want to see them?"

"No," said Ben. "I can't. I wouldn't know what to say."

"Neither do I," said Sally. She went away to see to whoever was calling her. Ben was on his own, left to his thoughts. He did not know what to think. His mind jumped between the last conversations he'd had with Harrison, things Donald Hinton had said about faith, and things that Sally had said and done about the hospice. He thought of the fun plans he had made for Christmas, and they seemed like such a waste of time. No, that wasn't true. One of his schemes seemed to be more important than ever before right now. You should live before you die. Ben had helped Harrison live.

He was aware of someone standing next to him. He looked up and saw little Cherry standing there. She had just become a resident here.

"Don't be sad, Magic Man," she said. "Harrison isn't ill any more. He's in heaven." She climbed onto his lap, digging a bony knee into his leg on the way up, and gave him a big hug. It made him feel even more like crying, but he was determined not to show his emotions in front of this child. Unfortunately, he did not want to throw her off, either, so he was stuck there with her for a few minutes, at least until Sally got back.

"I see our own pastoral care officer has given you some of her time," said Sally when she returned from whatever duty she had. "Cherry's been visiting everybody and comforting them."

"She's," started Ben, then he couldn't say any more. He didn't want the tears to come, not yet, not with the child there. Cherry climbed down from his knees and went off to 'care' for someone else.

"I'm going to go," Ben said after a while. "I'll give you a ring. And I will keep my phone turned on, night and day, from now on." Sally wanted to keep him there, but he would not stay.

He almost ran out to the car park. The cat scooted out of his way as he left the building, got into his car and started driving. Half way between the hospice and Newbridge he had to stop the car and wipe his eyes before carrying on his journey, because he could not see to drive. It was not five o'clock yet, so Emily would probably not be home, although she often left early on a Wednesday, especially with the darker nights and poorer weather.

Ben parked outside her house and waited for her. While he was waiting, he pulled his phone out of his pocket and turned in on. The battery marker on the screen showed it still had plenty of power, but he would charge it up tonight, anyway.

Emily turned up less than twenty minutes later, parking in her little parking bay on the road near her house. She recognised his car and walked across to him. He opened his car door and got out. He tried to say "Harrison's dead," but struggled. She worked it out anyway, took his hand and led him into the cottage, where she placed him in the two-seated sofa and curled up next to him. He rested his head on her shoulder and finally cried properly. She rearranged her body to make him comfortable against her, and wrapped her arms around him. They hardly said a word to each other for the next hour or so as he sobbed in her arms.

"Steve told me," said Ben, eventually, after he had cried himself out. "He said that place would break my heart."

"And you carried on visiting Harrison anyway."

"I didn't know. Steve knew, but I didn't work out how it would feel."

"Would you have stopped visiting Harrison if you knew what it would feel like now?"

"Yes. No, but if I…" he stopped and thought about what he was feeling, what he was about to say. "I might not have started visiting him in the first place."

"That would have been a shame," said Emily. "For both of you."

"What do you mean?"

"Weren't you telling me, at the weekend, about the good you thought you had done him? That you felt pleased that you were able to be of some help?"

Ben started to nod. Then he decided he wouldn't do that any more, as his head was in the perfect place resting against Emily and he didn't want to dislodge it.

"Well I think," said Emily, "that he was good for you, too. You were out of the college, and got a taste of a world outside your own."

"A sour taste, as it turned out."

"Not at the time."

Ben's telephone buzzed in his pocket. He managed to pull it out without moving his head.

"Ben April," he said.

"Hello, Ben," said a rich, melodious male voice. The vicar's voice was unmistakable.

"Donald," said Ben, aware that he sounded neither rich or melodious, or even interested.

"Sally said she thought I should give you a ring. You must be feeling bad, right now."

"Yes. Thanks for ringing," Ben said flatly. He had no idea how he was feeling, or what to say to Donald. He wanted to hang up, because it was all Donald's fault. But that wasn't really true. He wanted Donald to go away – Ben wasn't one of his 'flock', after all.

"I think you might like to know that I spent the last few hours with Harrison and his parents. He took a bad turn suddenly quite late in the evening. I came out at about midnight, and stayed with him. At the end, he was at peace with himself and with the Lord."

Ben might not have believed in God, but he understood roughly what Donald meant. It wasn't some Vicar's preaching that helped him understand, though, it was a five-year-old girl.

"Is that what Cherry meant when she said he was in heaven?"

"Cherry is an amazing child," said Donald.

"How do you do it?" said Ben. "How do you keep on caring and getting on with things, how do you keep on believing in God, when this happens to all of the children in your care? To *all* of them." The size of St Mark's capacity for love suddenly hit him.

"How could we carry on *without* believing in God?" said Donald. "I'm with Cherry on this one. Harrison is in a better place."

"Is that why you called?"

"That, and to tell you that the funeral has been set for next Wednesday at St Mark's Church, at two in the afternoon."

"I'll be there," said Ben. He actually never wanted to see St Mark's, Reverend Donald or the hospice ever again, but he didn't hesitate to say yes to the funeral.

"I wonder if you would like to say anything about Harrison in the service?"

"Me?"

"You were close. His parents asked."

"In that case, tell them yes." Why did he keep saying yes when he wanted to shut that the hospice out of his life?

"There will be a little reception afterwards at the hospice."

"At the hospice? That's an unusual place to hold a reception."

"It's where most of his friends will be," said the vicar.

"I don't think I will be able to make the reception," said Ben. Not if it is at the hospice, he thought.

"Oh, I'm sorry about that. I wonder if you can get a message to Miss Darkchilde?"

"She's right here," said Ben.

"Can I speak to her?"

Ben had to sit up to hand the phone over to Emily. He decided to stand up, in fact. He ached. His chest ached.

“The Reverend Donald Hinton wants a word,” he said, and while they were talking, he went out to her kitchen to make them both a hot drink. She was finished when he returned, and handed back the phone to Ben, who did not ask what they talked about – he hoped that the vicar had not asked her to try and persuade him to go to the reception.

Ben stayed late. He was beginning to lose his fragile emotional state, but it was being replaced by a feeling of numbness. The only thing he could feel was how grateful he was for Emily’s love. He didn’t think of love very often. He had always told himself that he simply didn’t understand it. He believed he was a loving, caring person, but he never analysed how or why, or what that ‘love’ really meant. Now that he was inside Emily’s love, as it were, its power was the only thing he had to hang on to.

The next few days were hard. Thursday and Friday were thankfully busy days, with lessons full of fast magic tricks and presentation ideas. Although he was a comedy magician, most of his class this year seemed to prefer the more serious stuff, so they spend some time looking at different presentation styles, and what worked in different settings. Ben was glad of this, because it exercised his tired mind and he did not feel much like comedy.

The sign on the door changed twice, but Ben didn’t appreciate the jokes right now. On Thursday afternoon, Ben spent some time on his own in the cellar classroom. On his own, that is, except for Mark.

People with Asperger’s syndrome, Ben knew, were not good at reading people’s body language. However, they were not completely insensitive, and Mark Tyler could not fail to notice the gloomy mood that Ben was in. The lad was very clumsy in his attempts to comfort him, but Ben appreciated it nevertheless. When he first thought of teaching as a profession all those years ago, he thought he would have to be the strength to help his pupil’s weaknesses, but he had discovered it was a shared experience, and, certainly in this College of the Arts, the students were adults who could become his friends.

On Friday, only a few of his students came to the classroom. The magic for the Christmas show had been sorted, and there was preparation to be done in other lessons. In addition to that, most of the young people didn’t know how to talk to the bereaved Ben, so they didn’t talk to him at all. One exception to that was John.

"I'm sorry about Harrison," John said when he came by just before lunch on Friday.

"Thank you," said Ben. "Have you spoken to Sally?" He asked because he was aware that he had not called her himself.

"Yes," said John. "We spoke for a long time. That is, she talked, I listened, mostly. It was, well, strange."

"Strange? How?"

"It's a sad situation, but somehow I felt, well, privileged to be part of it – to be the person that Sally wanted to talk to."

Ben thought about what John had said, and he began to look at what he had done over the last three months or so with Harrison in a different light. Ben had been angry that it had happened like this, that God, or the vicar, or circumstances, had done this to him. He had not really considered it a privilege. Perhaps John's perspective was a better one, in the end.

Emily arranged to spend Sunday with him. She was not going to be around on Saturday because she had things to arrange.

"I need to go to the music shop in Stevenbridge to pick up music and a soundtrack for 'Into the West'," she said.

"'Into the West?'"

"The vicar of St Mark's asked me to sing it at the funeral next week. Apparently, it was Harrison's favourite song."

"I know. It's a strange song to be a young person's favourite."

"I've heard it a couple of times. It's very beautiful."

"It's about death," said Ben.

"It's about the elves leaving Middle Earth for distant, beautiful lands."

"When the singer says 'you're here in my arms, just sleeping', she's in denial. He's not just sleeping; he's going away forever."

"And passing over to a better place."

Ben felt like arguing angrily, like saying he didn't believe in heaven, or a God who could strike down a child like that, but, in all honesty, he rather hoped that Donald was right and he was wrong. On Saturday, he moped about his little granny flat, not wanting to go to the college or anywhere, but not really wanting to be there, either. Without Emily, he felt lonely.

Over the next few days, Ben only spent a token amount of time at the college. He felt it would be a good idea to work on what he wanted to say at Harrison's funeral. He wrote five minutes of fantastic stuff, including his own humour, reminiscing of favourite moments, commenting on Harrison's changing attitudes over the few months he knew him, saying clever things to help and encourage Harrison's family. Then he threw it all away and started again. He read and re-read what he had written several times, dismissing it as either sentimental or arrogant. It was his fifth rewrite that he finally decided to go with, but even then, he was not sure.

On the following Wednesday, he got to the church early. He was still not sure whether to deliver his little speech from memory or if he should read it. The service was fairly short, and Ben was a little distressed to note that he would get up and do his bit just after Emily sang her song. It was sure to affect him.

Emily sang in her usual excellent manner, her voice clear and not faltering over the words. She sang as if she was singing just for Harrison, and it seemed to Ben as if the young lad was there, listening to her with a tear in his eye. But when she got to "here in my arms, you're only sleeping", and he noticed the tear track down *her* cheek, and it took all he had to hold back his own tears. He was on next.

Then Ben got up and stood at the lectern. He looked down at the light pine coffin standing on simple wooden trestles, and was surprised at how small it was. Surely Harrison had been bigger than that? He thought of all of the children in the hospice, and faltered.

He looked up to see the friends and family, quite a reasonable number, all looking as devastated as he felt, and the words he had chosen simply did not seem appropriate. He shook his head at the scrap of useless paper in his hand.

"Sorry," he said to them all, and sat down again. He almost walked out of the church – and he might have done if it wasn't for Emily being there.

Harrison was buried in the graveyard on the outskirts of Stevenbridge. Apparently, St Mark's had once received a very large donation from the family of one of the first residents of the hospice, and had bought land adjoining the graveyard which they dedicated to patients at the hospice. Many of the children who died there had been buried here.

During the committal, Emily stayed close to Ben and kept her arms around him. Ben drove home from the cemetery alone afterwards, taking a longer route out Stevenbridge in order not to have to drive past the hospice. He wasn't sure whether he was just sad or really angry – he just knew he didn't want to go anywhere near that place ever again.

20.

The printed cloth that Ben had ordered weeks ago was finally ready on the Wednesday morning of the following week, the last day of term and the day of the Christmas show. Ben rushed in to Stevenbridge early to pick it up, knowing that it would make him late for work. He telephoned the Professor from the magic shop and explained most of what he was up to.

It was well after eleven in the morning when he turned up at the college. He hurried down to the cellar, where only Mark was waiting for him. The sign on his door said, ‘For Sale: Parachute. Only used once. Never been opened.’ That was something from the Internet, thought Ben. They are running out of ideas.

Ben looked at the sign, and smiled at Mark.

“Where are the others?”

“The professor s-sent a m-message. He s-said you’d b-be late. They are in the theatre, g-getting ready.”

“Leaving you to put this sign up.”

“It w-was already here.”

“When *did* you put it up, then? Last night?”

“I d-didn’t p-put it up. I left b-before you did yesterday,” said Mark, but he sounded a little guilty. Nevertheless, he wouldn’t lie, so Ben worked out the rest of the notice-on-the-door conspiracy.

“So Martin did it after you and I had both gone home.”

“You knew,” said Mark.

“I worked it out. He would have asked you to type it up on the computer, because you’re good with computers, and he can’t read or write very well. But the ideas were his.”

“You’re n-not angry?”

"No, I love it. The two of you working together – I couldn't suspect you because neither of you would be likely to do it on your own. It had to be a collaboration."

"I t-told him you'd like it," said Mark.

"When did you think of it?"

"It was M-Martin. It was all h-his idea. He just n-needed m-me to t-type it up f-for him and p-present it in a nice way. B-but he c-couldn't do it until he was ready t-to admit he c-couldn't read or write."

"You know when John and Rich were bullying you at the beginning of term?" said Ben. Mark nodded, and his head drooped again as he remembered. "Well, I reckon it showed Martin he had friends. They were rotten, we were understanding. The bad time you went through helped him to know who he could go to."

"I'm g-glad Rich was caught. But J-john's not so b-bad. N-not n-now."

"Sometimes people need to take a look at a world outside their own," said Ben. He wasn't sure he believed his own words however, because, even as he said it, he knew in his heart that he never wanted to see the 'outside world' of St Mark's Hospice again.

"Look," said Ben, who always found it difficult to get rid of Mark. "I've got something to prepare. One of my surprises for the show tonight. I wonder if you could leave me to it for a few minutes." He realised that Mark would probably take that 'few minutes' literally. "I mean half an hour or so."

"Is it something Pamela's doing?"

"No, this is all me."

"B-but it's a st-st-student show. You won't be p-performing."

"Sorry, it's still a secret."

"I've g-got to help ups-stairs, anyway. S-see you later."

Mark left him to his work, and he took out the cloth ready to include with the equipment Martin was going to use in tonight's show. He sat down with a needle and thread, and stopped.

Nothing happened in his world for a few minutes. A tear formed in his eye for no particular reason. He reflected on who he was and what he had done. The funny man, the comedy magician, had gone for a while. His friendship with Harrison had changed him, and his death had changed him more. He may have wanted nothing more to do with St Mark's, but at the same time he considered himself weak for thinking that way. He wondered again how people like Sally and her father could live with that *all the time*, making friends with people, with children, and then losing them. Then again, he thought, how could they *not* do it?

He eventually did his sewing, and as he was finishing, he heard someone at the door. He put the cloth away quickly. It was attached where it should be attached for the trick to work. He did not want anyone in the college to know about it other than the two other people who had to. The person at the door was not one of those two. In fact, if everyone else in the world knew about it, this was the one and only person from whom it should be kept secret. It was Emily.

"You should be in your classroom, shouldn't you?" said Ben.

"And hello to you too," said Emily. "And no, it's lunchtime. It's well into lunchtime, in fact. You're late."

"Again."

"You were late in this morning," said Emily.

"I had to arrange something."

"Did you visit the hospice?"

"No."

"*Will* you visit the hospice?""

"Not today."

"Ever again?"

"No. Yes, I will. We've arranged to go on Christmas Day, next week."

"You're still doing that?"

"I made a promise," said Ben.

"If you broke that promise, everyone would understand."

"No," said Ben with as much strength as his weak heart could muster. "I am going to be there."

Emily came into the room from her place leaning against the doorway and gave him a big hug. He held on to her for several minutes as if she would disappear forever if he let go. When he finally, reluctantly, did let go, he looked down into her eyes and smiled.

"Thank you. I suppose we had better get upstairs. Wait a minute – what about you?"

"What about me?"

"Christmas Day – you said you would perform, too."

"I certainly will," said Emily. "I made a promise."

Lunchtime was more or less over, but because of the nature of this particular day, with everyone preparing for the show, the dining room would stay open for a while longer. A few people were still eating, and one or two, including Ben and Emily, drifted in late.

Shelley made a point of coming up to Ben and saying something. Normally she was comfortable with Ben and spoke to him with confidence, but this time she faltered a little.

"I'm sorry to hear about that boy at the hospice," she said. It had been two weeks since he died, and this was the first time Ben had seen Shelley since then. He realised that he had spent a lot his time here at work out of the way in his classroom, doing only necessary things, and had not been out and about in the college like he would normally intend to be.

"Thank you," said Ben. "How are things with the new president of the student union?"

"That starts next term," said Shelley, relaxing as she realised he did not wish to talk about Harrison. "I'm just looking forward to Christmas first."

"Doing anything special?" asked Emily.

"Xander is taking me home to meet his family this Christmas."

"Now there's a Christmas present," said Ben. He had seen how the two of them were just about inseparable this term. Shelley smiled.

"Yeah," she said. "We've got on really well this term. He wants me to meet his fiancée."

"What?" said Ben.

"Didn't you know? He's getting married in the summer. He wants to persuade his lady to let me be a bridesmaid."

Ben was beginning to get the impression he didn't know anything after all. He had interpreted Shelley's and Xander's friendship as something more romantic. When they were sneaking off together, they were obviously playing their part in the student soap opera, as Emily called it, and not going off for some private romantic time at all.

"I thought…" Ben started, and then he stopped himself, because there was no need for him to reveal to Shelley his stupid mistake. However, it was too late, and Shelley was too sharp to misinterpret the expression on his face.

"You thought me and Xander were together?"

"Well," said Ben, making excuses for himself. "I've hardly seen you *except* together. In fact, when I first saw you sneaking off together behind the trees I thought you were…"

"Yes?" said Shelley.

"Yes?" said Emily.

"You know," said Ben.

"No, I don't," said Shelley.

"Neither do I," said Emily. "You'll have to explain yourself. In detail."

"I thought you were going off for a little private time together," said Ben. He was developing a certain fear of when two women got together. It was Emily and Shelley, or Emily and Juliette, or Emily and Sally. Funny, he thought, how it was always *Emily* and someone.

"Private time?" said Emily. "What does that mean?"

Shelley and Emily shared a little laugh at his expense, and then the student went off to find Xander and tell him all about Ben's little misunderstanding. Emily stopped teasing him in the absence of another woman to share the joke with, and started paying him some more 'proper' attention.

"You haven't gone back to the hospice since Harrison died? At all?" asked Emily.

"No."

"What about Sally?"

"What about her?"

"Haven't you spoken to her? She cares about you, you know."

"I've talked to her on the phone, to confirm I would be there on Christmas day. And she doesn't care about me. She stopped caring about me when she found out about me and you."

"No, Ben love, that's not what I meant," said Emily. Ben loved it when she called him 'Ben love'. "She doesn't want a *relationship*; she cares about you. She cares about you *now*. She's probably seriously worried about you."

She leaned over towards Ben and reached out with both arms. Ben was surprised at Emily's display of affection in such a public place, but she only wanted to reach into his pockets to pull out his phone.

"Call her," she instructed. "Now."

He dialled her number.

"Hello, Sally?"

"Ben! How are you?"

"Not so bad," he said. "Well…" There was a moment's quiet understanding between them. Calling up someone on the telephone to share a moment's silence was strange. Then Sally perked up.

"I'm just getting ready to visit you," she said.

"Visit me?"

"Not you, *Ben*; you the *college.* John's invited me to your show tonight."

"Of course," said Ben. "That's brilliant. I'll see you then."

Ben, in fact, did not see much of her that night, as she spent the whole time with John. But they said hello at the beginning, and shared a meaningful moment where they both seemed to be remembering Harrison in each other's company without actually mentioning his name. Then they went off, Sally to her seat with John and Ben to his various preparations. After the show, John took her away without seeing Ben, in spite of what happened at the end of the evening.

Ben enjoyed the Christmas show, although more than half the people performing were not students that he knew all that well. Juliette had opted not to sing, as she was frequently the 'star of the show', at least where Emily's singing class was concerned, and she felt it would be good to give some of the younger students a chance. It was also intended that she should take part in one of Ben's schemes later in the show, although nobody except Ben and Martin knew that. There was a superb duet between a boy and a girl from the singing class, though, which he enjoyed immensely. He also enjoyed the large dance group which included Shelley Hickman. They performed their own, rather original interpretation of a piece from Riverdance. However, he was restless because of the surprises he had planned. He was looking forward to Pamela's unusual performance shortly, and even more to the shock he had in store for everyone at the end of the show.

About an hour into the show, a large canvas was brought on to the stage. It was supported by a strong framework made by the stagecraft class, so that it stood firm and almost wobble-free in the centre of the stage. Pamela Grice came onto the stage dressed in a painting smock, assisted by two tall lads who carried her paints and brushes onto the stage. The backdrop of the canvas had already been painted. It was a snow scene, with hills in the background and the vague outline of a couple of houses and one or two trees roughly sketched in the foreground.

Pamela acknowledged the audience in the way Ben had taught her, and then turned her back to face the canvas. They had experimented with putting the huge canvas at an angle so that Pamela didn't have her back to the people watching, but nothing worked, so they went back to the original plan. The music started up, and Ginny, one of the girls from Emily's class, started singing "Walking in the Air" as Pamela started painting. Her sweeping arm movements were dance-like, thanks to Mrs Cleese's tuition. Pamela was not in her class, but she had given a little help and support to this project because it required the combined skills from a number of different lessons to make it work. In fact, a large number of different classes and students were involved in this scheme of Ben's. Surprisingly enough, the only class not involved was Ben's own magic group.

As the song unfolded, Pamela used the larger paint brushes in great arm-stretching sweeps to illustrate the story that the song told. In less than five minutes, she drew the snowman flying through the air with a child in tow, and all the features of the song seemed to be there. She embellished the trees and the houses, adding detail to the scenery with fast-paced dabs of her various, different-sized brushes. She had not quite finished when the song ended, but the extra half-minute or so was just as spellbinding as the rest, and she finished her display to a standing ovation.

The finished picture was stunning, considering that the detail in it had been added in only five minutes. It seemed to contain a huge amount of substance, and created an atmosphere that was enhanced by the song that Ginny had just finished singing.

As she took her bows, she blew a kiss to Ben, and bowed particularly low to Bryn, who was beaming like a proud father at her achievement. He was always light-heartedly complaining about his subject never being showcased in one of their shows (Ben always assumed it was light-hearted, anyway), so now his big moment, as well as Pamela's, had come. Pamela graciously signalled for her companion, Ginny, to come onto the stage from the side so that she, too, could receive the audience's appreciation.

The picture stayed on stage for a few minutes during the break. The interval was only a few minutes long, giving the audience a chance to stand up and take a stretch, but no drinks were served and everyone was eager to get on with the next part of the show.

In the second half, there were a few more short pieces from one or two other classes, including a well-read classical poem, and a film piece prepared by the media class.

Towards the end of the show, Martin took to the stage, and started performing a trick that was familiar to the members of the magic class. He took two large blue silk handkerchiefs and waved them at the audience. There were a couple of knowing laughs as the sequence started. However, this was not going to go exactly as they were expecting.

As he tied the silks together, he asked for a volunteer from the audience. A number of the boys put their hands up, including John Stockton.

"No," he said, "I mean I want a young lady assistant." A number of boys tried to persuade certain girls to put their hands up. Eventually he chose Juliette, who was the only other person besides Ben who knew what this performance was *really* all about, and had insisted that she be included.

She had dressed for the part, wearing a top which was a little daring – considerably more daring than the kind of reserved, refined stuff that she would usually wear. Ben could only assume she borrowed it from someone like Shelley, as it was not really her kind of clothing, and would be unlikely to find its way into Juliette's wardrobe. Nevertheless, the low-cut garment showed off her excellent figure really well, and would be just the misdirection that Martin would need.

He explained to the audience that he needed to put the silks that he had just tied somewhere so that they were in full view. He looked at Juliette's top. "I can't think of a fuller view than that!" As he made a lunge for her, she took a step back holding up her hands in mock denial. He stood up straight, and rubbed his cheek as if she might have slapped him. A number of the students laughed at that reference to what had happened earlier in the year, even though most of them had not witnessed the original event.

She put her hand out to take the silks, and he held back, as if wanting to do it himself. She was persistent, all smiles, her fingers beckoning to him to hand over the silks. Finally, he relented, handing them over to her, acting disappointed. Ben recalled the discussion that

Martin had about verbal and visual comedy with Steve Goss, and was interested to note that, although he had said he preferred verbal comedy, he carried off the visual stuff really well. Juliette tucked the tied silks in the front of her top. Martin then proceeded to pick up a small yellow silk handkerchief from his little table, and stroke it through his hand, making little jokes as he proceeded to feed it into his closed fist. He told the audience what Ben had told them in the first week of term, that making something disappear was okay, but making it reappear somewhere else was…

"Magic," and, upon that word, he opened both empty hands to show the audience. Then he turned his head slightly towards Juliette. She shook her head, as if to warn him away. Stories about this trick and what would happen next had got around the students, so the laughter (and a few cheeky comments) from the audience built up. Then Martin faltered.

"I'm sorry," he said. "I can't do this."

Everyone shut up. There was silence in the theatre. Sometimes, one of the students would falter during a show, and a great deal of sympathy rattled round the rest of the college as they watched. Only Ben, Juliette and Martin himself knew that this time, it was all part of the act. Martin turned to Ben.

"I wonder if you would finish the trick for me?" he asked the teacher. "I know you're not supposed to perform in a student show, but I'm sure the professor wouldn't mind."

"Certainly," said Ben, not hesitating to take the stage. He stood in front of the audience of teachers and students, and explained.

"Just in case you think Martin has messed up, I think I should tell you that he has kindly allowed me to steal his thunder."

He turned to Juliette.

"With your permission?" he said.

"You have my permission," said Juliette. This was a private joke, as, apart from Ben, only Juliette, Emily and Mark knew about the Fifth Element reference. Ben reached for the dangling ends of both of the blue silks, and gave them a pull. They came away from Juliette's top, revealing the yellow handkerchief tied between them, but not only the handkerchief. This time, instead of a bra, there was a large white cloth, printed with words. He held the cloth so that the words could be read clearly.

They read, 'Marry me Emily'.

The audience remained silent for a second as they all tried to work out what was happening. Then there was a huge eruption of cheering and clapping, which took several minutes to calm down. At the end, when it finally went quiet again, Ben was still standing on the stage with the proposal in his hands, but nobody was looking at him. All eyes were on Emily, who looked embarrassed.

She recovered quickly, and smiled.

"I'll tell you tomorrow," she said in a loud, clear voice which got further applause.

The professor had been kind enough to allow Martin's piece to be the grand finale of the show. He did not know exactly what Ben had planned, but he had trusted his teacher enough to know that it would be a great finish to the show. There was a crowd around Ben and Emily at the end as people began to get up and leave. That is to say, there were two crowds, one each for them, which kept them apart. Emily's class and some of the other girls crowded round her, while most of the lads gathered round Ben, although Pamela managed to squeeze her short body through them in order to say 'thank you' to him for arranging the show piece.

"It was brilliant," she said. "I was terrified, but…"

"But you loved the experience," Ben completed for her.

"It was the best," she said.

He wanted to chat to her some more, but he also wanted to try to connect with Emily. He craned his neck to see if he could see over the heads of the students.

Professor Kennington also met him among the crowds, to shake his hand and thank him for his part in the preparation of the show. He did not have to squeeze past the others, because they parted for him. He kept Ben talking for a while.

"That was an interesting and unconventional finish," the professor said, clinging on to his hand as if he was trying to hold him in place.

"Thank you, sir," said Ben, still turning his head to see if he could see Emily. The professor did not let go.

"I was impressed with what you did for young Pamela, too," the professor continued. "Combining the different media to present a fabulous show, it was quite a confidence builder for her."

"Yes," said Ben, becoming more distracted.

"I have a confession, Ben."

"What?"

"I said I have something to confess," repeated the professor. "I saw Emily before I came over to you. She wanted me to keep you talking for a few minutes to distract you, but I'm not really very good at that."

"What?" said Ben.

"I think 'why' would be a better question there, Ben."

"What? Why?"

"Because she wanted to get away," said the professor. "I'm afraid she is going to make you stew a little, waiting for an answer."

Did he just do something really terrible? Had the emotional roller-coaster of the last few weeks given him the wrong impression of where his relationship with Emily was going? He had misread Xander and Shelley, after all. He had believed that Harrison would recover just days before he died. His friendship with Emily had been as close as two friends could be, and the romantic times that they shared, few as they were, seemed to indicate that their friendship could be so much more. He had even cried on her shoulder! Surely he had read the signs correctly.

But their friendship had been based on communication. They could talk about anything, and they could sit in silence and still understand each other. Now he had kept the secret of the printed silk and the on-stage proposal from her, and sprung it on her by plotting with her own star pupil. Was that, after all, the wrong thing to do?

She had gone home by the time he had a chance to look for her. He got out his mobile phone, and started to pull up her number, then decided against it. It had to be her move, now, after all.

He got home, went to bed, and didn't sleep. He spent a bit of time worrying about how he had presented his proposal, and what Emily's answer would be. He imagined possible outcomes and conversations with her, some of which ended happily and many that didn't. He tried to look in his minds' eye at the expression on her face when she had said 'I'll tell you tomorrow'; had she been smiling? He certainly thought so at the time, but the lights were on him, not the audience, so it was hard to tell. The tone in her voice implied she was going along with the fun of the moment, and that she intended to say 'yes'. Maybe she was keeping him waiting to get her own back for asking her in such a way. Perhaps, when she had slept on it, she would change her mind and say 'no' after all.

He was full of hope, then despair, then the tiredness of the last two weeks caught up with him and he drifted off to sleep, then he woke up in a panic, and then reasoned himself back to sleep again.

Although he finally slept quite deeply, he still woke up early in the morning, eager to get into the college and find out what was going to happen next.

21.

It was Thursday 22nd December. The term was over, and everyone was going home for Christmas. Ben got into work early in the hope that he would get to speak to Emily before she came to say goodbye to her class today. She had not arrived as early as she usually would, so he had gone down to the cellar to do a bit of tidying up. The sign on the classroom door read "Say Yes Emily". He decided he would leave it there. He really, *really* wanted to see her. Perhaps she would come down here to see him and take the advice on the door.

The problem with doing a bit of tidying up was that he had been doing a bit of tidying up for the last couple of weeks. He had spent as much of his time at the college down here as he could because he did not want to be at home on his own, but neither did he want to be in the company of the students 'up there'. He had not returned to visit the hospice, and thought of doing so filled him with sadness bordering on despair. Apart from fulfilling his promise on Christmas Day, it was not his intention to go near that place again. However, when he was at the college, he found there were times when he did not want to be among the people there either, so he had come down here to do a bit of tidying up.

It was late morning before Emily came and found him in the cellar. She gave him an all-encompassing hug and a loving kiss on the lips. Her students had gone home without knowing her answer – she had said to them she would tell them when the new term started. Some of them were already speculating that she would say 'no', or she would have said 'yes' straight away.

"Why?" she asked him, still holding him in her arms. Of all the words in the English dictionary he wanted to hear from her right now, ‘why’ was not on the list. It seemed she was determined to keep him waiting. Perhaps, he thought, she *was* going to say ‘no’. Surely not.

“Why what?” asked Ben.

“The proposal.”

“Oh, that,” said Ben. “I wanted to find out your real surname.”

“And you think I would tell you if you proposed?”

“It’s the magic sentence.”

“What is the magic sentence?” enquired Emily.

“It goes like this: ‘I, Ben April, take you, Emily…”

“Darkchilde,” said Emily. “And I’m not changing it to April. You’ll have to change yours.”

“To…?”

“Darkchilde. I said. It’s my name, my real name. I *like* the name Darkchilde.”

“I’ll have to change mine?”

“That’s right.”

“So what you’re saying is, yes, you’ll marry me?”

“You’re not getting off that lightly. First you have to tell me the real reason you asked.”

“You know why I asked.”

“That’s not an answer,” insisted Emily.

“Because I want to marry you.”

“Say it,” she insisted. He knew what she meant, and, even now he would have to admit that he did not understand love and was reluctant to use the word until he knew what he was talking about. Unfortunately, he did not expect *ever* to understand the word.

Ben thought of keeping this going for a bit longer, but he had to relent, so he said what she surely didn’t really need to hear. Perhaps it was not about what she needed to hear so much as what he needed to say. So he stood facing her, and took her hands in his.

“I love you, Emily Darkchilde. I love you and I want to spend the rest of my life with you.”

“You knew I’d say yes,” said Emily. “I was always going to say yes. And I loved the way you asked; even though I was so embarrassed I rushed home after the show yesterday as fast as I could.”

“I wondered why I didn’t see you,” said Ben, feeling remarkably calm considering what had just happened.

“I’ve got a great date for the wedding,” Emily suggested.

"When?"

"Your special day. The first of April," she said. She did not give him a chance to come back with a smart reply, because she kissed him. She kissed him with the kind of kiss that gave him no doubt of her feelings for him.

The rest of that Thursday and all day Friday and Saturday was a whirlwind of activity. Christmas Day was on the Sunday. Ben telephoned his mother as soon as he had a moment to spare on Thursday to tell her the news.

"She said yes," he said, excitedly and not explaining himself. "She kept me waiting all night, but she said yes."

"I can't help feeling I've just come in half way through a conversation," said his mother, all calm and showing no signs of excitement whatsoever. "Did you start telling me this story before I answered the phone?"

"What?" said Ben.

"Don't keep saying 'what'. You've said 'what' ever since you were a child. You're a teacher now. You should at least speak properly."

"I'm getting married."

"And that's your excuse for not speaking properly?" said his mother. Then she did a double take. "Who to?"

"I thought I might marry Professor Kennington," said Ben, exasperated. He loved his mother, but he was sure she took lessons at annoying him from Emily. "You always said he was a nice man."

"I hope you are both happy together," she said. "You and Emily, I mean, not you and Professor Kensington."

"Kennington," said Ben. He was sure she knew his name, and only said Kensington to annoy him. "And if you knew it was Emily, why did you ask who?"

He woke up early on Christmas morning, and he felt like a child eager to open his presents. He was actually looking forward to going to the hospice. Something had happened to him between the time Emily said 'yes' and now. Something had changed in him. When Emily had forced him to use the word 'love' to her, it was not just about romance. It was something different, stronger even.

Or perhaps it had started before Harrison died. Perhaps the hospice taught him something about himself and about love every time he had visited over the last few months. He did not hate the place like he had told himself he should. It was a good place to be, full of love and encouragement for needy people.

Harrison had benefited from Ben's encouragement and support, but, as Emily had already said, Ben had benefited more from Harrison's friendship, as well as from Sally and her father's love and devotion to their project. He met up with Emily at her house, and they loaded her stuff into his car. After the hospice, he was going to take Emily to his mother's home in Birmingham, where they would stay until they went to the New Year party that her father would host in Southampton. The next few days would consist of lots of parties as people celebrated their engagement. It was going to be hard, Ben thought with some amusement, but they would cope.

When he parked in the hospice car park he paused before getting out of the car. Emily had already started unloading her stuff, but she stopped and looked at him for a moment.

"You okay?" she said quietly.

"I think so."

He looked at the front of the hospice. It was decorated for Christmas, as if a child had done it. It looked far more beautiful in its ragged appearance than it would have if they had left it to adults. The outside day was a little overcast, so the lights from the inside seemed to be brighter and more joyful, casting an aura around the area that seemed to speak of love and joy and all sorts of other corny Christmassy stuff you see on corny Christmassy films that Ben thought were so awful this time of year. But this wasn't awful – not any more. It wasn't about death – it was about making the most of whatever life you had left.

Inside the hospice, Sally greeted Ben and gave him a huge hug. In the wordless action, Ben managed to release some of his grief over Harrison's death, comfort Sally for *her* grief, and apologise to her for avoiding the place. They kept on hugging until Emily said, "Okay, that's enough."

They set up in the usual place. The show started more or less on time. Ben did a bit of magic, and then Emily sang to the children. She had learned the words and recorded the backing music for 'Frosty the Snowman' especially for this show.

One of Harrison's friends asked her to sing 'Into the West', but she politely turned him down, saying that a Christmas party was probably not the right place to perform that song. She did promise, however, that she would visit them again and sing it another time.

Ben did another set of tricks, mostly with funny or silly magic involving sponge balls, collapsible boxes and colourful handkerchiefs. He performed 'Sally's Bottom' again, partly for the children who had joined the hospice since September, partly because the ones that had been there in September asked him to do it again and partly because Emily would have had a go at him if she didn't get to see him 'do that thing with her bottom'.

They ate a fabulous Christmas dinner together, and Sally got to speak to Ben, trying to have a private conversation with him while surrounded with children.

"I'm really sorry you took Harrison's death so hard. You were a good visitor, and we'll miss you."

"Were?" said Ben. "Is that it, then?"

"Are you saying you would do it again?"

"I've thought about it a lot. I thought for a while that I never wanted to see this place again. But now I am not sure I'd know what I would do without it."

Cherry came up to him and stood by the chair where he was sitting.

"Hello, Magic Man," she said.

"You'll continue to be a visitor here?" said Sally.

"Will you be *my* visitor?" said Cherry before Ben could answer. "I would like someone to be my friend when my mummy can't be here."

Sally's big eyes shone and a little tear began to form. "Cherry needs someone like you, Ben. Why don't you spend a few minutes with her? We can talk about visiting after your Christmas break."

Ben agreed, and Sally left him to Cherry. She knew what she was doing, thought Ben, as she watched the short care assistant busy herself around the tables, looking after all the children in her care, smiling and laughing with them and pouring out her love to them all as she wished them a Merry Christmas. She knew that Cherry would win him over. He was not even going to put up a fight.

The adorable little girl kept asking for tricks. Emily untangled herself from the older teenage boys who couldn't take their eyes off her and came to join Ben and his new companion.

"Competition?" she said to Ben.

"Sorry, Emily," said Ben, putting an arm around Cherry. "I've got another woman. Cherry appreciates me for what I am. She doesn't get together with the other girls and gang up on me."

"We can soon change that," said Emily.

Little Cherry asked for another trick.

"I think you've used up all my tricks," said Ben with a smile.

"I want to be a magician when I grow up," said Cherry. A wave of emotion suddenly came over Ben again like it had every now and again when something reminded him of Harrison. He choked up. *But you're not going to grow up*, he thought. *You'll be dead before...*

"Oh, no," said Ben with a laugh in his voice he didn't feel. "Competition! I'll go out of business."

"We could be a double act," she suggested.

"I could be your beautiful assistant," suggested Ben.

"Silly," said Cherry. "Men aren't beautiful."

"They are sometimes," said Emily under her breath.

"I could be *your* beautiful assistant," said Cherry.

"That's sounds like a good idea," said Ben. "Let's start work on our show straight away."

About the author

Peter Cooper is a magician, puppeteer and award-winning ventriloquist. He is a founder member of King of Hearts Creative Outreach, which serves to build up confidence in children and young people, and is engaged in community development and Christian communication.

www.khcreative.org.uk